THE ANGEL'S VOW

THE ANGEL'S VOW

R.L. PEREZ

WILLOW
HAVEN
PRESS

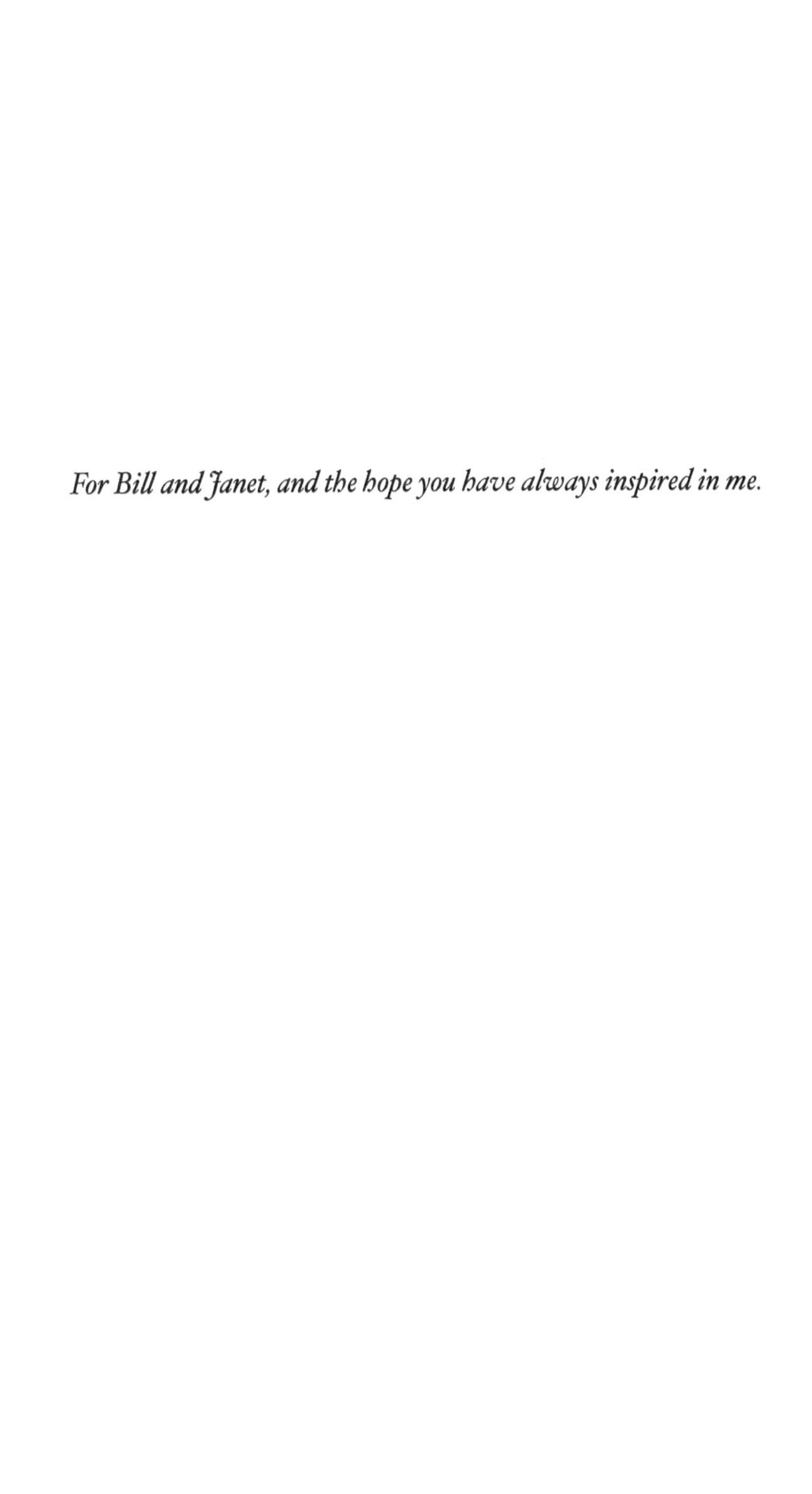

For Bill and Janet, and the hope you have always inspired in me.

CHAPTER 1

VINCE

Nausea was the first symptom of losing my Nephilim magic. Followed swiftly by vertigo. The spinning and swaying. The complete lack of balance and gravity.

For days, I lay on what felt like a sturdy cot, surrounded by darkness and shadows. I was so ill I could barely make out where I was. From what I could tell, we were underground. I never saw the sun.

Mom was patient with me. Her steady gray eyes often watched me with an otherworldly insight as if she saw something I couldn't. It unsettled me.

Or maybe it was just being around her again. It felt surreal. To go from having a dead mother to sharing the same air with her again was almost too much.

Mom sat by me even as I puked my guts out. And when I shivered, she layered quilts on top of me, tucking me in like I was a child again. Every move I made, she was there. It was almost like she was making up for lost time.

When the sickness finally faded, I moaned, "Why is this happening to me?"

Mom stroked the damp hair out of my eyes. "Your body is undergoing a huge change. It's just adjusting to it."

"B-but I still have my warlock magic, right?" I asked.

Mom didn't answer right away, which only made me panic. I searched inward for the familiar crackly presence of my Teleportation abilities, but I felt nothing. I wasn't sure if it was because I was sick or because I'd lost my magic.

"It's not that simple," Mom finally said. "Things work . . . differently down here."

"The Underworld?"

Again, Mom hesitated. I wished she would stop doing that.

"Kind of," she said, her eyes guarded. "We exist in what's called the Astral Realm. The space between worlds."

I merely blinked at her.

"Our magic is now tethered to the Underworld, so we have to stay close. But because we aren't dead, we can't exactly live *in* the Underworld. It would upset the balance between the spirits beyond."

I gazed at the ceiling as my head spun. My stomach contracted, threatening to heave again. But then the feeling faded. As I squinted, I made out a dark spherical dome built into the ceiling.

"What does that have to do with my warlock magic?" I asked.

"It doesn't function in the same way here. The forces that power your magic are completely different. Time is different, the air is different, even the food is different. It's almost like you're living on a new planet. Your body—and your magic—have to adjust."

A new planet. Though the idea made my mind quiver, it didn't seem that far-fetched, given everything I'd seen: time travel, people in two places at once, friends living inside my head . . .

My thoughts soured as I thought of Luke, my best friend. We'd known each other for years, but he'd kept his magic a secret, making me believe he was a clueless mortal.

It didn't matter. Now that I lived in this weird Astral Realm, I would probably never see him again.

Or Cora.

My stomach tightened for a different reason as I remembered our goodbye kiss. And how desperately I'd wanted to stay with her.

But she had responsibilities to her demon coven. And I had to live here as a Reaper because I'd refused to join the Nephilim. I couldn't be a part of the clan. Not after Hector's corruption. Hector had vanished, but the clan leaders would just follow in his footsteps.

Even though all I wanted to do was see Cora, I could never live with myself if I pledged fealty to the corrupt Nephilim clan.

"What exactly does it mean to be a Reaper?" I asked, shifting my gaze to Mom. Thinking of Cora was too painful right now. The wound was still fresh.

Mom pressed her lips together, her brow furrowing. The faint scar above her eyebrow tightened from the motion, and I wondered for the millionth time how she'd gotten it. She was still my mother—she smelled and sounded the same—but so much time had passed, it almost made us strangers.

"I can't answer everything for you now, Vince," Mom said. "It's a lot to take in. One step at a time, okay? For now, let's digest the fact that you live in another realm and your body needs to adapt."

I nodded, but something snagged my thoughts. My head turned to face Mom. "You said *time is different*. What did you mean by that?"

Mom sighed, her eyes sparking with part frustration, part amusement. "Time passes differently here."

I swallowed. "How differently?"

"I'm not sure. We don't travel to the mortal realm often. But it's much slower down here."

We don't travel to the mortal realm often. My mouth felt dry as I turned the words over in my head. She hadn't said *we never go there.* Just not *often.*

Which meant I could go back. I could see Cora.

"Vince," Mom said. The warning in her tone reminded me of the days when she caught me doing something I shouldn't—like digging into her stash of chocolates in the pantry.

My eyes snapped back to her. "What?"

"You're thinking too much right now. You need to relax."

My racing heart made me feel nauseous again, so I changed the subject. "Where's Jocelyn?"

"She's fine. She's sick, like you. *Unlike* you, she's actually resting like she's supposed to." Mom widened her eyes meaningfully.

I exhaled, my head throbbing as I fixed my gaze on the strange spherical ceiling again. I wished Jocelyn were here. She had recently become a Reaper, like me. It would've been a relief to talk to someone who understood how confusing and disorienting this all was. Having Mom here was a comfort and I wouldn't trade it for anything . . . but it was overwhelming. She was so different. And she knew so much more than I did.

I didn't know how to act around her. How to think. Having her here made me circle through dozens of questions about where she'd been. If she *could* go to the mortal realm, why hadn't she come to see Dad and me? Why couldn't we go back to the mortal realm permanently? What powers did a Reaper actually have?

I squashed these questions down as the ache in my head intensified. I closed my eyes, grimacing against the pain.

Mom pressed a cool washcloth against my forehead. "Maybe you need a distraction. Tell me about your life. Tell me about . . . about your dad." Her voice cracked, and I opened my eyes to look at her. Her eyes were tight, but her face remained composed. I could tell she was in pain, but she was trying to mask it.

As I watched her, I wondered how long she'd been dying to ask me about Dad. How many hours had she sat with me while I'd been sick? She hadn't said a word about him.

But I saw the curiosity and desperation sparkling in her eyes. She needed to know.

"He's—he's good," I said in a strained voice. "Well, sort of. Actually, I . . . I don't know how he is." My heart twisted. I'd never been away from my dad before. We'd always been together.

Now, he was on his own. No job. No magic. No one to protect him.

My throat felt tight, and I couldn't speak.

Mom pressed her hand against mine. "It's okay, Vince."

I shook my head. "No, it isn't. Maybe—maybe I should've stayed with him. If I'd pledged, maybe we could've fixed things with the clan, and—" I stopped, realizing how pitiful my words sounded. There was no *fixing* what Hector had done. He'd wanted to isolate our Nephilim clan from the world in order to "preserve" our light magic from being tainted by others.

I couldn't live in a place like that. And neither could Dad.

"He doesn't blame you," Mom said quietly. "I know that much. He trusts your decisions, Vince. He trusts *you*."

My eyes fixed on her. Anguish swirled in her expression. She knew exactly how it felt to be torn away from her family.

"Why didn't you come back?" I whispered.

Mom blinked. "What?"

I hadn't meant to ask it. The words just spilled out before I could stop them. But now that I'd said it, the question burned within me. I *had* to know. "You said you don't go to the mortal realm *often*. But—but you do sometimes?"

Mom stared at me, her gaze so distant I felt like she was looking right through me. "When Reapers—when *we* travel to other realms, our magic calls us back here. The separation is . . . excruciating."

"And you didn't think the pain was worth it." My words sounded bitter.

Mom's eyes widened, and she shook her head quickly. "Vince, *no*. It isn't that. I've only been to the mortal realm twice since I became a Reaper. And each time was dire. I only travel there for extreme magical emergencies. If I'd been delayed in any way, the repercussions would've been devastating. I—I couldn't allow myself to be selfish like that when lives were at stake." Tears glistened in her eyes, and she swallowed. "I tried, though." Her voice broke, and her face crumpled as tears streamed down her face. "I tried using my Nephilim powers the first time I went back. I tried getting back to you. It—it didn't work. And I was in so much pain that someone had to come fetch me and bring me back. I couldn't get back on my own." She inhaled a shuddering breath. "I'm so sorry, Vince. I never wanted to abandon you."

The tightness in my chest loosened at the sight of her grief-stricken face. I couldn't be angry with her. None of this was her fault.

It was Hector's. And instead of tracking him down, I was stuck here.

My nostrils flared, and with the blazing anger inside me came another onslaught of nausea. I gritted my teeth and closed my eyes, waiting for it to pass. In a tight voice, I asked, "What . . . repercussions?" When Mom frowned at me, I added, "You said . . . devastating reper-cussions."

"Oh." She hesitated. "It's Reaper responsibilities. You'll learn soon enough."

Her constant hedging only made me *more* nervous. I was almost certain I would feel better if she just told me instead of making me fret about it.

"How many Reapers are there?" I asked. Surely, she could answer *that* question.

"Oh, hundreds. But we don't all stay in the same place. Some are here in the Astral Realm. Others are in the Underworld as Soul Reapers."

"Soul Reapers?" My brow furrowed.

"Much more complicated than normal Reapers. But don't worry, you don't have to deal with that."

"I thought you said only dead people could live in the Underworld."

"Soul Reapers *are* dead."

What the hell? My head was spinning again. "What determines where the Reapers go? Why am I here instead of the Underworld?"

"The strength of your Nephilim powers determines where you go. If you're here in the Astral Realm, it's because your magic pulled you here. This is where it's been summoned."

For some reason, a chill swept up my spine at her words. "Summoned by *whom*?"

"Not who—what. This realm has a life force of its own. Like I said before, magic works differently down here. It's almost like it's *alive*. It must be nurtured in order to grow and thrive. When we travel to other realms, our magic turns to a sickness because it knows it doesn't belong there. If you're here, it means your magic is most compatible with this realm."

"Is it?" I choked out a laugh. "Because my vomiting might say otherwise."

Mom offered a wry smile. "It's normal, I promise. It's just the shock of being in a new environment."

I grunted as I finally tried sitting up. My head still pulsed with agony, but my nausea was gone. I exhaled in relief. Mom pressed a hand to my shoulder, her brows knitting together.

"I'm fine," I said. Blinking away the fogginess in my brain, I squinted at my surroundings. It wasn't just the ceiling that was spherical—it was the entire room. It looked like we were inside a giant metal ball. "What *is* this place?"

"Tunnels," Mom said with a smile.

"Where did they come from?" I gazed at the perfectly sculpted walls that gleamed from the few lanterns surrounding us. Another cot sat opposite mine, which my mom was sitting on. Had she slept here with me? The thought made me feel warm and uneasy all at once.

"The tunnels have been here for ages as a go-between

for the different realms. We speculate the first Reapers built them for protection."

My eyes widened. "Protection from *what?*" What else lived in this realm besides us?

Mom's mouth clamped shut, her eyes guarded again. She'd shut down. I knew she wouldn't say any more.

I opened my mouth to insist she tell me, to say I wasn't a child who needed to be coddled, when a shrill scream echoed from outside the tunnel. The sound rang against my ears, making my skin crawl.

I stiffened. "What was that?"

Mom immediately stood and strode toward the door. Before she got to it, it swung open, and a woman with gray hair and pale blue eyes rushed in. Her inky black wings fanned out behind her, and dark feathers floated in her wake. For a moment, I was struck by the *magnificence* of her wings. I still wasn't used to seeing dark wings.

"What happened?" Mom asked, her tone ringing with authority.

"We've got another one," the woman said breathlessly. "You need to come quick."

Mom glanced at me.

"Another *what?*" I demanded, rising to my feet. My legs wobbled, but, thankfully, I didn't fall over. I pressed a hand against the cool metal wall to steady myself. "Mom, just *tell* me. What the hell's going on?"

Mom bristled—whether from me swearing or the way

I challenged her, I couldn't tell. She lifted her chin, her eyes glinting. "Another magical aura has been stolen."

CHAPTER 2

CORA

I REALLY JUST WANTED TO KILL SOMEONE. LIFE HAD been so much simpler when that was my only goal.

Instead, I sat behind a desk with a stack of papers so high I could barely see over it. I was drowning in bills and notices and contracts. So many papers I felt like my eyes were bleeding. When I closed them, I just saw printed words blurring together.

Kill me now.

The door to my office opened. Ordinarily I would welcome the distraction, but these days, I feared it would mean something *else* needed my attention.

I wanted to sleep. I wanted to hunt. I hadn't killed someone in months, and it was making me restless.

Rubbing my eyes, I groaned, "What *now*?"

"Silas is here to see you," Benny hedged. I'd known it

was him even before hearing his voice. He was the only one who had the gall to enter without knocking.

"Again?" I dropped my arms on the desk with a loud thump.

Benny shrugged. "He wants to renegotiate the coven's contract with his pack. He thinks you're trying to cheat him."

I gritted my teeth, my fingers curling into fists. "I'm *not*. That's all we have to offer."

"I know. But he doesn't believe that."

I sighed. "Can't *you* talk to him? Werewolf to werewolf?"

"I tried. He won't answer to me." He raised his eyebrows. "Do you think I do nothing here?"

I rolled my eyes. "Don't start."

"I *am* trying to fend off the wolves for you, Cora. Both literally and figuratively. But with a new coven leader, it's like a drop of blood in shark-infested waters. They're circling. Waiting for you to screw up."

And I already had. *Plenty* of times. Riots happened every other night in Hinport. Coven leaders made offers I rejected, and they retaliated by killing one of my men. We were one gunshot away from a civil war. And I'd only been coven leader for six months.

"I should just kill everyone," I muttered, letting my head drop on the desk. "One of my elixirs is rumored to have the power of an atomic bomb. We could just wipe out the city."

Benny offered a wry smile. "More would come. You know that."

I did know that. Half our problems were because new demon covens had come to town, hoping to take advantage of an inexperienced leader like me.

I was a killer. Not a negotiator or a liaison or a politician. The few demons who had sworn loyalty to me were now wishing they hadn't.

Except, it seemed, for Benny.

"You want my advice?" Benny asked, crossing his arms and leveling a hard stare at me.

I slowly lifted my head to look at him, though all I wanted to do was pass out on the desk. "If I say no, will you leave?"

Benny ignored me. "You're the *Blade of Hinport*. You used to be the most feared person in the city."

"I know that," I snapped.

"Be that person *now*, Cora. These demons are walking all over you because they don't respect you. You need to demand that respect."

I frowned. "When I was an assassin, I demanded respect by killing people. Is this your way of encouraging me to go forward with my atomic bomb plan?"

"You demanded respect by setting an example. After

your first few kills, everyone knew who you were and they knew not to cross you."

I stared vacantly at the open door behind him. Voices echoed in the hall. Phones rang nonstop. I'd hired several secretaries, but it was never enough.

These past months of toeing the line between killer and diplomat were exhausting. The problem with sitting on the fence was that the demons didn't respect me because they didn't see enough of either side of me.

Wistfully, I remembered the days when I would walk the streets of Hinport and people would dive out of my way, eager to let me pass freely. They avoided direct eye contact because they didn't want to challenge me.

Lilith, those were the days.

Resolve hardened in my chest, and I stood. My legs ached from being cramped behind a desk for so long, and my fingers were throbbing from papercuts. But a familiar fire surged within me, one that had been smothered for too long.

I strode past Benny and into the hallway, ignoring people who called out to me or asked me questions. My steps were forceful. Motivated.

No one would stop me.

I reached the lobby where Silas, the gray-haired werewolf alpha, sat waiting for me. His large nose looked even bigger with his nostrils flared in irritation. He glanced up when I approached, his yellow eyes gleaming.

"About time," he snarled. "You think you can weasel your way out of—"

I cut off his words by punching him in the throat. He made a hoarse gurgling sound and stumbled backward so violently he hit the wall and a picture frame shattered. I drew my blade and held it up to his throat, pinning him against the wall. His eyes widened in fear, his breathing sharp and ragged.

"I made you an offer, you dog," I spat. "If you want to renegotiate, you talk to Benny. If that's not good enough for you, then I'll let my knife do the talking." I pressed the blade into his neck, and a bead of blood trickled from his skin. "Understood?" I cocked my head at him, narrowing my eyes.

To his credit, Silas gritted his teeth. His trembling betrayed his fear, but he had the gall to look me in the eye and say, "You're making a *huge* mistake. Don't you know how powerful I am?"

"To me, you're just another demon."

Silas's nostrils flared. "I'm the most powerful alpha on the east coast. You think you can threaten me like I'm one of your goons?"

I leaned forward, baring my teeth at him. "Just because you're a bigger dog than the others doesn't mean you get special treatment when negotiating contracts. You work with Benny. His word is as good as mine. If you don't abide by those terms like everyone else, then you and my blade are gonna get *real* friendly."

Silas's yellow eyes flashed. "That blade can't kill me, you little bitch."

I grinned. "I know. Killing you instantly would take all the fun out of it." I pressed the dagger harder, and three narrow lines of blood ran down his neck. Silas hissed in pain. "Shall we?" I asked.

Silas licked his lips. "You don't want to do this."

"No, I *really* do." My eyes widened for emphasis. "Do I need to prove it to you?"

Conflict warred in his eyes. I read the venom and hatred swirling in his gaze, but it mingled with genuine fear. "N-no." He swallowed. "No. I understand perfectly."

I smiled and withdrew, then turned to face the crowd that had gathered to watch. "Anyone else want to challenge me?" I asked, spreading my arms wide. A few drops of Silas's blood flicked from the motion, and several people flinched. I glanced at each person, but no one met my gaze.

Just like old times.

I dropped my arms. "Perfect. I'll be in my office. If anyone enters without permission, I'm slitting their throat."

I stormed back down the hallway, and people darted out of my way, eager to avoid a run-in with my trusty dagger. Benny's eyes glinted, his face lifting with a smirk, but I ignored him as I returned to my office and slammed the door shut.

It didn't solve my paperwork problem, but it got my blood pumping again. And that was all I needed.

CHAPTER 3

VINCE

MY VISION BLURRED, BUT I FORCED MYSELF TO REMAIN upright as I said, "What do you mean by *stolen magical aura?*"

The gray-haired woman looked from Mom to me and back again. "You haven't explained it to him yet?" The severity of the woman's expression and the authority in her tone made me stiffen.

Who had authority over Mom? She'd been the *leader* of our clan.

"He's been sick," Mom said defensively, but the argument sounded weak.

"I'm *fine*," I snapped. "Will someone please tell me what's going on?"

Both women bristled at my outburst. The older woman's nostrils flared, and Mom's eyes turned steely.

"He can't come," the older woman muttered.

"The hell I can't!" I surged forward. Fire burned in my veins, sending a bolt of clarity in my mind. Energy crackled around me as I approached the woman, dwarfing her by at least a foot. "Go ahead. Try and stop me." I thought of Cora, always fearless in the face of those who challenged her. I lifted my chin, trying to channel that same energy and courage.

"Vince—" Mom said.

"If you leave me here, I'll just try to follow," I said loudly. "I'm sick of being coddled. I need to know what's going on here."

"You don't give orders around here," the older woman said curtly.

My eyes narrowed. "And who are *you?*"

The woman blinked and looked at Mom again. "Have you told him *anything?*"

Mom's mouth opened wordlessly, then closed, her expression a grimace.

I gaped at her. *Mom* was speechless?

Who *was* this woman?

The gray-haired woman drew in a breath, her cold eyes fixed on mine. "I'm Gwendolyn Peters."

My brow furrowed. Gwen Peters was a legend among the Nephilim. A powerful leader and liaison between covens.

Until she'd been killed by a demon coven thirty years ago. Someone had ordered a hit on her, and many demons had eagerly taken the challenge.

I shook my head. "Gwen Peters died."

The woman's jaw went rigid. "Another deception. Like your mother, I was stripped of my powers and banished here."

I squinted at her. She *did* vaguely resemble the picture of Gwen Peters, but it was hard to tell because of the wrinkles and gray hair. "You—you age here?"

"I told you time passes differently," Mom whispered.

I swallowed. Nephilim usually didn't age. It's why Hector and the rest of the officials looked no older than thirty-five, though they were hundreds of years old.

A knot formed in my throat. This meant Mom would get old in this realm. She could eventually die of old age.

My eyes felt warm. Another scream filled the air, and we all jumped.

Gwen cleared her throat. "We don't have time for this." She briskly walked to the open door. "Are you coming?"

I stood there, speechless, until I realized she was talking to me. "Yes." I joined Mom, and together, we followed Gwen out of the room. The giant metal door creaked shut behind us.

We emerged in a wide tunnel with various paths that

were sure to get me lost. Lanterns hung on the tunnel walls, guiding our way. It looked like a giant sewer—but cleaner. Though, if the walls were metal, I supposed it was more of a bunker than a sewer. The walls were curved and spherical like the ceiling. A damp, musty smell tickled my nose. With each step, a ripple of pain quivered through my head. I gritted my teeth, trying to focus on following Gwen. She turned down different paths in the tunnel, winding this way and that as if purposefully trying to confuse me.

I was just about to ask how much farther we'd be walking when another scream pierced the air—and this one was much closer. My ears throbbed, and my skin prickled. This was no ordinary human scream.

This was something otherworldly.

A magical aura has been stolen. What did that *mean?*

We stopped in front of a door that thrummed with power. I stilled, staring wide-eyed at the door. Energy pulsed under my skin in response to the magic waiting on the other side.

Mom grasped my shoulder. "Stay close to me," she murmured.

I swallowed and nodded.

Gwen pushed open the door with a loud creak. A burst of magic exploded around me, clouding around my face like a mist. I sucked in a breath, my head spinning.

Low voices echoed around me. Mom took my hand and guided me forward, and I clung to her like a lifeline. My vision was foggy, but the voices around me persisted. Who were they talking to?

After a moment, I realized they weren't talking—they were chanting a spell.

Another strangled scream tore at my eardrums. It was raw and anguished.

Gradually, my vision cleared, and I made out a wide circle of Reapers surrounding a girl lying on a slab of concrete. I squinted. No, not a girl.

A *spirit*.

She was completely transparent. I could see the concrete through her body as if she could pass right through it. She writhed and struggled as the Reapers continued their chant, their dark wings billowing behind them from the magic in the air.

Mom ushered me to the corner of the room and whispered, "Stay here." Then, she followed Gwen to the circle of Reapers. Mom's wings sprang out as easily as if she'd lifted her arm. She and Gwen inserted themselves into the circle, clasping hands with the other Reapers and joining in their chanting.

I sucked in sharp breaths, leaning against the cold wall for support. The magic still clouded around me, fogging up my mind. I could barely think straight. I shut my eyes, screwing up my face in concentration.

Focus, I told myself. *You can overcome this. Just listen.* I inhaled shakily, counting my breaths.

After five breaths, I could make out the words the Reapers were chanting.

"Souls of the dead, restore her essence. Souls of the dead, restore her essence."

They repeated the same sentence over and over. The words sent a chill sweeping through me. Energy quivered within me, tickling the muscles in my back. In a burst of power, my wings exploded behind me. Dark feathers tickled my face. I sucked in a breath, my eyes wide. It felt as if something heavy had been lifted from my chest. And now I could *breathe*.

I glanced over my shoulder. My heart lurched at the sight of black wings behind me.

I was so accustomed to white wings.

Another scream filled the room, this one weaker than before. The girl on the concrete arched backward, her mouth tearing open and her face taut with agony. When her body relaxed against the concrete, she didn't move again.

The chanting stopped.

Something in the air went eerily still, and the magic surrounding me vanished. Everything was frozen.

Then, the Reapers dropped their hands and backed away from the girl. Each face was filled with regret and disappointment.

My mouth felt dry. Had the girl died? The thought sounded silly, since I was fairly certain she was already dead.

Mom's eyes met mine, and her face slackened in shock. A mixture of emotions filled her face, but she quickly composed herself. Her eyes roved over my wings, spread out behind me, and pride glinted in her expression.

I wasn't sure how I felt about that.

Gwen leaned forward, whispering something to the other Reapers. A few of them nodded and approached the girl on the concrete. In an instant, the girl vanished, and a mist pooled from the center of the concrete, swirling in the air. Moisture brushed against my face as the mist rose higher and higher until it vanished completely.

My heart sank to my stomach. Something told me the mist was the girl's spirit.

And it was gone now. Leaving nothing behind.

Mom appeared by my side. Her piercing eyes questioned mine. "Are you all right?"

I suddenly found it hard to breathe. Each inhale was a rasp. "I—I feel . . ."

She nodded. "I know."

But she *didn't* know. *I* didn't even know what I felt. It was like my body responded to the magic here without my permission. Like it knew more than I did about what was going on.

My mind was a mass of confusion. But the magic within me was at peace. It baffled me.

A small smile lit Mom's face. "Your magic has awakened."

I nodded numbly. "Yeah." I stared at the concrete. Slowly, the Reapers filed out of the room, leaving Mom and me standing alone.

I looked at her. "What *was* that?"

Mom hesitated before answering. "A spirit who had passed on. Her magic was ripped from her before she died. When she arrived here, she was suffering from the loss. We couldn't save her."

My brow furrowed. "Save her from . . . what?"

"Extinction."

I shook my head, not comprehending.

"A soul is tethered to magic. They are bonded. When a soul is on the brink of death, it hovers between realms, and its link to magic is fragile. If that magic is forcibly removed, some souls do not recover from the trauma. The girl's spirit couldn't exist without her magic. So, it disintegrated. Her essence returned to the magic in the air around us."

My heart turned to cold stone in my chest. It sounded like a fairy tale adults told their children about what happened when people died. *Returning to the magic in the air* was just a kind way of saying she ceased to exist.

She died a permanent death and would never return. Never live again.

It all felt very final. I wasn't sure if I'd ever believed in heaven and hell, but in this moment, I realized I always believed in something beyond death. An afterlife. Death was never *it*.

"How did it happen?" I asked, my voice a whisper.

"We don't know. It's only just started recently. Souls have started arriving without their magic. Someone is robbing them. A brutal theft." Mom's face hardened with fury. "Whoever is doing this knows exactly when to strike."

"What do you mean?"

"Magic is most potent just before death. It's like a magical aura knows it needs to bond with its host in order to make the transition to death easier. Whoever is stealing magic knows this—and they are striking at the perfect time. They're siphoning the magic to gain more power, and the souls are suffering for it."

A chill raced down my spine. *Someone is stealing magic from the dead.* "Who has the power to do that kind of thing?"

Mom offered a wry smile. "Someone like us."

I stilled. "You think it was another Reaper?"

Mom shook her head. "No. Reapers are bound by the

vows we swore when we first came here. It couldn't be a Reaper. But someone like us—someone with the power to travel to different realms—could have done this. This wasn't the work of a mere demon. It has to be someone who is familiar with other worlds."

Bound by the vows we swore. I licked my lips, suddenly feeling uneasy. "What vow?"

Mom blinked. "What?"

"You said you swore a vow."

"Oh, yes. Before Reapers can begin working, they must swear a vow to ensure they don't abuse their powers."

Sickness swirled in my stomach. I was reminded of the Ceremonial Rite in my Nephilim clan where we had to pledge fealty to the clan—and forswear all other forms of magic.

Had I just left one prison to enter another? Would the Reapers try to squash my warlock magic too?

Mom seemed to read the terror in my face. "It isn't like that, Vince. It's not like a pledge. A vow is a promise to uphold the law. It doesn't limit your magic at all, just what you *do* with it."

That still didn't sound much better.

Mom sighed in exasperation. "The vow keeps you from harming souls, Vince. It protects them from the very thief we're trying to find. As a Reaper, you're given an enormous power that could be abused by the wrong people. The vow just preserves the sanctity of our duty."

I was suddenly very wary of what this "duty" entailed. "What duty is that?"

"We reap magic. When a soul arrives from the other side, we reap their magic from their soul so both can co-exist in harmony."

I frowned. "How is that different from stealing magic from a soul?"

"The soul is *willing* when we separate them from their magic. And it only happens *after* death. Whoever is stealing magic is doing it just before the caster dies."

"But you said a soul is bonded to their magic . . ."

Mom nodded. "Yes. We still allow the magic to live with the soul. But they are no longer confined to one body. The magic can return to the air but still flow with the person's soul. It's no longer restricted to one host."

When I gave her a perplexed expression, she chuckled.

"Think of it like a flower. This thief we're trying to stop, he's ripping the flower from the ground forcefully—in a way that won't allow the plant to survive. But what *we* do is much gentler. We nurture the plant. We make sure we keep all the roots when we pull it from the ground. We put it in a fresh spot with plenty of soil and sunlight. The thief isn't exerting caution like we do. He doesn't care what happens to the souls as long as he gets their magic."

My brain was starting to hurt. "I understand why you held back so much before. This is a lot to take in."

Mom nodded and squeezed my shoulder. "You need to rest. We can talk more about it tomorrow."

She guided me out the door. Just before we left, I glanced over my shoulder at the empty slab of concrete.

The girl's screams still echoed in my mind.

CHAPTER 4

CORA

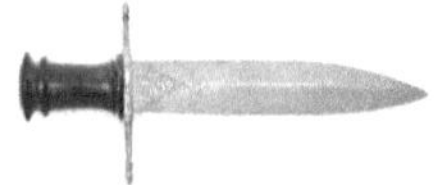

I DREAMED OF VINCE AGAIN—HIS WINGS SPREAD OUT behind him, his eyes ablaze, his face an unholy mask of fury.

He was power. He was vengeance.

It was absolutely breathtaking.

I awoke gasping for breath, a cold sweat on my face. It took half an hour for my heart rate to settle, but even then, I was still wide awake.

It had felt so *real.* And it reminded me of the vision I'd had of him after we'd both drunk the Seeing elixir.

It's just odd, that's all, I'd said.

That we're dreaming about each other? Vince had asked.

Yes.

His gray eyes had pinned me in place, unyielding like steel. And in that moment, I'd known I was doomed. Even if I didn't want to admit it.

My heart twisted, and my chest ached. A knot formed in my throat, and I found it hard to breathe again.

I wanted to believe this was another vision, foreshadowing that I would see Vince soon.

But it wasn't. For one thing, I hadn't taken my Seeing elixir in months.

For another, his wings had been white in my dream.

My eyes felt hot as I turned on my side, burying my face in my pillow. I gritted my teeth against the agony that quivered through me down to my bones. I was the Blade of Hinport, for Lilith's sake. And I couldn't handle a little heartache?

Pitiful.

Part of me wanted to argue that I'd been busy. Too busy to think about Vince—which had been a blessing at the time . . . but now it was catching up to me, crashing over me like violent waves.

Another part of me thought, *Hell, it's been months since I've gotten laid. Maybe I'm just lonely.*

But I knew that wasn't it either. All the men I'd slept with had been mere distractions.

Vince was the only one I loved. And I hadn't even shared my body with him. The thought wrenched through me, reminding me of what I couldn't have with him.

Damn him. Damn him and his determination to do the right thing and sever himself from his clan.

And damn myself for falling for him.

"Cora? Did you hear me?"

I blinked, my gaze shifting to an irritated Benny. Exhaustion tugged at my body. I sighed, rubbing my eyes for the millionth time. "Sorry. Say that again."

Benny pinched the bridge of his nose. "Kip and the others. They're giving us trouble."

I clenched my teeth, thinking of Kip and his buddies. They'd been Damien's best friends. I had no doubt that if they were released, they would stage a coup and take over the city by means of blackmailing and coercion just like Damien had. "What kind of trouble?"

"I mean, they're fighting the guards. Riling up the other prisoners."

Prisoners. Our coven had faced so much unrest lately that we were constantly arresting people. It made us as unpopular as the *actual* police.

I waved a hand. "Give them another beating."

Benny leveled a hard stare at me.

I raised my eyebrows. "You had something better in mind?"

"How long do you intend to keep them around?"

I frowned. "I don't know." My eyes snapped to him. "You think I should kill them?"

"I think you need to send a message."

I was standing before I realized it. "Consider it done."

Benny sighed. "Cora."

"What?"

"You can't execute them yourself."

"But you said—"

"Right now, the coven needs to be reminded who has the authority. *Not* who has the power. Order someone else to do it."

My mouth opened and closed. Order someone *else* . . . to do the killing?

The idea sounded as strange as if Benny suggested I take up tap dancing.

"I can do it, if you need me to," Benny said.

Something jolted within me, and I cocked my head at him, my eyes narrowing. "Do you think I'm an idiot?"

His head reared back. "What? Of course not."

"That I'm just some feeble, inexperienced leader you can manipulate?" I stepped around my desk to face him.

He had the good sense to look afraid before he spoke. "I'm just trying to help you."

"Out of the goodness of your heart?" I rolled my eyes. "Why do I find that hard to believe? What do you want out of this, Benny? What do you have to gain if I order Kip's execution?"

"Same thing as you."

I crossed my arms and clicked my tongue.

Benny dropped his arm against his thigh. He hung his head back and stared at the ceiling in exasperation as if help would drop out of the sky. "Mother of Lilith, you are *so* paranoid, Cora. I'm not trying to double-cross you. I'm not trying to manipulate you. You've never been a leader before, but I have. I'm just trying to coach you."

His words stirred something inside me, but I kept my expression carefully composed. "You've been a leader?"

He nodded. "An alpha."

I stilled. *Alpha.* My skin prickled as my instincts told me to be wary of him. Alphas were dangerous and powerful.

But . . . they also couldn't be dethroned unless they were killed. So how had Benny survived?

"I stepped down," he said, answering my unspoken question.

I glared at him. "Stop that."

Benny raised his hands in surrender.

I rubbed my forehead. "Seriously, Benny, if you want me to trust you, you can't just go reading my mind whenever you want."

Benny's lips twitched. "I wasn't."

I stared at him.

He smiled. "Like you, I have to limit how often I use my powers. If I use them too much, it alerts the wrong kind of people. Besides, not everyone here knows about me." He widened his eyes with emphasis.

I waved a hand. "Don't worry, I won't tell."

"I know you won't."

"Why did you step down as alpha?"

Benny watched me, his yellow eyes unreadable. A grimness set in his face. "My wife died."

I wasn't sure what I'd expected, but it wasn't that. My mouth fell open, and my stomach turned over. All I could say was, "Oh."

"Someone from my pack got her. She didn't survive the transformation. I couldn't bear to be around wolves anymore, so I left."

That would explain why he'd been a lone wolf when he joined my coven. I swallowed as a sick feeling filled my gut. "I'm so sorry."

Benny's lips pressed together into a thin line. His eyes were haunted but still guarded. Like he'd grown accustomed to masking his feelings.

I could relate to that.

"What happened to the guy?" I asked. "The one who bit her?" I didn't know why, but I had to ask.

Benny lifted his chin, his gaze darkening. "I killed him."

I nodded once. "Good." Because if the asshole was still alive, I would've killed him myself.

Benny held my gaze for a moment, and I felt something shift in our relationship. We weren't necessarily friends, but there was a certain understanding between us now. A mutual acceptance of the darkness that lived in both of us.

Something in me deflated, and I sat on the edge of my desk, feeling fatigued again. Benny slowly sank into the chair opposite me.

"Look, if you want to succeed as coven leader," Benny said, "you need to stop thinking like an assassin and start thinking like someone with authority. You were close to Damien. What would he have done in this situation?"

"He would've ordered me to kill whoever was disturbing the peace." The words tumbled from my mouth automatically.

Benny nodded. "Exactly. So, who's your hitman?"

My mouth twisted as a sour taste climbed up my throat. I didn't trust *anyone* in this coven, not even Benny. So how could I assign someone to kill for me without worrying they'd turn around and kill me next?

Power pulsed to life inside me, and a slow smile spread across my face. Benny raised an eyebrow, his eyes curious.

"I know just what to do," I said.

CHAPTER 5

VINCE

I followed Mom down the winding tunnels, our pace slower than when we were with Gwen. My head was still reeling, and I wasn't paying attention to where I stepped.

"You probably have a lot of questions," Mom said softly, her voice echoing in the vast tunnel.

I swallowed. My mouth felt dry. "Not yet." My voice cracked. "Still processing."

Silence passed between us as we continued walking.

Then, I blurted, "Can I still Jump?"

Mom raised her eyebrows. "Yes. You still have access to your warlock powers. But they'll work differently down here."

"You keep saying that, but what does it *mean*?"

"It means the rules and laws of magic aren't the same as in the mortal realm. It will be like starting over."

I suppressed a groan. I'd worked so hard to figure out how to Jump through time. Now I had to do it all over again?

"I can help you, Vince," Mom said with a soft smile.

I frowned. "But you're not a Jumper."

Mom laughed. "Not with Jumping. With adjusting to how magic works here."

A lump formed in my throat, but I forced a smile.

To be honest, all I wanted was to talk to my dad. He'd been a Jumper before. He coached me when I first tried using my powers. He knew exactly what it felt like.

I ached to talk to him about this. My heart twisted so painfully I thought I might be sick again.

Mom glanced at me, concern etched into her face. Before she could say anything, muffled footsteps echoed ahead of us in the tunnel. I stiffened as fear gripped my body, though I wasn't sure why.

A pair of Reapers appeared. The first was a tall, wiry man with dark eyes and a blank expression. And the second was—

"Jocelyn!" I cried, rushing forward to embrace her.

Jocelyn gasped and clutched me tightly, laughing into my shoulder. "Vince! Thank Lilith you're all right." She drew away to look me over, her blue eyes shining. Her red hair was frizzy and disheveled. "I was so worried about you." Her face was paler than normal, no doubt from the same sickness I'd endured.

"Me too." Even as I said the words, regret swelled within me. I'd completely forgotten about her with the whole *magic-stealing* ordeal. "Are you all right?"

Jocelyn nodded and cast a wary glance toward the Reaper next to us, who remained stoic. "This is, uh Ellis. My mentor."

"Hi." I extended my hand, but Ellis didn't move. His eyes were distant and unfocused.

I looked uncertainly at Mom. "Is he all right?"

Mom's face had gone blank as well, but when I turned to her, she offered a pained smile identical to the one I'd given her earlier.

I saw right through it.

"He's fine," Mom said. "Some of the Reapers down here get a little closed off over time."

Alarm pulsed through me. What did *that* mean? Jocelyn and I exchanged fearful looks, and I knew we were thinking the same thing.

Would that happen to *us*?

"Don't worry, he's perfectly capable of teaching you," Mom said quickly, misreading our unease.

An awkward silence fell between us. I cleared my throat and changed the subject. "Where are you headed?"

"Ellis is going to show me the sleeping quarters now that I've finally recovered." Jocelyn grinned sheepishly.

Mom nodded with approval. "Excellent. Once you both get settled, we can swear you in and get you to work." Her voice was chipper, but her words seemed ominous and filled me with dread.

Swear you in.

Was there anything in my life that didn't require some kind of permanent oath? Something to restrict me? Did such a life *exist* for a Nephilim?

"Where are you two going?" Jocelyn asked, her eyes darting between Mom and me. Her eyes lingered on my mom for a long moment, her expression awestruck.

This had to be baffling for her. She'd grown up believing my mother was dead too.

I looked at Mom, waiting for her to respond. I'd figured we were going back to the room we'd been in before, but with Jocelyn headed to the sleeping quarters, now I wasn't so sure. Perhaps the room I'd slept in had only been temporary while I was ill.

"I just need to grab something real quick for Vince." Mom smiled tightly. I frowned, sensing the lie.

"See you soon, then?" Jocelyn asked, her eyes filled with hope.

I nodded. "Sure." But my eyes remained on Mom. She watched Ellis lead Jocelyn down the tunnel, away from us. Then, she turned to me.

"You can't tell anyone about what you saw," she said in a whisper. "About the magic thief or the Reaping circle or any of it."

My eyes widened. "Why not?"

Mom pressed her lips together and glanced furtively up and down the tunnel. "Not here. Come on."

She led me down the tunnel and took a left at a narrower passage. A few doors lined the wall, and Mom pushed one open before ushering me through. The room was about the same size as the one I'd been sick in, but this one had no cots—only a few metal chairs. It seemed cold and uninviting.

Mom sat down in one chair and gestured that I do the same. Though I longed to remain standing and pace the room, I obeyed. My legs bounced with my anxiety.

Mom took a deep breath and leaned forward. "What I said about some Reapers becoming closed off . . . Well, it's a bit more than that. Some people, when they've been down here for so long, they don't react well to being cut off from humanity."

My brow furrowed, and my heart rate quickened. "What does that mean?"

"It means . . . sometimes, people forget to *feel*. To think like a human. They've been surrounded by death and auras for so long that they've forgotten what it is to be alive."

Horror wrenched through me. My head reared back. "Are you saying this realm is *killing* Reapers?"

Mom shook her head quickly. "No, not like that. Their bodies are fully functional, as is their magic. But they don't . . . respond to situations in the right way."

My mouth opened and closed again as I stared at her, bewildered.

Mom groaned and rubbed her forehead. "Let me give you an example. Let's say Ellis had been in the circle of Reapers with the girl who lost her magic. I imagine he would've attempted to bring her back, like the others. But I also fear he would've given up sooner. Logically, the attempt was futile. But emotionally, Reapers are drawn to the souls we protect. It's part of what motivates us to do our duty. Love for the souls we help.

"Ellis would not have loved that girl. He would've seen her as a task to check off on his list. And once the logical side of his brain registered that she was a lost cause, he would've given up and moved on to something else. He wouldn't have kept up the effort like the other Reapers had."

The idea of becoming an empty, emotionless shell left a sick feeling in my gut. My mouth twisted in a grimace. "But . . . the girl was lost anyway. Right?"

Sorrow filled Mom's gaze. "Yes. But sometimes, we *can* bring them back. Sometimes, even if the odds are against us, we can rescue a soul."

I sucked in a shaky breath. "If Reapers can't do their jobs, why don't you send them back? Help them get their humanity back by going to the mortal realm?"

"It doesn't work like that."

"Why not?"

"I told you, Vince. Once you're here, your magic is bound to this realm. Traveling to other realms is possible, yes, but it's extremely painful. And Reapers like Ellis have no *desire* to go there. If it were part of an assignment, he would do it, but he would come back immediately. Not just because he's drawn here, but because he doesn't want to be anywhere else."

A prison. This place was a prison for him. And he didn't even realize it.

Mom took my hand, and I resisted the urge to shake her off. "This doesn't happen to everyone, Vince. Just a few of our Reapers are like this. But it would probably be best if you kept this to yourself—the magic thief, the loss of humanity, all of it. Reapers like Ellis might not react in the best way, and Reapers like you might start to panic. I don't want there to be discontent among our people."

I stared at her as something hardened in my chest. I truly *had* just exchanged one prison for another. And now my own mother was asking me to lie to keep her secrets.

For the first time since I'd gotten here, I felt I'd made a grave mistake in leaving my clan.

CHAPTER 6

CORA

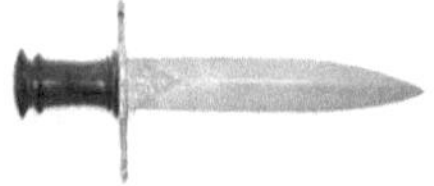

THE CONFERENCE ROOM BUZZED WITH ANTICIPATION. Beside me, Benny stood as erect as I was, though I felt his uncertain gaze boring into me.

I refused to look his way. I knew he had his doubts.

But I felt in my gut this was the right thing to do. This would secure my place in the coven.

It was time to stop hiding.

A crowd stood before us, anxious and restless. And to my left were the four prisoners that had caused so much trouble: Kip, Tucker, Pete, and Conrad. Over the past few months, they'd managed to kill a guard or two in prison. And they'd refused to abide by our coven's new rules. They wanted the freedom to beat up random demons in the street, to pick fights they knew they could win just to boost their egos. It was something Damien

46

had been lax with, but I would have none of it. We didn't need *more* reasons for the other covens to turn against us.

This was their last chance. But I knew by the look on their faces that they would refuse. I wasn't exactly surprised. They'd been Damien's most trusted officials in the coven.

Aside from me and Benny, they were the only ones left.

The thought sent a mixture of sadness and triumph through me. Sadness as I remembered the days when things had been easy and simple. Triumph because Damien's reign would finally end today. And then, the coven could start anew.

When the last member of the coven entered the room, the doors shut behind him, and silence fell. I clasped my hands in front of me and stepped forward to address my people.

"Welcome," I said loudly, spreading my arms. "I know things with the coven haven't been easy lately, but I am grateful for your loyalty and the hard work you've put in. I assure you, things will be changing soon. The transition won't be easy, but it will be worth it. I swear to you I will help this coven thrive again."

"You killed Damien!" a voice bellowed. "How can we trust you?"

Other voices murmured their assent. Beside me, Benny stiffened.

Fire burned in my chest, though I'd expected some resistance. My hands curled into fists at my side. "Damien betrayed us all. He was willing to sell coven secrets for his own benefit. He aligned himself with a *Nephilim clan* to take out members of his own coven."

"So *you* say," snapped another voice in the crowd. "Where's your proof?"

I'd expected this too. I nodded to Benny, who turned to the desk behind us and grabbed a file before lifting it in the air for everyone to see.

"These are Damien's financial records," I said. "All the hits he ordered in the past year, deals he struck with other covens, everything. Any of you are welcome to look through his file and see for yourself. There are transactions to Hector Moses, who was a Nephilim clan leader, as well as proof of extortion of members of our own coven." Members like *me*, I wanted to add. But I figured that wouldn't sit well with this crowd.

It didn't matter. If the demons here were determined to hate me, they could either leave or wait for me to kill them myself. I couldn't force loyalty on my people.

More distrustful murmurs rippled through the crowd. I was losing them.

I cleared my throat loudly and gestured to the four prisoners. Kip's eyes were hard as steel as he glared at me. Pete had the gall to look nervous. His eye-patch was lopsided, and his one eye was wide with fear. Conrad and Tucker almost looked bored.

"These men have had six months to accept me as their leader," I said, my voice ringing in the room. "They have refused and have brought too much tension to our already suffering coven." Slowly, I turned to the prisoners. "This is my final offer. Will you pledge to follow my rules? To accept me as your leader? To live among us in *peace?*"

The crowd stilled, the muttering dying completely as we all waited for an answer.

"Go to hell." Kip spat on the floor at my feet. The others grunted their agreement, glowering at me with eyes full of venom, their expressions unyielding.

I stared at them, my face nothing but a hard mask. Facing the crowd again, I said, "I've been more than patient, waiting for these men to come around. But now, their time is up. Today, they will be executed."

A stunned silence filled the room. Heads turned, but no one made a sound.

"This is a demonstration of what will happen to those who turn against me." My voice was lethal. Here, I channeled my inner assassin. The woman most feared. "And this is the only warning you will receive. If you wish to leave and find another coven, I won't stop you. But you will *not* threaten me or my people. I take care of my own." My voice hardened as I slowly gazed over each member of the crowd, challenging them.

No one would look me in the eye.

A sliver of satisfaction wormed its way into my chest. Power filled me, swirling rapidly, waiting to be unleashed.

I took a deep breath, allowing the tension in the room to simmer just a bit. *Let them fret. Let them squirm.*

I lifted both hands, closed my eyes, and summoned my Bloodcaster magic.

Purple sparks exploded from my hands. The crowd gasped collectively, and some of them shifted as if contemplating fleeing from the room. The lights flickered and went out, leaving only my magic to light the room. I closed my eyes, focusing on the four prisoners, picturing their faces clearly in my mind. Within me, my magic churned hungrily.

Death, I thought.

I slashed my hand through the air. A jet of purple flames sliced through each prisoner like a blade. They crumpled without a sound.

It was so quick that some in the crowd didn't see what happened. I dropped my arms, and the lights flickered back on. Several demons craned their necks to look at the prisoners, who lay motionless on the floor.

I felt Benny's eyes on me, though it was hard to tell if he was pleased or disappointed.

He'd told me I couldn't kill them myself.

But this was different. I'd hidden my identity as a Bloodcaster my whole life. Now, it was time to reveal the truth about myself. I'd only ever killed with a weapon. Never with my own magic.

This coven already suspected who I was after my battle with Damien. This only confirmed it.

I was a blood witch. And I was to be feared.

CHAPTER 7

VINCE

THE SLEEPING QUARTERS REMINDED ME OF MILITARY bunkers. Dozens of bunk beds filled a wide room. No privacy. No bathroom. Mom showed me the washroom down the tunnel, and my head ached with the thought of stumbling my way down there in the middle of the night when nature called.

With every passing hour, I became more and more uncertain about being here.

I spent the next several hours following Mom around, trying to memorize the confusing map of tunnels to follow. Occasionally, we passed other Reapers. Some wore blank expressions like Ellis, and it made me shudder. I'd hoped to pass Jocelyn again, but no such luck. I was desperate to find someone *sane* to talk to about all this.

"What about Hector?" I blurted, interrupting Mom discussing the schedule of meals.

She blinked, her brows knitting together. "What about him?" Her voice was hard.

"You Reapers clearly have a lot of power," I said. "Can't you use your magic to find him? He's still out there."

An unreadable expression crossed Mom's face. "You mean *we* Reapers."

It took a moment for me to realize what I'd said. I shook my head. "Right."

Mom sighed. "We don't deal with mortal messes anymore, Vince."

Indignation roared within me. "But he's a *monster*. Look at what he did to you! What he almost did to me and Dad! How can we just let him go?"

"We're not *letting* anything happen. The magical authorities will take care of him. It's not our problem."

I scoffed. "Yeah, right. He's one of the highest-ranking Nephilim in the world. I doubt the Council will do a damn thing." Last I'd seen, the creepy Timekeepers had shown up and taken him away. He could've been anywhere by now. Luke made it clear Hector couldn't be killed because it would threaten the timeline. Whatever that meant.

Mom grabbed my arm suddenly, her expression cold as ice. "Vince, listen to me. Everything you left behind in that realm *doesn't matter anymore*. Your duty is to the souls of the dead now. That's what a Reaper does. If we fretted over every mortal squabble, we'd never get our job done."

My jaw went rigid, and her words sent an icy shiver through me. How could she say that? I'd left behind my *father*. How could she say he didn't matter? Or Cora? They were the most important people in my life. And so was Mom.

But now, I wasn't so sure she felt the same way.

"Is that the real reason why you never came back to us?" I asked in a quiet voice. "Because Dad and I didn't matter once you became a Reaper?"

Mom's head reared back. "What? Vince—"

"That's what you said. Everything in the mortal realm doesn't matter."

Her mouth opened and closed. Regret filled her eyes, but it mingled with resignation. "I—Yes. I won't sugarcoat it, and I won't lie to you. The work I do as a Reaper is much more important than living a life with you and your father in the mortal realm."

I wrenched my arm free of her grasp. My brain was numb with shock, and for a moment, all I could do was stare at her.

"Don't look at me like that," she said in a low voice. She ducked her head, her nostrils flaring. She seemed angry. But when she looked at me, her eyes were full of sorrow.

Not anger. *Shame*.

"Is this my future?" I asked in a weak voice. "Am I doomed to forget everyone I loved? To stop caring about them at all?" My voice broke on the last word, and I shook my head.

"It's much bigger than that. Just *listen*—" Mom reached for me again, but I stepped away from her. Hurt shone in her eyes. She swallowed. "I still care about you."

Her words sounded so feeble that I laughed without humor. "Right. Very convincing. It's a miracle you've convinced *yourself* all these years."

"No, you don't get to judge me like that," Mom said, her voice harsh. "You have *no* idea what I've been through or what I've done."

"You're right. Because you never bothered to reach out to us! Maybe if you had, we would've had some kind of closure, knowing you'd so easily forgotten us." My heart broke as I said it because no matter what Mom had done, Dad and I would never have gotten over that loss.

Which made this sting worse, knowing Mom was happily fulfilling her duties as a Reaper without a care in the world.

"I *told* you, things are different down here," Mom said. "This realm doesn't work the same way! Over time, you adapt to that way of thinking."

"I don't *want* to!" I shouted, my voice ringing in the tunnels.

"You don't have a choice!" Mom cried. "This is your

life now, Vince. This is what's expected of you. It will be easier with time, and soon you'll forget all about your mortal life."

I gaped at her. "If I'd known that's what I was signing up for, I *never* would've agreed to become a Reaper. I don't want to leave behind my mortal life! You keep telling me I'll adjust, that my magic will change, that *I* will change. But *I don't want to*!"

I stormed away from her, unsure of where I was headed. But I couldn't be around her right now. Fury boiled in my veins, consuming me like a raging fire.

Did she expect me to just hop on board the Reaper train until I turned into an emotionless shell like Ellis? Until I became a willing and obedient servant, imprisoned by the will of whatever the hell sort of magic lived down here?

I couldn't do this. Becoming a Reaper had been a huge mistake.

But I hadn't pledged a vow yet. Maybe I could get back to the mortal realm somehow. Surely, I could find a way.

I left the sleeping quarters, moving toward where I thought the washroom was. But the farther I walked, the more lost I became. The washroom was supposed to be a few paces away from the bunkers, but I'd been walking for ten minutes and hadn't seen it.

My furious stomping faded to a slow trudge, my anger

ebbing. My breathing was still hard and fast, and I longed to grab my crosse and ball and head to the field to play out my frustrations.

Another thing I hadn't considered. I would never get to play lacrosse again. These tunnels didn't really seem like they'd accommodate any physical recreation.

Damn this place. Damn my own stubborn will, thinking I could change things by becoming a Reaper.

I couldn't do anything here. And Hector was still running free. My Nephilim clan was in turmoil, and I couldn't do *anything* about it.

And Lilith knew where my dad was. I hoped he'd found a job and a life. That he wasn't suffering.

"Vince?"

I jumped, whirling to find Jocelyn a few steps behind me, her face blank with shock. I glanced behind her, expecting to see Ellis's creepy face. But she was alone.

"What are you doing here?" we both said at once.

Jocelyn laughed, but I couldn't even crack a smile. Her grin faded, and she stepped closer to me. "What's wrong?"

I shook my head, running a hand through my hair and leaning against the cold metal wall behind me. "I just—I can't do this."

"Do . . . what?"

"Be here. Be a *Reaper.* I'm worried I made a huge mistake, Joss."

Jocelyn was silent, and I couldn't look at her. She'd come here because of me. If I hadn't shattered the façade the clan had built about Reapers, she would've happily pledged to stay.

"What makes you say that?" she finally asked. There was something uncertain in her voice. Something I couldn't place.

I swallowed. "Everything. Mom keeps saying we're going to *change* once we've been here long enough and have adapted. But I don't *want* to change. I don't want to become a zombie like Ellis!"

Jocelyn flinched. "I know."

"She's trying to convince me nothing in the mortal realm matters anymore." My words sounded harsh and bitter.

Jocelyn's blue eyes snapped to me. "I'm guessing it didn't work."

I shot her a flat look, and she chuckled.

"I get it, Vince." She sighed and leaned against the wall next to me. "But we made our choice. We have to accept whatever comes with it."

I stared at her. "Do you really believe that? Don't you think there's a way we can go back? We haven't sworn in yet."

Jocelyn raised an eyebrow. "We can't go back. We might not have sworn in, but by refusing to pledge, we severed ourselves from the clan. There's no coming back from that."

A lump formed in my throat, and I leaned my head back, closing my eyes against the ache in my chest.

"What would you do?" she asked. "If you could go back?"

Be with Cora. The words almost left my lips, but I shoved them back down. Instead, I said, "See my dad. Hunt down Hector. Make things right with the clan."

Jocelyn nodded, her gaze contemplative. "Well, maybe you can do some good *here.*"

I frowned at her. "What do you mean?"

"There might be things *here* that you can make right. Maybe cutting out the mortal realm is something that can be fixed." She shrugged. "Maybe there's a way to merge the two realms so it's easier to access."

I went still at her words. *Merge the two realms.* My blood raced with excitement at the idea.

Suddenly, Jocelyn laughed. "You've got that look. Easy now, Vince. I said *maybe.*"

"But I'm a Jumper," I said. I couldn't hide the eagerness in my voice. "If anyone can do it, it's me, right?"

Jocelyn seemed doubtful. "You must think very highly of yourself."

I shoved her arm. "Come on, Joss." When she continued to look uncertain, my hope faded. "What do *you* think about this place?"

Jocelyn grimaced, gazing around the musty and damp tunnel that surrounded us. "I agree with you. It's weird. But . . ." She exhaled. "Change is always difficult. I don't think I've given it enough time to form an opinion. Yes, there are things that give me pause, like—like Ellis." She shuddered. "But there were worrisome things about the clan. You and I know that better than anyone."

My gaze settled on the dark, stony ground, my thoughts far away. Was I really just being a petulant child, resisting change? Was that how Mom saw me?

But no. My instincts screamed at me that this was wrong. It was something more than my resistance to change. Especially if there was a thief skulking around, robbing souls of their magic.

But maybe Jocelyn was right. Maybe I *could* do something about it.

"Whatever you decide, I'm with you." Jocelyn's eyes were earnest. "If you want to try to find a way back, I promise I'll help you."

My lips tugged with a soft smile. "Why would you do that? You don't owe me anything."

Jocelyn's eyes warmed. "Because that's what friends do, Vince."

CHAPTER 8

CORA

"Have you seen this?"

Benny dropped a stack of papers on my desk. I took a long sip of my coffee, still blinking exhaustion from my eyes. It was too early for this.

I swallowed and said, "Good morning to you too, Benny."

Benny crossed his arms, his eyes flashing. My smile faded. This had to be serious.

Setting my coffee down, I leaned forward and leafed through the stack of papers. When I realized what it was, I laughed and relaxed in my chair. "That's nothing."

"They're *threats*, Cora."

"And I've been threatened before. It's no big deal."

"As a coven leader, it is."

I sighed. He was right. After my little display in the conference room last week, half a dozen demons had opted to leave the coven. As promised, I didn't stop them. The ones that remained seemed too terrified to get within five feet of me.

Which was fine by me.

"They're afraid of you, Cora," Benny said.

I spread my arms. "And?"

Benny rolled his eyes. "A leader should be feared, yes. But they should also be respected and admired. Trusted."

I snorted. "Damien wasn't."

"He was definitely more likable than you are right now."

My smile vanished. Rage boiled through me. How dare he imply that *Damien* was better than I was? Damien was a manipulative pig who thought only of himself.

Before I could retort, Benny lifted his hands in surrender. "*I* like you more than I liked Damien. But your coven doesn't know you like I do. Damien was friendlier. More personable. He let the coven see that side of himself."

I raised an eyebrow. "Are you saying I should go around shaking hands and kissing babies?"

"I'm saying you need to let these people know you. They only see you as a monster who kills people. And while that's good for inspiring fear, it's not great for inspiring loyalty."

I groaned and rubbed my forehead. I *really* didn't

need this right now. Waving a hand, I said, "I'll . . . consider it. But for now, we have bigger problems." Sliding open the drawer next to my feet, I pulled out the coven ledger and handed it to Benny. "Look at the highlighted portion."

Benny took the ledger and frowned, his yellow eyes roving over the numbers. Slowly, his face went slack with shock, then red with fury. "I—" His hard gaze met mine. "Someone's skimming."

I nodded. "Did this happen with Damien?"

"Years ago. He killed the guy."

"Right. That's definitely on my to-do list. But first, we have to *find* the guy."

Benny's eyebrows lifted. "Any idea who it could be?"

I laughed. "Take your pick. I've got lots of enemies."

"Yeah, but who would be stupid enough to steal money from under your nose? Especially after you outed yourself as a Bloodcaster?"

"The ledger indicates it's been going on for a while. We just didn't catch it until now."

Benny leafed through the pages of the ledger, his eyes darkening the longer he looked. "Merciful Lilith. This started *before* Damien died."

"Yeah."

Benny exhaled through his lips. "Who do you think it is?"

"My guess is it's one of the new partners he signed on.

Someone green enough to think they would get away with this."

Benny nodded. "I'll do some digging." He hesitated, his eyes guarded.

"What?" I asked.

"It's just—getting to know the coven better would help you weed out anyone untrustworthy."

I groaned. "Yeah. I know."

Benny's lips spread in a thin line and he nodded again, stiffly this time. "Right. Well, I'd better get to work on this." He lifted the ledger before leaving the office.

I stared at the spot where he'd stood, something uncertain wriggling in my stomach. Benny had seemed reluctant to leave. Had I forgotten something? I mentally sifted through everything we'd discussed, but my head started throbbing, and I couldn't see straight.

"Later," I muttered, leaning forward to go through the mountain of paperwork.

A small *pop* echoed next to me, and I lurched to my feet so violently the desk almost toppled over. Several stacks of paper fell to the floor, but I ignored them, my heart thundering loudly in my chest.

In front of me, his giant dark wings casting shadows on us, stood Vince.

My pulse roared in my ears. I couldn't breathe. Couldn't think.

He was *here*. With me. Right now.

My throat was dry. My arms felt restless at my side. I wanted to run to him, but I remained locked in place.

"Vince," I whispered numbly.

He strode toward the door, and for one wild minute, I thought he was about to leave. But he closed it softly, then turned to face me, his expression grim.

I took in his appearance from his black combat boots to the leather jacket and T-shirt. His hair was shorter than when I last saw him. And a long, thin scar ran from his eye to just above his lip.

The sight stole my breath. This was a warrior, battered by combat.

This wasn't my Vince.

"I don't have much time." He drew closer to me, his steps loud and commanding. His voice was deeper and gruffer.

"Are you really here?" I asked.

He nodded. "But not in the way you think."

I frowned, and then comprehension dawned. "You're a Mimic."

He nodded again.

Something in me deflated. This wasn't the Vince I knew. This was Future Vince. Vince from a different timeline.

So he hadn't found his way back to me.

Vince's eyes softened, and he took my hands in his. His palms were rough and calloused, but they still felt soft against my skin. I closed my eyes, relishing the touch.

"I haven't seen you like this in a while," he murmured. His breath brushed my forehead as he leaned in, pressing his lips into my hair.

I suppressed a shiver of longing. Why did this feel so wrong? Almost like I was cheating on *my* Vince. Taking a breath, I drew back and asked, "Seen me like *what?*"

Vince's brows knitted together. His eyes turned guarded and wary. He shook his head. "Nothing." He cleared his throat. "I'm here to warn you."

I crossed my arms and raised my eyebrows expectantly, trying to squash the desperate ache of longing that was ripping my body in two.

Vince sighed. "You'll see my Mimic soon. The Vince you know."

My heart stuttered, my mouth falling open in shock. *The Vince you know.* My Vince. I would see him soon. Swallowing, I looked at Future Vince, resisting the urge to beg him for more information. When? How? For how long?

"You need to send him back," Vince said.

All hope within me shuddered and died. My chest caved inward. "What?" I breathed.

"He needs to go back to his realm, Cora. When he comes to you, he'll try to stay. You can't let him."

His words gutted me like a knife. My heart twisted painfully. "W-why not?"

"I can't tell you that."

Anger swelled within me, and I stepped closer to him. "Yes, you can. You can't just show up out of the blue when I've been desperate to see you for *months*, drop a warning on my lap, and expect me to just be your obedient little puppy!" My voice rose with each word.

Vince blinked, his head rearing back.

"Now, you tell me what's going on right now, or I swear to Lilith I'll chain him here myself when he shows up." My nostrils flared, and fury coursed through me, fueling my fire.

Vince's eyes darkened for a moment, flashing with something I'd never seen in his face before: a raw, bloodthirsty anger. It chilled me to the bone.

But his expression smoothed quickly, and he nodded stiffly. "Fine. That's fair." He took a breath. "The Reapers need his Teleportation powers. Something big is coming. Something bigger than even the mortal realm. He's one of the few who can travel back and forth. Without him, the Reapers will be trapped. Souls can't move on. Magic is being stolen. The gate between realms is being torn apart."

I stared at him, horrified. It sounded like the apocalypse. "How are we supposed to stop it?"

Vince offered a wry smile. "I don't know. It's still

going on now. But I felt the pull to the timeline. I had to come here to warn you. If I didn't, Vince would stay here, and the Reapers would be cut off forever."

It's still going on now. My eyes widened. "How—when—what year are you from?"

Vince was silent for a moment. "It's been a year since I became a Reaper."

My heart stopped for a full beat. *Six months. In six months, Vince will look like this.*

How did he get his scar?

How did this apocalypse begin?

Had it *already* begun?

"What—what can I do to help?" I asked. "My blood, my potions, surely I can find a way to—"

"No," Vince said sharply. "You can't. This is beyond your magic, Cora. Just make sure my Mimic goes back."

A lump formed in my throat, and I nodded. I wanted to shout at him. To scream that I was powerful, that he had no idea what my magic could do, that I *knew* I could find a way to help. But I also wanted to draw him closer and kiss him so fiercely that my knees would go weak and he would moan with pleasure.

"I know this is hard," Vince said softly. I couldn't tell if he could read the misery on my face or if he knew because he felt the same thing. He clenched his teeth, the veins and tendons standing out in his neck. A violent shudder rippled through him. He teetered, and I caught him by the shoulders.

"Vince!" I cried in alarm.

He shook his head, his eyes distant, and righted himself. "I—I'm out of time. I can't be here any longer." His gaze locked onto mine. "Remember, Cora. I need you to remember. I need you to do this for me."

I nodded. "I will."

With a small *pop*, he vanished, leaving me feeling as empty and cold as if I'd lost Vince all over again.

CHAPTER 9

VINCE

IIT HAD BEEN SEVERAL DAYS SINCE MY FIGHT WITH Mom. We didn't speak of it, but things were cooler than usual between us. I got the impression she didn't know how to handle arguments with me. It was certainly different from when I was a little kid.

I kept close to Jocelyn, even when Ellis was there, giving me the heebie-jeebies. We shared meals, and I sat in on their training. Ellis thought it was important to start mentally preparing her for Reaping duties even before we'd sworn in.

I knew Mom was okay with it because she often sat in on the training sessions to watch. I wasn't sure if she was monitoring me or if she was genuinely curious about how things were going.

Training was really just a form of meditation mingled with yoga, but it was unlike anything I'd ever experienced before. Ellis showed us various back and arm stretches to flex the muscles of our wings—even when they weren't out. By the second training session, Jocelyn's black wings had appeared, garnering applause from Mom and a wide grin from Jocelyn.

I wanted to feel proud. But I couldn't. I felt even worse knowing my own wings had popped out on their own. By accident.

It felt very final to me. Even though I hadn't sworn in yet, it made me feel like I'd sealed my fate as a Reaper.

But, as Jocelyn often reminded me, that ship had sailed. There was no turning back.

"Where do you think all this food comes from?" Jocelyn asked as she spooned soupy porridge into a bowl in the dining quarters.

I sniffed my own food, frowning. It smelled bland. "No idea."

"The magic in the air," said a voice behind us.

I glanced over my shoulder and suppressed a groan. It was Mom.

Jocelyn, however, seemed eager to bring my mother into the conversation. "How does that work?"

"As Reapers, we participate in the circle of life of all magic. When you swear in, your magic is returned to the air of this realm just like everyone else's. It helps power what we do here."

"Like electricity?"

Mom nodded.

Jocelyn exhaled in half shock and half wonder as we found seats at a small table. To my dismay, Mom sat down with us. Jocelyn immediately dug into her food, but I sat up straight, eyeing Mom with suspicion. She caught my gaze and cocked her head at me, a question in her eyes.

"Am I bothering you, Vince?" Her voice was cold.

Irritation flared within me, a normal occurrence these days. How dare *she* treat me with hostility? She'd been the one to admit I hadn't mattered to her. Even while I spent my childhood grieving her.

I didn't answer. Instead, I dropped my gaze and took a bite. The porridge was warm and mushy. Not my favorite texture, but the taste was bearable.

Jocelyn, sensing the tension between Mom and me, quickly dived in with a question about the dark wings and if they differed from white wings. The answer, of course, was no, but Mom replied anyway to keep the conversation going.

I wasn't sure if I should feel grateful for Jocelyn keeping the awkwardness at bay, or angry that she was giving Mom more opportunities to linger.

When another lull hit the conversation, Mom asked carefully, "I was wondering when you two would feel comfortable pledging your vow to the Reapers."

Never, I thought bitterly, but I swallowed down the retort.

Jocelyn pressed her lips together and met my gaze with unease. I felt a small surge of relief, knowing I wasn't the only one here with doubts.

"It's all right if you aren't ready," Mom said quickly. "But just know that life here will be very boring for you until you *do* swear in."

"What happens if we don't?" I couldn't hide the bite in my tone.

Mom's eyes flashed. "Then you'll be trapped here as a powerless Reaper."

"Powerless?" I raised my eyebrows. "So, you'll strip us of our powers?"

Mom's face paled. "What? No! I just mean that until you swear in, you won't have access to all the Reaper abilities."

Interesting. So, I could still use my warlock powers even if I hadn't sworn in yet . . . I kept my face carefully neutral as I took another bite.

"Has anyone ever refused to swear in?" Jocelyn asked, her voice hushed.

"No. But some have taken quite a while to come to terms with it. We're willing to wait as long as it takes. No rush." She widened her eyes pointedly at me, no doubt emphasizing how different this place was from my former Nephilim clan.

I still wasn't so sure.

More silence. This time, Jocelyn was too preoccupied to fill it. Her brow was furrowed, and she chewed on her lower lip as she gazed distantly around the room. I could tell her thoughts were elsewhere.

Mom cleared her throat and rose from her seat. "I'll, uh, leave you to enjoy your meal." I felt her gaze on me for a long moment, but I avoided it, focusing instead on my food. Finally, she turned and left, and I exhaled with relief.

"How long are you going to stay angry at her?" Jocelyn asked in a whisper.

I shook my head. "I don't know. An apology would be nice. But I guess that's asking for too much."

Jocelyn snorted. "Parents are never wrong, Vince. You might be waiting an eternity for that apology."

I looked at her, but she dropped her gaze. I thought of her own father, Peter Wilkes, who had worked so closely with Hector. The whole panel of clan officials had been narcissistic and patronizing. I could only imagine what it was like to have one of them as a parent. I could easily envision Peter never admitting failure. Just like Hector.

Something within me softened. "I'm sorry. I shouldn't be complaining. It must be so hard for you, Joss."

She offered a wobbly smile. "It's okay." She paused and took a deep breath. "I just feel so . . . conflicted.

Like, I know I *shouldn't* miss my dad, given everything he did and all the lies he spread. But I can't help it." She shrugged, her eyes moistening. "He's my dad. He'll always be a part of me."

Warmth filled my throat. I reached forward and took her hand in mine. "I'm here for you."

Her smile turned more genuine, and she sniffed. "Thanks."

Ellis and Mom badgered us twice more that day about when we would pledge. Each time they asked, I grew more irritable. I was starting to understand why all the Reapers in the past had eventually given in. Maybe they'd just wanted everyone else to shut up and stop pestering them.

After the third time, I finally gave in. "Two days," I snapped at Ellis. "I'll pledge in two days."

"Me too," Jocelyn said at once, her eyes meeting mine. She nodded slightly as if to say, *I'm with you.*

Ellis merely gazed at us, his expression as blank as ever. Then, he turned and walked away. I pictured his steps disjointed and robotic like a giant machine, but he moved with grace and agility just like all the other Reapers.

"You seemed to give in pretty easily," Jocelyn said with raised eyebrows as she sat down on her bunk bed.

I glanced around the sleeping quarters to ensure we were alone before I knelt on the floor next to her. She perked up, her eyes glinting with excitement as if we were about to share secrets together.

"I'm going to try to Jump," I whispered.

Jocelyn's face turned white. "*What?*"

"I have to know if I can before I commit to staying here. I have to know if there's a way back on my own."

Jocelyn shook her head. "Vince—"

"Aren't you tired of your life being decided for you?" I hissed through clenched teeth. "You either swear in with the clan or swear in with the Reapers. There are no more choices! Just two very different prisons."

"But isn't it like that for everyone?" Jocelyn asked. "Every magical being has rules to follow, Vince."

I suddenly thought of Cora, and my chest ached with the usual yearning I felt when she crossed my mind. Cora played by her own rules. I'd always envied that. Most demons were rule-breakers. It didn't seem very fair to me.

Soft footsteps approached. My head whipped around, looking for eavesdroppers, but it was just another Reaper. A tall, bulky blond named Jonas. He dug through the bag by his bed, ignoring us completely.

I swallowed and leaned closer to Jocelyn. "Do you want to be there when I try it?" I breathed.

Jocelyn's eyes were alight with a mixture of curiosity and fear. Slowly, she nodded.

"Meet me in the dining hall after lights out," I said quietly.

She nodded again, and a slow smile spread across her face. I realized I was only inches away from her. Her breath tickled my cheeks, and her eyes stirred with desire.

No. The word coursed through me before I could even process anything. Slowly, I drew away from her and dropped my gaze. My chest tightened, and my stomach spun. I wasn't sure what to feel. I liked Jocelyn, but not like that.

And even if I *did* like her in that way, my heart and head were still consumed by Cora.

Emotion climbed up my throat, choking me. I barely muttered a hasty goodbye before I bolted from the room, eager to escape the thoughts and confusion raging within me.

A restless, anxious energy swept through me for the rest of the day. There was no way to measure time in the tunnels. And even if there was, it probably wouldn't be accurate, given everything I'd learned about this realm. I performed the usual stretches with Ellis, even though my legs ached to sprint away, to exert myself with vigorous exercise instead of these slow, careful movements. I longed to run, to sweat, to strategize, to *play*.

If you figure out how to Jump back home, then you will, I told myself. I clung to the idea as the hours trudged by.

I sat with Jocelyn at dinner, though neither of us could eat much. We remained quiet, our eyes drifting around the room before settling back on each other, wordlessly communicating the gravity of what we were about to do.

Why did I feel so afraid? I wasn't breaking any rules. Mom had said it herself: we were welcome to use our magic here. This was supposed to be how Reapers were different from the Nephilim clans.

Even so, ripples of unease coursed through me like a dark omen of things to come.

At long last, the Reapers retired to the sleeping quarters. Some lingered, chatting or reading, and I resisted the urge to shout at them. I lay stiffly in my bed, my gaze fixed on the bunk above me, waiting. Agitation surged inside me. I gritted my teeth. My head throbbed.

Finally, the lights went out. Still, I waited. The beds creaked as the others got comfortable. Gradually, soft snores filled the room, echoing in the dark chamber.

My blood thrummed with anticipation as I eased out of bed. My eyes had adjusted, and the faint glow of the lanterns in the hall lit my path as I dodged the beds to escape the bunker. I waited in the tunnel just outside the sleeping quarters. When I heard the soft patter of Jocelyn's footsteps, my heart skittered.

She appeared, her red hair wild around her face and her eyes alight with excitement. "Ready?" she whispered.

I nodded, and together we crept down the tunnel. Each noise made me jumpier, reminding me that I was doing something I shouldn't. But my determination fueled me. I *had* to try.

We'd been here long enough to find our way to the dining hall without getting lost. The space was dark and empty like a vast abyss that would swallow us whole. I suddenly felt uncertain about using this area to practice Jumping. But we couldn't exactly use the living quarters, and this was the closest space where we wouldn't disturb anyone.

"What do we do first?" Jocelyn asked, her voice trembling.

I swallowed. If I wanted to time travel, I needed an anchor. From within my pocket, I pulled out a balled-up T-shirt—the same one I'd worn when I first arrived here. It smelled of sweat and pine trees and *home*. The bitter nostalgia clamped down on me, unyielding. Emotion built up in my throat, and I sucked in a deep breath. I'd worn this shirt on the last day I'd seen my dad.

I closed my eyes, gripping the fabric tightly in my fist as I imagined that day.

Just let me go back, I pleaded. *Let me see Dad and Cora one more time. Please.*

"Stand back," I told Jocelyn. I heard her scuffle away from me. I took another breath and envisioned the lacrosse field. The morning dew still clung to the blades of grass beneath my feet. Sweat and dirt coated my skin like a second layer. Adrenaline pulsed through me. In my hands, I gripped my crosse, my palms calloused and ready.

I searched the field, looking for my teammates. Usually, when I went into my imagination like this, the faceless opponents and teammates surrounded me. Luke had been the only one familiar.

Now, it was only me. No one else.

Unease spread through me. Could I still do this without other players? I swung my crosse tentatively, but nothing happened.

There was no ball. Everything here was just . . . empty. Like a switch had been turned off.

No, I thought in horror.

I gazed around the field, desperately searching for something. *Anything.*

"Hello?" I called.

"Looking for this?"

I whirled around. My heart lodged itself in my throat. Across from me stood Luke, though he wore street clothes, his face and arms clean of dirt and grass. In his hand, he held the lacrosse ball. His eyebrows lifted expectantly.

My throat felt dry. "Luke," I said. Seeing my old friend reminded me of my former life—before time travel, before Hector's betrayal, before the Ceremonial Rite. Relief swelled in my chest, and I took a step toward him.

Luke smiled and lifted his chin, his dreadlocks bobbing. "Long time." His eyes were guarded, and the smile didn't quite reach his eyes. I wasn't used to seeing his face look like that. He'd always been the goofball.

Now, he was something else entirely.

"What—what's going on?" I asked, gesturing to the empty field.

"Your powers don't work the same way anymore."

I was getting so sick of people saying that. "What does that even *mean*? They still *work*, right? How do I do this?"

Luke shrugged, and my frustration mounted. "I'm just a guide. I've never Jumped before."

"Some help you are," I muttered.

Luke sighed. "You had to use an anchor before, right? To ground you like gravity. Well, in your realm, gravity works differently. You have to abide by those rules and find a way."

In your realm. The Astral Realm was *not* my realm. It wasn't my home.

"How does gravity work differently?" I asked. "If it didn't work, I'd just be floating."

"Unless there's something else grounding you."

I remembered what Mom had said about reaping magic from a soul. The magic returned to the air where it could be used freely by everyone. She claimed my warlock magic would do the same thing.

Magic surrounded the Reapers like a living thing. A blanket of power and energy.

"It's magic," I said softly. "Magic grounds us."

Luke's brows knitted together.

"Can I use *magic* as an anchor?" I asked.

Luke immediately shook his head. "No. If magic is your anchor, you risk damaging *all* the magic in the realm. You'll mark it, just like you marked Hector."

I flinched, then cursed myself for it. I didn't regret what I'd done to Hector. He'd been about to kill me. Frustration mounted within me. "You know, you're spouting a *lot* of rules without offering anything helpful."

"Don't shoot the messenger, man."

The words were so easy, so *normal,* I found myself grinning without realizing it. Remembering my situation, the smile slid off my face. "Why are you here, Luke?"

"I told you, you and I are bound."

"Yes, but *why?*"

"A spell was cast, binding us together. I don't know the details—I was really young when it happened. But even if I wanted to, I couldn't withdraw from you."

A spell was cast. Who would've done that? Who had that kind of power? And *why* would they do it?

I dropped my crosse and rubbed my forehead. "Look, I just want to get out of here. Can't you help me at *all?*"

"I already told you I *don't know.* You're the Jumper. And I've never been to the Astral Realm."

"Well, what do your creepy Timekeepers have to say about it?"

Luke's gaze shifted slightly, his eyes tightening. Ah, finally, a reaction. "They don't say anything about it."

"I find that hard to believe."

"Contrary to what you might think, the world doesn't revolve around you, Vince. Once you left the mortal realm, you were no longer on their radar."

I frowned. "So Timekeepers can't travel to other realms?"

Luke hesitated. "I didn't say that."

Something sparked in my mind. Of *course* Timekeepers could travel to different realms. Their powers were similar to mine. And Luke all but admitted that they could.

"Can you bring one of them here?" I asked eagerly. "Maybe one of them can show me—"

"Vince, *no*!" For the first time, Luke looked nervous, his gaze floating around the field as if expecting someone else to show up. "You can't talk about them. They'll *hear* you."

I wanted to laugh. But the severity of his words sent a chill racing down my spine. *They'll hear you.* Suddenly, I looked around too, the back of my neck prickling like someone was watching me.

I swallowed and drew closer to Luke. "What am I supposed to do? Just go back to the Astral Realm and sign my life over to this prison?"

Luke's lips spread into a sympathetic grimace. "That's the path you chose."

I lifted my arms and let them fall. "That's hardly a *choice*! Imprisonment in Hector's clan, or imprisonment with the Reapers!"

"Don't be so dramatic. It's not a prison. And you weren't a prisoner in the clan, either. You still had a *life*. Now, you'll just have to learn how to make one here."

I shook my head, staring at him numbly. "So, you won't help me at all?"

"I'll always help you, Vince. But I can't do the impossible. You have to tap into your magic your own way."

I remained silent, something in me deflating. Luke held my gaze, offering a sympathetic smile.

"Why did you lie to me?" I whispered. "All those years growing up when I thought we were friends."

"We *were* friends."

"So, why didn't you tell me? I told you *everything*." My chest ached as I spoke, and I swallowed hard.

Luke sighed, his cool exterior fading. Sorrow gleamed in his eyes. "The Timekeepers forbade me from telling you. They said it would alter the timeline if you knew. I'm really sorry, Vince. More than anything, I wanted to tell you."

I found myself nodding, though I didn't know why. If anyone could understand being bound by rules and laws they didn't understand, it was me. I wasn't sure when, but I'd already forgiven Luke. My predicament with the Reapers made all my other problems seem small in comparison.

The field around us faded. I could feel my consciousness drifting between Luke and the dining hall with Jocelyn.

"No," I said desperately. "I need more time. Luke—"

"It'll be all right, Vince." Luke's voice grew faint.

"I—I wish you were here. *Really* here with me."

"So do I."

I closed my eyes, trying to ward off the tears that threatened to spill.

"Choose your own way," Luke said, his voice like a

whispering wind. "Stop seeing a prison and start seeing the possibilities."

He vanished, leaving me standing in front of Jocelyn, my eyes burning as they adjusted to the darkness. My palms were slick with sweat, and I was breathing heavily.

"Did it work?" Jocelyn asked.

A hard lump formed in my throat. Despair crashed through me, dragging my heart down like an anchor.

"No," I whispered numbly. "No, it didn't work."

CHAPTER 10

CORA

I COULDN'T SLEEP. ANYTIME I CLOSED MY EYES, I SAW Vince's face. That expression, hardened by grief and trauma. The long, jagged scar on his face.

One year. That was all it took to alter him so much. To think his goodness, his innocence was so fragile that it could be shattered in merely a year made me shiver.

But who was I to talk? I'd seen it all. I'd been a killer most of my life.

Deep down, I knew I couldn't judge Vince. I didn't know what he'd been through.

But part of what had initially drawn me to him was his innate kindness. His determination to see the good in people. Even in a monster like me.

Had whatever trauma he'd endured changed that? Would he see me differently now?

You're an idiot, Cora, I thought irritably. *Of course he won't see you differently. You changed, too, and you still love him.*

I'd just given up on sleep and tossed aside my blanket in frustration when my cell phone rang. It was loud, shrill, and obnoxious, and it made me jump, reaching for my dagger. Once I realized what it was, I relaxed, and anger rose up inside me. Benny had insisted I get this stupid phone in case of emergencies. I usually never carried one. It was just one more way for people to find me when I wanted to stay hidden.

I took a deep breath, pressed the phone to my ear, and grunted, "What?"

"You'd better get here. Quick." I recognized Benny's gruff voice.

I straightened, and an icy chill of foreboding swept over me. "Get *where*?"

"The office." A small *click*, and Benny hung up.

My mouth fell open as I stared numbly at the phone. The office? What the hell was going on there in the middle of the night?

Urgency pulsed through my veins. I quickly dressed and armed myself before darting out the apartment. It didn't take me long to reach the set of office buildings the coven owned. And even before I got there, I knew something was off.

Smoke filled the air. Well, more than usual. On this side of New Jersey, the air was always filthy. But sparks and ash floated in front of me, and the closer I got, the thicker the smoke became.

I quickened my steps, practically sprinting down the sidewalk. My pulse thundered in my ears, a warning rhythm that something was very, very wrong.

I rounded the corner, and my heart shuddered. My eyes widened, my body stiffening in shock. My blood ran cold.

The office building was on fire.

A small crowd filled the parking lot. Many of them wielded weapons. A gunshot fired in the air, and I lunged forward.

"Stop!" I roared, racing toward the mob. I quickly found Benny and hurried to his side. A long, bloody gash lined his cheek, and white fur coated his arms—a sign of his transition to wolf form.

Benny normally had no problem keeping his cool. If his wolf was starting to emerge, I didn't want to think about what the crowd had done to him.

I looked him over, searching for any urgent injuries.

"I'm all right," he said, answering my unspoken question.

"Why didn't you call sooner?" I demanded, tugging him away from the crowd. Several men grabbed Benny's arm, intent on keeping him there, but I raised my free hand and shot a burst of purple magic. The demons flew backward, releasing their grip on Benny.

"I thought I had it handled," Benny said.

I gritted my teeth and shot him a sharp look. "Even if you *did* have it handled, you still should've called me."

Benny was panting. He met my gaze, but his eyes were tired and resigned. "I know."

"You can't just walk away from us!" roared a voice behind me.

Fury exploded within me. I released Benny's arm and whirled to face the angry crowd. "You want to stop me?" I shouted. "I'd like to see you try. Go ahead!" I raised my arms expectantly.

The man—Finn, a dark warlock—hesitated. He wielded a pistol, and his fierce gaze was contorted with rage. But he knew he couldn't take me.

"Is this what you wanted?" I yelled, gesturing to the burning building. In the distance, sirens echoed, but I knew it was too late. The offices would be reduced to ash. "Are you satisfied with your little temper tantrum? Or do you still need to let out some frustration?" I stepped forward, drawing my knives and stakes before dropping them to the ground with a loud clatter. "I'll even make it easier for you. Now, I'm unarmed. Have at it."

A few demons glanced at each other warily as if sensing a trap.

"Well?" I practically screamed. "Why else are you here, if not to fight me? Why would you torch this place if you didn't have a problem with me? It's all out in the open now. Let's hear it!"

Some of the demons shifted uncomfortably. Then, a loud voice cried, "You aren't fit to lead us."

The voice was deep but distinctly female. I squinted, trying to see through the crowd. The coven didn't have many women in it.

A spark of bright purple hair caught my eye. It was Piper, a dark witch who'd joined the coven just before Damien's death. I didn't know much about her, just that she was powerful and could hold her own in a fight. If anything, I admired her—until now.

I raised my eyebrows. "Oh? And why not?"

"You're a merciless *killer*," she snarled. "You don't see the problems right in front of you. All you see are your next targets."

"Who do you think *assigned* those targets?" I snapped. "You think I was just killing for fun?"

"That's not the point," another man said. "Killing is all you know how to do. But Damien, he *knew* us. He cared about us."

"He was willing to turn you over to the Nephilim!" I argued.

Shouts mingled as several demons cried out in outrage, clearly unconvinced of my claims of Damien's betrayal. I had to scream until my throat was raw to get them to quiet down.

"Okay, clearly you have a problem with me," I said hoarsely. "So you decide to *burn down the building*? How does that help?"

"You think we're stupid enough to confront *you*?" Piper screeched. "You demonstrated your power with the execution. We knew you'd only see a confrontation as another opportunity for spilled blood."

More voices shouted their assent. I went very still. Though anger still quivered through me, something small and logical pierced through the haze of my thoughts.

You did this, the voice said. *You wanted them to fear you. Well, good job. Now, they do.*

But they didn't respect me. Benny was right. I didn't know them at all. And they didn't know me.

So, naturally, they relied on their fear and let it completely take over.

A hard lump formed in my throat. A desperate urge rose within me, the desire to *fix* this. But it seemed broken beyond repair. What could I do?

"Cora," Benny groaned beside me. I glanced at him and found him leaning against a lamppost for support, clutching his side. The sirens in the distance grew louder.

Many in the crowd shifted restlessly, no doubt nervous about the authorities showing up. It was no secret that most of the demons here were criminals. It was why we lived in Hinport, after all.

I had to do something about this. *Now.*

"Look." I licked my lips. Even *I* could hear the note of desperation in my voice. "I'm still new at this. You're angry, I get it. You're confused and worried. I may not have been listening before, but I *am now*. Come back here at noon tomorrow. I'll be here to listen to your complaints."

"You expect us to believe you won't hurt us?" Finn scoffed.

"Yes," I said sharply. "Because I swear it. And if I *do* hurt any of you, you have my permission to gang up on me and execute me yourselves."

I heard Benny's sharp intake of breath behind me, but I ignored him.

Some of the men looked at me doubtfully.

"I may be powerful, but I can't take on twenty at once," I added.

Mutters rippled through the crowd. The sirens were so loud they blared against my ears. Already, demons were peeling off and disappearing into the street, afraid of being caught.

"Give me a chance," I begged. "Please. I just want what's best for the coven."

More demons rushed off. But within the crowd, a strong voice shouted, "I'll be here."

It was Piper. Shock flared within me, followed by an unfamiliar emotion: gratitude.

After Piper's comment, several others followed. An

echo of agreement passed over the crowd, and I exhaled with relief.

Bright blue and red lights flashed, and the crowd scattered.

I grabbed Benny's elbow and tugged him into the shadows. Summoning my magic, I murmured,

"Magic above and powers that be,

Conceal us from this enemy."

A faint purple glow emanated from my hands before surrounding Benny and me. I gripped his arm tightly, keeping us pressed up against the building, concealed by shadows and my cloaking spell. Benny was stiff, his body tense and his breathing short and ragged.

I shot a glance at him, then noticed the stain of blood on his shirt. "Liar," I whispered. "You are *so* not all right."

"I'll be fine," he rasped.

"Let me heal you."

"I'm serious, Cora."

"So am I. I don't want you bleeding out on the street."

Benny looked at me, his face paler than usual. A sheen of sweat coated his forehead. "How long do we have to stay here?"

I looked at the two police cars. A fire truck pulled into the parking lot behind them. A few cops surrounded the building. One of them darted off in the opposite direction, no doubt trying to chase down the demons who had fled.

"I think we're good now." I tugged on his arm, dragging him down the alley between two buildings and away from the chaos behind us.

After taking Benny to my place to give him a healing elixir, I went back to the office building to assess the damage.

As I feared, all that remained was charred rubble.

I stared at the smoking husk that once had been the headquarters for our coven, and emotion unexpectedly built in my throat.

It was just a building. Nothing to be sentimental about.

But I remembered when Damien had bought this building. It had been a huge step for us. He and I had taken down a corrupt demon coven and started from the ground up. Buying this property had made it official.

I remembered the gleam in his eye, the proud smirk on his face that I once mocked.

Now, a new kind of emotion filled my chest. Regret. A deep, raw ache for what had once been. The eagerness that Damien and I shared. Our aligned goals and dreams for the coven.

When had it all changed?

The day Damien had ordered the hit on Vince had changed things for me. But for Damien, it must've happened before then. Gradually. A little power here and there, mixed with greed and ambition. He'd probably thought he was doing it all for the good of the coven.

Just like me.

It was a lie we told ourselves. It was really for *our* own good. Nobody else mattered.

My eyes stung. I wanted to blame the ash in the air, but the moisture blurred my vision, and a tear slid down my cheek.

Killing is all you know how to do. But Damien, he knew us. He cared about us.

The coven had been right. I didn't know them or care about them. I hadn't even bothered to try.

My whole life had been a battle. Year after year, I struggled to keep myself hidden from the world. To isolate myself from everyone for my own safety.

That had to end if I wanted to lead these people. Opening up about my magic had been the right idea, but I'd executed it horribly. I'd used it to inspire fear instead of respect.

I didn't *need* these people to fear me. They already did.

But they didn't know me. And for me to succeed, that had to change.

For the next few hours, my body was restless. I itched to hunt. To fight something. And the tighter the ball of energy grew within me, the more I realized this had contributed to the problem.

I'd been an assassin for so long that I'd depended on it as a form of release. And when I became coven leader, that release had been taken away. I hadn't found anything to replace it with.

So, I'd relied on that part of me even when I shouldn't have.

I needed a new outlet.

After briefly returning to my apartment to change, I laced up the running shoes I rarely wore and started sprinting. My feet knew the neighborhood well—all the alleys and shadows that would keep me concealed. But today, I didn't care who saw me.

I was certainly no runner. Within a few minutes, my legs started to burn and a stitch formed in my side. But the pain was bracing. Like a splash of cold water. I reveled in it.

My legs pumped harder. Farther. Sweat poured down my face and neck. My breathing turned sharp and winded. The more I ran, the more tension I released. Push, push, push. Faster, faster, faster. Each breath was a slice in my lungs. The cool air was biting against me, but my body felt burning hot.

I ran until I couldn't breathe. Until black spots

danced in my vision. Until the cramps in my side and legs were so severe I almost fell over. When I stopped, my legs still felt like they were in motion, carrying me away. I doubled over, clutching at my side and resisting the urge to collapse right there.

It felt liberating. Exhilarating. The familiar thrill of the chase coursed through me, but it was different this time. There was no threat; no danger. Somehow, I assumed I needed both in order to feel this way.

I was wrong.

Like Vince, I found solace in the exercise. In pushing myself and relishing the exertion.

My chest ached with a new kind of pain, but I welcomed that too. *Vince.* His hardened expression swam in my mind, and I closed my eyes.

Dive into the pain, I told myself. *This is your release, Cora.*

And so I did.

I didn't have time to change or shower before meeting my coven. So, I arrived at the smoking remains of the office building in my tank top and shorts, still covered in sweat. I was sure my face was beet-red and my hair a tangled, sweaty mess. But I didn't care.

A few people had already gathered in front of the building, including Benny. I recognized Finn and another warlock named Perry. They stood off to the side, casting dark looks toward Benny. The werewolf looked better than when I left him, but his face was still haggard. He turned when he saw me, his eyes wide as he took in my appearance. Something darkened in his eyes as he drew nearer.

"What happened?" he demanded. "Are you hurt?"

I choked out a laugh, still winded from my run. "Hardly. I went . . . running." The words sounded so forced, so strange coming from my lips.

Benny noticed. His head reared back, and his eyes narrowed as he scrutinized me as if trying to tell if I was kidding.

I just grinned at him, but that only made him more suspicious.

"You sure you're all right?" he asked.

I nodded, feeling freer than I had in days. Part of me wanted to explain it to him, to share this feeling of euphoria with someone. But another part of me wanted to keep it to myself. My own private sanctuary.

So, I said nothing else to Benny and instead turned to Finn and Perry. They, too, eyed me warily.

"Perry. Finn." I nodded at them. "Thank you for coming."

Surprise flitted across their faces, and they glanced at each other for a moment. Finn recovered first and nodded stiffly, his jaw rigid. But Perry watched me for a moment longer, his expression unreadable.

He knew I was different. I wasn't sure what to make of it, either. I wasn't the reserved, isolated, intimidating killer they'd seen last night.

This was a completely different Cora. And it was frightening and exciting all at once.

A few minutes later, a dozen more demons arrived, including Piper. I made sure to greet each of them by name and offer a smile. Ordinarily, it would feel forced. But after my run, keeping a pleasant expression felt natural.

Endorphins, probably.

When I was certain no one else was coming, I stood in front of the building where the entrance had once been and cleared my throat loudly. The chatter around me faded, and everyone watched me expectantly. Though some of them glared with hostility, the air felt calmer. More collected. Even Piper watched me with a neutral expression. The venom from earlier had completely vanished from her gaze.

I drew courage from that before I spoke. "I know I don't deserve another chance. The coven has been a mess since I took over. And I'm sorry. You're right. I didn't know how to be a leader. In some ways, I still don't. But I'm willing to improve if you'll let me.

"Times are hard. Like I told you before, if you don't feel comfortable staying in the coven, I won't judge you for leaving. But unlike before, I promise not to rule by fear and violence. Those of you here with me right now have remained loyal to the coven, and you'll be rewarded for that.

"I want this to work. I want to help restore this coven to its former glory. But I can't do it without you. I *need* you on my side.

"One more chance. That's all I'm asking for. If you leave, that's fine. But if you give me one more chance, I swear I'll make this work. We can rebuild this coven together, one step at a time."

I fell silent, unsure of how to finish my speech. The words had poured from my mouth on their own, but now that I was done, reality crashed back into me. A wave of uncertainty rose up inside me. *I can't do this,* a small voice said in my mind. *I can't.*

"I'll stand with you," said a voice. I didn't need to look up to know it was Benny.

Though I'd expected his loyalty, I still offered a small smile.

Then, to my surprise, Piper chimed in, "Me too."

Finn, Perry, and the others all murmured their assent.

The hostility in their eyes was gone, replaced by a cautious optimism. There was still tangible tension in the air.

But for now, we were united. And this coven still stood a chance.

CHAPTER 11

VINCE

I STOOD IN THE KITCHEN OF OUR TINY HOME IN Ravenbrooke. Dad stood in front of me, his eyes kind and full of affection. "You're not clearing your head," he said gently.

"I'm trying!"

"Vince, don't get mad. Focus."

I gritted my teeth, biting back a growl. How could I focus when I was getting so frustrated?

Dad sighed, but it wasn't out of impatience. He watched me with a calm, steady gaze, and for some reason, this only made me angrier.

"Tell me, when do you feel most calm?" Dad asked.

I glared at him. "What does that have to do with anything?"

"Humor me."

I groaned. "When I'm sleeping."

"Besides that."

I rubbed my forehead. "I don't know, uh, when I'm watching TV? Or reading?"

Dad nodded, his eyes contemplative. "Let's go do that." He led me from the kitchen and into the living room. Though bills and papers were strewn all over the coffee table, he still sat me down on the sofa and took a seat next to me. As casually as if it were a normal Saturday afternoon, he clicked on the TV. One of our favorite sitcoms was on.

Dad relaxed against the couch, crossing his arms and lifting his feet on the coffee table. Though I stared hard at him, his gaze remained idly on the TV.

My nostrils flared, and I glowered, determined to remain upset. But silence fell between us, and I found myself listening to the dialog. Each time the laugh track hit, something within me loosened just a fraction.

We sat there watching for ten minutes. When I laughed out loud, Dad muttered quietly, "Picture the field, Vince. See it in your mind. Now, go there."

I stilled, my body still relaxed on the couch. Focus, *a voice inside me said.* Focus.

Keeping my body loose and casual, I slowly closed my eyes and pictured the lacrosse field Dad often took me to. I breathed in and out again. Before realizing what was happening, I was on my feet. I turned in place. A small pop *rang in my ears—*

I woke with a jolt, my heart thundering in my chest. My eyes opened, and I imagined I'd find Dad sitting right next to me, his eyes gleaming with pride.

But no. Dad wasn't here. I would never see him again.

Instead, Mom's pale face loomed over me. She softly shook my shoulders, and I faintly registered she'd been trying to wake me.

Disappointment and grief flooded my chest. I turned away from her, feeling like a petulant child.

But I didn't care. Right now, her face was the last one I wanted to see. I longed to dive back into the memory of Dad teaching me how to Jump on my own for the first time. I'd been ten years old. The memory was as clear as if it had happened yesterday. I just wanted to go back. To be with him, even if our home was a dump and the clan treated us like dirt.

"It's time, Vince," Mom murmured, jolting me from my anguished thoughts.

My heart stopped for a full beat.

It's time.

Time to swear in. Time to plunge my life onto another path I didn't want. Away from the people I loved.

Time to resign myself to living in this realm forever.

I wanted to scream. To throw things. To grab my mother by the shoulders and knock some sense into her. How could everyone here be so *insane*?

"Vince," Mom said again. A hint of impatience touched her tone.

I slowly turned to face her. When I met her gaze,

uncertainty stirred in her eyes, followed by raw emotion and vulnerability.

She was nervous for me. And in her eyes, I saw the devastation from the distance that had grown between us.

This wasn't her fault. And I *had* agreed to swear in.

That had been before my failed Jump. I'd been so sure I could leave.

But Luke had been right. I had to accept this choice I'd made.

With a heavy sigh, I sat up, my body stiff and my mind still reeling from the vivid dream. A hard lump formed in my throat. For the millionth time, I wished my dad were here. He always emphasized that this was *my* life. *My* choice. And I should always make those choices regardless of how he felt about it.

Make your choices, Vince, Dad had said. *But face the consequences too. Every choice has repercussions you don't always know about. Face them like a man, head-on.*

I swallowed and inhaled a shaky breath. Over Mom's shoulder, I saw Jocelyn. Her hair was a wet curtain down her back as she slid on a light jacket. I assumed she'd just showered. Her movements were shaky, and when she turned, her eyes caught mine.

Her lips quivered, but her chin lifted. Determination gleamed in her eyes. She nodded at me.

I nodded back.

After I'd dressed, Mom led me and Jocelyn past the dining hall. At first, the tunnel seemed unfamiliar. But once we arrived in the small room with a slab of concrete in the middle, I realized I'd been here before—when that girl's spirit had vanished into nothingness after her magic had been stolen.

The memory sent a ripple of emotions coursing through me, but guilt was at the forefront. Guilt over my own childish resistance. My petty desire to have the life I wanted.

Meanwhile, souls were falling into extinction, never to be seen again. The elusive magic thief was still cutting away these auras.

While I'd been whining about going home, the souls were suffering. Souls who needed my help.

I squared my shoulders, my resolve hardening within me. I remembered Luke's words: *Stop seeing a prison and start seeing possibilities.*

Perhaps I was here for a reason. Perhaps I *could* make a difference.

Cool fingers slid against mine. I started, turning to find Jocelyn right next to me, offering a hesitant smile. I swallowed and squeezed her hand.

Her presence comforted me. I wasn't alone in this. It reminded me of the Ceremonial Rite when we'd made the same choice together.

"Which of you will go first?" a strong voice rang out. I

looked around and found Gwen Peters standing in front of the circle of Reapers, her cold blue eyes shifting between me and Jocelyn.

"I will," I said at once. Jocelyn looked surprised, but I nodded before stepping forward. In a way, I felt responsible for Jocelyn being here. Though I knew she'd made the choice, I didn't think she would've if I hadn't done the same.

"Lie on the altar." Gwen gestured to the slab of concrete in the middle.

I stared at it. *Altar.* As in . . . for sacrifices? My stomach churned at the thought.

The circle of Reapers watched me expectantly. I took a deep breath and strode forward before carefully reclining against the rock. The cold stone pressed into my back and made me shiver. I stared at the dome-shaped ceiling, trying to ignore the goosebumps springing along my arms.

Footsteps shuffled around me. I wanted to glance around to see, but my vision was limited. The Reapers surrounded me, their black wings rippling against each other. I searched for Jocelyn's familiar flame of hair but couldn't find her.

My eyes settled on Mom. She watched me with a blank expression. I wasn't sure what I'd hoped to find in her face—pride? Uncertainty?—but it wasn't that. Her empty gaze only reminded me of Reapers like Ellis.

My future.

No, I told myself, closing my eyes. *I will make a new life here. And I will find a way to save myself. To save others.*

I was not defined by this—being a Nephilim or a Jumper. I was Vince Delgado.

And here, in front of all these Reapers, I silently made my own vow to never lose sight of who I was.

"Join hands," Gwen's voice rang out.

I kept my eyes closed as the Reapers murmured around me, their voices echoing at one ethereal voice.

"Black wings and powers from the otherworld,

Hear and welcome us into the fold,

This Reaper who pledges to serve and work,

To care for souls and never shirk,

To only use his powers for good,

And to help every soul he should."

A ripple of magic sparked in the air. My skin prickled, and I suppressed a shiver.

"Repeat after me, Vince," Mom said softly.

I nodded, keeping my eyes shut tight.

"I, Vince Delgado, pledge a vow to this clan of Reapers."

Grateful my voice didn't shake, I repeated the words.

"I swear to use my magic to heal and not hurt."

Again, I repeated.

"To continue the natural order."

My voice sounded wooden as I said the words.

"To part souls from their magic and restore balance to the realms."

I trembled as I repeated after Mom.

The rock underneath me quivered. My eyes snapped open as I expected the ceiling to cave in, crushing me into oblivion. Sparks ignited in the air. Ash stung my nose, mingled with a foreign power I didn't often smell around Nephilim.

Dark magic.

Something tickled just behind my shoulder blades, and in a flash, my dark wings spread out behind me, lifting me off the concrete and pitching me forward. Feathers fluttered in the air around me.

Then, a blistering pain surged within my body as if my insides had been set on fire. I stiffened, my hands forming fists at my side. The strange presence cut into me, slicing through bone and flesh. I cried out, my voice echoing. Dark spots filled my vision. My fingernails dug into my palms.

Power exploded within me so violently that I screamed. The sound was shrill and rang in my ears.

And then . . . a burst of clarity. I saw my warlock powers—a glistening blue orb that hovered above me, illuminating the dark room. And next to it, a crimson ball, much smaller than the blue one.

My Reaper powers.

The redness gleamed like a predator sizing me up.

The color was ominous to me; I'd never seen a caster with red magic before.

The magic of the Underworld, a voice whispered in my head.

The magic of death.

I swallowed, and in a flash, the two orbs disappeared, darting back inside me. At first, I thought I'd imagined it, but something sharp sliced through my gut as if the magic had literally *cut* its way into me. I gritted my teeth, biting back another scream.

Then, as if someone had flipped a switch, the magic in the air vanished. My ears still rang and my body shook from exertion. But the pain was gone. Nothing but a cold sweat and my own sharp gasps remained.

Gradually, my vision cleared, and I made out the figures of the Reapers surrounding me. Their hands lowered, and Gwen's voice rang out, "You are one of us now, Vince."

My mouth felt dry. Gwen watched me expectantly, but what was I supposed to say? *Thanks for infusing me with the magic of death. Really appreciate it.*

"Stand up, Vince," Mom whispered.

I rose to my feet. My legs felt like lead, but I forced myself forward. My head was spinning, and I barely remained upright. A flash of red caught my eye—Jocelyn. I stumbled toward her and found her lingering in the corner, away from the circle, no doubt because she wasn't a full Reaper yet. Her eyes were wide and her face pale.

"Are you all right?" she asked, looking me up and down. I patted my chest and stomach, searching for wounds. I was certain something had cut me open and pierced through my innards.

But I was fine. Had the pain been my imagination? Or had it been healed right away?

Jocelyn stared at me, her eyes fearful, and I realized she was waiting for an answer. I cleared my throat. "Yeah. I'm fine. I think."

"Your turn," said a bored voice from the circle of Reapers. It was Ellis, and he watched Jocelyn with a blank expression.

Jocelyn shivered and stepped forward before lying on the concrete just like I had. I backed into the corner, rubbing my arms and trying to ward off the sudden chill that surrounded me. My wings had receded at some point, and I hadn't noticed. But right now, I was more focused on trying not to throw up to worry about it.

The Reapers began chanting again, but I was barely paying attention. Magic had come to life inside me, sweeping through my body like a current. What had once been familiar and comfortable was now foreign and frightening. It churned, buzzing expectantly as if waiting to be unleashed.

It was horrifying.

Jocelyn started repeating after Ellis just like I'd done with Mom. Her voice trembled, and it sounded like she was about to burst into tears.

I closed my eyes, pressing my lips together. I knew what would happen next. My back pressed against the wall, as far as I could possibly go, as if putting distance between me and Jocelyn would lessen the horror of it all.

It didn't. When the screaming began, it tore right through me.

And the deadly magic inside me laughed with delight.

CHAPTER 12

CORA

A FEW DAYS LATER, I MADE MY WAY THROUGH THE neighborhood. It took monumental effort for me to slow my pace. Normally, my strides were quick and purposeful because I had no reason for delay.

Not today. Today, I was a concerned citizen. Today, my people needed to see me and know I would stop for them.

My legs itched to sprint, and I thought longingly of that run a few days ago. So liberating.

Maybe I'll have to take up jogging, I thought. The idea was so strange that I almost laughed out loud. Cora Covington, the Blade of Hinport, the feared assassin—now a jogger.

It was ridiculous. Was this what normal people did?

I walked down the road between apartment buildings. Most of the coven lived right here in the same complex, which made things easier. It was still early, so I knew a lot of them weren't up yet.

But some were.

As I made my way down the sidewalk, I came across a pair of figures in the shadows, making their way to the staircase. They stiffened at my approach, and I tried not to wrinkle my nose at their strong vinegar smell.

Vampires.

"Hello, boys," I said brightly, offering a jovial wave.

The two men eyed me warily, their red eyes gleaming. For a moment, they did nothing but stare at me. Then, one of them ducked his head politely. "Ms. Covington."

This time, I *did* wrinkle my nose. "Call me Cora. Please." I shifted my weight from one foot to the other. "How—how are you?" The question sounded forced and awkward.

The vampires fidgeted too and glanced at each other. "We're well, thank you," said the second one. His hair was longer than the other's and fell past his shoulders.

I rubbed my arms, feeling deeply uncomfortable. Normally, our coven didn't have any predators like vampires or werewolves. But after Benny and his fellow wolves pledged loyalty to me, several other demons took that as a sign and joined up as well. After Damien's death, I couldn't exactly say *no*. I needed all the support I could get.

But I was uneasy around vampires. And it was painfully obvious. It was time for me to change that.

I sighed. *Drop the act, Cora. They can see right through you.* "Can I just . . . ask you guys some questions? You're the newest members of the coven, so I wanted to make sure you're comfortable here."

The first vampire shrugged. "Sure."

"Where do you feed?"

The second vampire flinched, and the first elbowed him.

My eyes widened. "I—did I say something wrong?"

"Of course not," the first vampire said quickly. "It's only—" He stopped, his mouth clamping shut.

I waved my hand impatiently. "Tell me. I promise I won't attack you or anything."

He swallowed and continued, "There is a prejudice against our kind. Most assume we feed on the innocent. But we don't. Hunter here was just reacting instinctively."

"Okay. So, how *do* you feed?"

"We have Donors," Hunter said. "Willing participants. We exchange blood."

I knew how Donors worked, but I still nodded encouragingly. "In Hinport?"

"No. Ravenbrooke."

My heart jolted. Damien once had me wipe out vampires who fed on people from Ravenbrooke because it posed a threat to us. Branching out to other cities was dangerous. Hinport was a gem because demons could live out in the open. But Ravenbrooke was different. Magic had to be hidden.

The first vampire read my alarm and jumped in hastily, "We're very discrete. And our feedings always happen here in the city. The Donors come to us."

I forced myself to nod again. "That's good."

"Dex," Hunter muttered, pointing to the sky. The sun peeked out from behind the buildings. Dex and Hunter shrank against the wall, clinging to the shadows.

"Oh," I said. "The sun. Right. Sorry to keep you. Thanks for answering my questions." I turned away, then paused. Facing them once more, I asked, "Can I visit you again? Maybe after sundown?"

Dex blinked, but a small smile spread on his face. "Certainly. Thank you for your time, Cora." He and Hunter vanished into the shadows, and I heard their quiet steps as they returned to their apartment.

It wasn't until silence fell that I finally relaxed. I hadn't realized my hands had been in tight fists until I released the tension and cringed at the cuts in my palm.

Sheesh, this was worse than killing. A million times worse.

I was *not* a people person.

"Two down, twenty to go," I muttered.

Vince was screaming, a raw sound of pure agony. Blood covered his face, and he held a shaking hand over a long, jagged gash on his cheek. He moaned, collapsing to the ground in pain. His dark wings fanned out behind him, but one of them was completely shredded. A halo of red magic encircled him, but I couldn't tell if it was his own Reaper magic, or . . . something else.

I wanted to reach out to him, to help him. But I could only watch. The sight of Vince, so wounded, so anguished, tore through my heart as if ripping it out of my chest. I wanted to sob with him. To hold him. To heal him. But I could do nothing.

Vince! *I tried screaming.*

Then, a dark shape rose from the ground, funneling in front of Vince and towering over him. Vince sucked in a ragged gasp, still clutching his face as he gazed up at the massive shadow. Magic churned in the air, and I suddenly felt ice cold. A low hiss emitted from the shadow, and Vince trembled.

"Please," he begged.

The shadow engulfed him. Vince screamed.

And I woke up, gasping for breath and covered in sweat. My chest wouldn't stop rising and falling, and each deep breath felt like knives in my throat. My head was spinning, my heart racing.

The dream had seemed so real. I'd taken my fair share of Seeing elixirs, so I knew what a true vision felt like.

It felt a lot like this.

I sat up in bed, wiping my damp hair out of my face and trying to calm my heart rate. It *couldn't* have been a vision. I hadn't taken that elixir in months—back when Vince and I had taken it together.

Nausea and fear churned within me, making me want to heave. What if it *was* real? I had powerful blood, after all. Perhaps this vision was strong enough to reach me even without an elixir.

I shivered, rubbing my arms and hunching over until my head pressed against my knees. I couldn't get the image of Vince's mangled face out of my head. His screams. His sobs.

My shaking fingers balled into fists. My nails dug into my palms. I couldn't take this. I was a killer. I was the leader of a demon coven. A silly dream shouldn't be able to rattle me like this.

Unless it isn't just a dream, I thought.

I went still, my breathing finally calm. My jaw ticked back and forth as I contemplated.

I glanced at the window. The sky was still dark, but faint purple rays peeked through the blinds. Dawn was approaching. I had a packed schedule, filled with frivolous things I had *no* desire to do, all to convince my coven I cared about them. It was important, I knew this. But I still didn't want to do it.

At this point, I knew I should probably just start my day. Get ahead of things.

But still, I remained frozen on the edge of my bed. Goosebumps rose on my skin as I circled through that haunting vision again . . . and again . . .

I had to do something. I *had* to.

Determination coursed through me as I jumped up from the bed and crossed the room to my stash of potion ingredients. Muttering to myself, I threw the ingredients together in my cauldron and waited for the hot plate to warm.

I would make a Seeing elixir and drink it. Then, if I had the vision again, I would know it was real.

And I didn't care if Vince lived in another realm. I would tear every world apart if it meant I could save him.

CHAPTER 13

VINCE

My strange new magic swirled within me constantly. It was like riding a roller coaster nonstop. At first it was exhilarating, even frightening. Now, a few days later, it just made me nauseous all the time.

As soon as Jocelyn and I pledged our vows, we were grouped with several other Reapers to undergo rigorous training before diving into our reaping responsibilities. The structured format made Jocelyn and me roll our eyes at each other, and I knew we both thought the same thing. We'd already finished high school, but now it felt like we were right back in it.

Except in a damp and musty, cave-like tunnel.

Our first teacher, a Reaper named Joey, gave us instructions on how to tap into our magic. Though a small, begrudging part of me wanted to resist this new power inside me, I resigned myself to try my best. I'd made my vow. I'd made my choice. Now, I had to live with it.

No point in fighting or complaining. I had to embrace it.

"The trigger is different for everyone," Joey said, pacing in front of the six of us in the small room. The space wasn't big enough for chairs or desks, so we sat cross-legged on large cushions. I felt like I was in kindergarten doing circle time. "The power within you has a presence," Joey went on. "A mind of its own. It won't grant you access unless you display the proper readiness."

He stopped pacing and clasped his long fingers together in front of him. His black wings rippled slightly, framing his bulky arms and shoulders. His dark eyes gleamed under the shadow of his curly black hair. "You must bond with your new magic. It's like it has a soul of its own. If you fight it, it will fight back. It can only bond with you when you complement each other." He held up his laced fingers, pulling them apart before bringing them back together. "You open up to it, and it will open up to you so you both fit together perfectly."

"How do we find out what our trigger is?" I asked.

Joey's eyes met mine. "You practice." His gaze swept over the other Reapers. "But I must caution you. An intense emotion is *never* a good idea. The power only responds to subtlety and gentleness. That is the way Reapers work. We do not thrust our power on anyone. It has to be freely accepted. As you practice, touch your emotions lightly. See what works and what doesn't. Anything too strong, and you put yourself and others at risk."

I remembered what Mom had said about the person who was stealing magic. The magic had been forcibly taken, which was a crime against humanity. But Reapers were supposed to coax the magic back into the atmosphere, guiding the magic like a nurturing hand.

It was almost laughable. Except, ever since I'd pledged my vow, I understood it more. We were like guardians, protecting the web of magic that surrounded us. The balance of magic in the web was a delicate thing. If we forced or pulled too strongly, it risked shredding the web completely.

Joey had us split into pairs and separate into different rooms so we could practice. Jocelyn and I partnered up and moved to the room adjacent to our classroom. We dragged our cushions with us and sat across from each other, keeping at least six feet between us in case things got messy.

"Want me to go first?" Jocelyn asked.

I almost volunteered instead, but knots formed in my stomach. Instead, I nodded quickly, wiping my sweaty palms on my pants.

Jocelyn exhaled long and slow, resting her hands on her knees as if in meditation. She closed her eyes and took several deep breaths. I resisted the urge to squirm as I watched her.

A minute passed. Then two.

I cleared my throat.

Jocelyn released a breath in a huff, her frame drooping. "Nothing?" she asked.

I shook my head.

"Damn." She rubbed her forehead.

"What did you try?"

"I just sifted through some mild emotions. Irritation. Fatigue. Anxiety."

I frowned, remembering something Cora had said when she'd helped me tap into my time travel ability. She told me to replicate the feeling of adrenaline I'd felt on the lacrosse field, and I'd laughed because it sounded too easy.

It was more than just mentally leafing through the emotions. It was putting yourself into that exact same mental place. For me, this was literal because of my connection to Luke.

I suddenly went still, my pulse racing. Luke had said we were bound. Could I use his magic to access my powers?

Would he let me? Even if he did, I had no idea the extent of Luke's power compared to mine.

I swallowed. "Let me try." I inhaled and straightened, closing my eyes just like Jocelyn had.

In my mind, I returned to the field. It was effortless. As easy as breathing. I'd come here so often that the transition was nothing.

For the first time, I wondered about it. I didn't know anyone else who could do this. I'd just thought my imagination was vivid, but now that I knew about Luke, I wasn't so sure.

On the field, I gripped my crosse. My body was covered in sweat and dirt. My heart was pounding as if I'd just run a mile.

It was all so *real*.

Something foreign stirred within me. My new magic. My heart lurched in alarm, my body on high alert. I had to calm down.

I gripped my crosse tightly. Faceless figures stood before me, some opponents and some teammates. One of them lobbed the ball toward me.

I sucked in a breath and caught it before racing forward, dodging figures as I ran. A thrill raced through me. My magic surged in response.

"Stop," said a voice in my ear.

I froze. The figures around me flickered and vanished like I'd turned off the TV.

Luke appeared in front of me, wearing street clothes like before. He crossed his arms and raised his eyebrows. "What're you doing?"

I sighed. "I'm trying to access my magic. Just practicing."

"I told you, it doesn't work the same way in this realm."

"That's not exactly helpful."

Luke shrugged. "I'm not a Reaper. Otherwise I'd tell you what to do."

My brow furrowed. Even *Reapers* didn't know what to do. Joey had said it was different for everyone.

I had to figure it out on my own.

For the first time, I gazed around, taking in my surroundings. The grass was freshly mowed. The sun hovered high in the sky.

But there was nothing else around. No crowd. No parking lot. Nothing but a wide expanse of grass.

"What *is* this place?" I asked.

"This is the bridge between your magic."

"What does that *mean*?" I was getting tired of Luke's less-than-helpful responses.

"Think of it as a Venn Diagram. You've always had two forms of magic—your Nephilim magic and your warlock magic. This mental place you're in is the space between them. The space where they overlap."

I stared at him. "Are you saying I used *Nephilim* magic when I time traveled?"

Luke nodded. "All your magic is a part of you. Your Nephilim magic fueled you in ways you didn't understand. It powered a portion of your Teleportation powers."

My head was reeling. "So . . . so if this place is the bridge between two sides of magic, why can't I use it now?"

"You can. This space hasn't changed. But your magic has. You can't access it by the thrill of the game anymore. You have to find a new access point."

A new trigger.

"But . . . the only reason I'm *here* is because of the adrenaline," I protested.

Luke smiled and shook his head. "Think again. You're here because this is your mental bridge. You're here for a reason."

A reason. A biting retort rose in my throat, but I swallowed it down. I was *so sick* of being *chosen*. I was sick of my choices being made for me. Of these greater powers and callings that took hold of my life with no mercy.

When did *I* get to decide my fate? My *life*?

I sighed. These frustrating thoughts weren't getting me anywhere. I relaxed my hands at my sides and took a steadying breath.

With my Nephilim magic, adrenaline had been my trigger. What had changed? My magic, obviously. But *what* about my magic had changed? *Why* didn't the same trigger work?

Nephilim had different responsibilities than Reapers.

Nephilim were free to roam the mortal realm. To make decisions that affected *everyone*—like Hector had. But Reapers were something . . . beyond. Something otherworldly. Their responsibilities weren't just to the mortal realm, but to *every* realm.

Distance. I needed to find distance. I thought of Ellis's blank expression and how Mom explained some Reapers lost touch with humanity.

It was because they *distanced* themselves from humanity.

A knot of emotions rose in my chest, but I had to focus on this trail of thought before I lost it. I couldn't stop. I was so close.

"Distance," I whispered. Once again, my gaze roved over the field, but I saw it with new eyes.

No crowds. No opponents. Luke wasn't wearing his gear. He was only here as my guide—not my teammate.

In the heat of the game, when strategy took over, when I had the ball in my crosse, I developed a sort of tunnel vision. I only saw one thing: the goal. The path I had to take.

Nothing else mattered.

Distance.

My mouth felt dry. I raised my crosse and surged forward, staring only at the goal before me. A faceless opponent appeared, but I didn't look at him.

I only saw the goal.

The crosse felt sturdy in my hands. I sucked in deep breaths. Luke shouted my name behind me, but I didn't listen.

I lunged, swinging my crosse . . .

"Vince!" a voice shouted.

I blinked. Reality slammed into me with full force, making my head throb. Darkness clouded around me, and the smells of the field vanished. Luke was gone.

Jocelyn sat in front of me, her eyes wide and her face pale. "What happened to you?" she breathed.

My mouth opened and closed. Something heavy sank in my stomach. *It didn't work.*

"I—I—" I broke off and swallowed. "What did I do?"

"You went into this sort of trance. Your eyes rolled back so they were all white. And you—you started twitching." Fear shone in her eyes. "I was about to run and grab someone for help. I thought you were having a seizure."

Blood pounded in my ears. I still felt like I was on that field, my gaze focusing on the goal. I had felt so *certain* . . .

Shaking my head, I flexed my fingers. Energy churned through me, violent and all-consuming. It demanded movement. I couldn't sit still.

"I—I have to—" I quickly stood up, turning away from Jocelyn and toward the exit.

Gravity shifted around me. Weight pressed in on me, crushing my chest so I couldn't breathe.

A small *pop* echoed in my ears.

My surroundings tilted. Ash filled the air. Deafening booms rattled the ground. My ears throbbed. My eyes stung from the particles in the air. I coughed, waving a hand in front of my face. An eerie red glow surrounded me, clouding my surroundings. I couldn't *see*.

Gradually, the glow faded, and I made out a figure sitting in front of me. Her head was propped against the wall behind her. Her face and shoulder were covered in blood.

Ice filled my chest. It was *Cora*.

She blinked up at me, her eyes widening. Her expression was dazed and weak. I'd never seen her like this before. The only time she'd been this weak was—

I froze, slowly gazing around. Demons and casters battled. Explosions of black and blue magic burst in the air like fireworks.

The Demon War. I'd time traveled. *Again.*

My gaze snapped back to Cora. She stared at me, her face pale and her eyes unsteady. I took slow steps toward her, my heart pounding in my chest.

"Vince," she whispered. Her voice was a low rasp. Darkness stirred in her eyes. As I stared at her, I saw the resignation in her face. The lack of fire and determination I always saw there.

She was dying. And worse—she *wanted* to die. The emptiness in her gaze was her decision to give up.

I wanted to rush and find my Mimic. To bring him back here before Cora gave up completely.

But something inside me went perfectly still as I watched Cora. I knew my Mimic would return and heal Cora—because it had already happened.

Now, *I* was here for a reason too.

Cora was ready to die. But it wasn't her time.

I held her gaze and murmured, "Not yet, Cora."

Startled, she blinked at me again. A burst of clarity shone in her eyes.

The air around me shifted again. I rose to my feet, my pulse thundering inside me as I Jumped again.

I had no control over this. Gravity claimed me, dragging me downward. Shapes and colors swirled around me, making me sick.

I slammed into solid ground, coughing and gasping for breath. Someone yelped, and I heard the scraping of furniture.

The first thing I noticed was the bright light streaming in through the window. Which meant I *wasn't* back in the tunnels.

I'd time traveled again.

Damn it all. I groaned and struggled to rise, but it was suddenly hard to breathe.

"Vince?" called a voice.

I stood, my legs trembling. My black wings were still outstretched behind me as I looked around. I knew this place. I'd been here once before—to say goodbye to Cora before I became a Reaper.

A hard lump formed in my throat as I focused on the figure before me. Her piercing blue eyes. Her inky black hair, which was a bit shorter than when I'd last seen her. And her face, drained of color as she gaped at me in utter shock.

"Cora," I whispered.

CHAPTER 14

CORA

I couldn't breathe. Once again, here he was in my office, standing there as if it were the most normal thing ever.

He looked different . . . but the same too. His magnificent black wings were stretched out behind him, almost taking up the whole space in the office. And his face was grim and closed off. Like he'd *seen* things. Experienced things he had to hide deep inside.

I knew that feeling well.

But . . . he didn't have that long scar on his face. Which meant *this* Vince lived sometime between now and six months from now.

"Are you"—I licked my lips, my mouth suddenly too dry to talk—"Is it really *you*? I mean—" I stopped again, closing my eyes. How was I supposed to ask if he was *my* Vince? If he was *present-day* Vince?

"It's me," Vince said, his voice uncertain as he gazed around the room. Disbelief was etched in his face, and he breathed heavily. Voices echoed in the hallway, and Vince whirled around, his body tense as if expecting a fight.

I rushed forward and closed the door. When I turned to face him, I sucked in a breath. He smelled the same, but a little different. Mint and soap and . . . the faintest whiff of woodsmoke. It made my head spin, reminding me of our time together last year.

"I just," I said, suddenly breathless. "I need to know . . . *When* are you from?"

Vince blinked and looked at me, his expression dazed. "I have no idea. There's . . . no way to measure time in the Astral Realm."

Astral Realm. So . . . not the Underworld?

Lilith, I was so confused.

But he probably was too.

I cleared my throat and took a step away from him. "What do you remember? How much time do you *think* has passed?"

Vince scratched his head, suddenly looking like the inquisitive student at high school again. "Uh, a few months maybe? Weeks? Hard to tell. It hasn't been very long since . . . well . . ." He grimaced and gestured to his wings behind him.

A few months. My insides turned numb. This was present-day Vince. This was *my* Vince.

Holy Mother of Lilith. He was *here*.

"When are *you* from?" Vince asked.

I stared at him. "It's been six months since you left." My voice was barely more than a whisper.

He gasped, the sound so faint I wouldn't have heard it if I weren't standing so close. His gray eyes grew distant as he concentrated on something I couldn't see.

"Why are you here, Vince?" I asked.

He swallowed. "I—I don't know."

Something hardened in my chest. His face was so lost, so confused . . . It was clear he'd arrived by accident.

Why did that slash through my gut like a knife wound?

Because I wanted him to find a way back to me.

This had been unintentional.

Vince ran a hand through his hair. It was cut shorter than I remembered, kept closer to his scalp than before when it'd hung just above his eyes. He exhaled through his lips. "And . . . this is the mortal realm?"

I frowned. "Yeah. Last I checked."

He looked at me as if just noticing I was there. "Lilith, *Cora*. It's really you." He swept me into his arms, and I let out a startled yelp. His strong arms encircled me, crushing me against his chest. But it wasn't unpleasant. His scent enveloped me, and I closed my eyes, burying my face in his shoulder.

He released me, his eyes filled with fire and longing

that made my stomach clench. His thumb grazed my cheek, my jaw, my lips. An involuntary shiver rippled over me, and I closed my eyes.

"How—how are you?" he murmured.

I inhaled and looked at him. "F-fine."

He smiled, and the sight stole my breath. "Stupid question, I know." He blinked and looked around. "I—I need to find my dad. Make sure he's okay."

"He's fine," I said immediately.

Vince stilled.

I waved a hand in the air. "I, uh, check in on him now and then. Though, it's been a while since our last lunch." I rubbed the back of my neck, feeling guilty as I remembered the mile-long to-do list I was drowning in and the responsibilities of the coven. Harvey needed a new Donor, and Wilson had a dispute with his neighbor I had to settle. New building contracts had come in that I needed to look over and sign, and Benny and I still hadn't tracked down the bastard who was skimming money from us.

The last time I'd seen José was over a month ago. He'd been more subdued than usual. I could tell the loss of his son was wearing on him. But he was optimistic. Still proud of Vince.

"He got a job as a legal assistant," I said. "He found an apartment near Glen Bridge. Nothing too fancy, but it suits him."

Emotion stirred in Vince's eyes. "You—you're keeping tabs on him?"

"Yeah. I mean, nothing creepy, just—just to make sure he's all right. That he's safe."

I couldn't read Vince's expression. Was he mad? Had I violated his privacy? Did he want me to leave his dad alone?

"Just say the word, and I'll back off," I said quickly. "I just figured—"

He grabbed my waist, drawing me toward him before his lips covered mine. At first, his mouth was firm and urgent, desperate and hungry. Then, his movements slowed and became achingly gentle. *Too* gentle. I clung to his arms, my hands trembling as his lips searched mine. I leaned into him. His tongue brushed against mine, and a bolt of heat seared through my stomach.

All the longing and restlessness that had built up in my chest after all these months was finally unleashed. An explosion of desire coursed through me, fierce and unyielding. I grabbed Vince's collar and pulled him closer. My arms wound around him, and my fingers clutched at the back of his neck. The intensity of our kiss was so powerful that we staggered. My back slammed against the wall. The force only further inflamed me, and I gasped before his lips were on mine again. His hips ground into me, pinning me to the wall. Though there was no space between us, I wanted him closer.

My fingers fumbled with the buckle of his jeans. A low groan built in his throat, and he grabbed my wrists, stopping me.

I looked up at him, panting. His eyes were dark with need, his lips swollen and pink from our make-out session.

I wanted to ask why he'd stopped me. Surely, he could feel this, this agonizing *need* building between us, uncontrollable and urgent. But the conflict in his face told me there was so much more than just our own feral desires.

"I'm sorry," I breathed, my face burning. "This probably isn't the best time for . . . I'm sorry." I ran a hand across my forehead, trying to control my pulse and the desperate heat between my legs.

Lilith, it had been a *long* time.

"Cora, it's—" Vince made a frustrated noise and ran a hand through his hair. "It's not that I don't *want* to." He sighed. "I do. More than anything. But I don't know why I'm here."

I forced myself to meet his gaze, to search his eyes. In his face, I saw confusion, doubt, and fear . . . and it sobered me. I had to remind myself this wasn't some conjugal visit. He hadn't *meant* to be here.

He hadn't meant to see me. It had just happened.

I swallowed. "Where were you trying to go?"

"I wasn't trying to *go* anywhere. I was trying to access my Reaper magic."

A hoarse laugh bubbled in my throat, and I gestured to his wings. "Looks like it worked."

He shook his head. "It's different from before. I had some kind of control the last time. But now, with this new magic, it feels like *it's* controlling *me*. It's terrifying."

I stared at him as memories stirred within me. Memories of when I first accessed my magic. First tested out potions from my blood.

I knew the feeling of being overwhelmed by your own magic.

"I don't need an anchor this time," Vince said.

My eyes widened. That *was* big news. "So . . . you can just time travel anywhere? Anytime?"

"I don't know."

Nodding, I dropped my gaze, unsure of what to say.

"Cora."

I blinked and looked up at him. His gaze had softened. His eyes were so tender that warmth automatically filled my chest. Raising his hand, he trailed his thumb along my cheek, down to my chin, and finally to my lower lip. He gently pried my lips apart, and my heart fluttered madly.

"For weeks, all I wanted was to find you," he whispered. "I tried so hard to leave. To get back to you. To keep my promise." He took a breath. "My magic works differently down there. It's—it's hard to explain." Frustration stirred in his eyes once more.

I placed my hands on his shoulders and forced him to meet my gaze. "Talk to me. We worked through this before, when you first time traveled. We can work through it again."

Half his mouth quirked up into a soft smile, which I returned.

Suddenly, he winced, hissing in pain. Ducking his head, he let out a strangled growl. His hand raised to his forehead, and his arms were trembling.

"What is it? What's happening?" I touched his shoulders, his face, trying to figure out what was wrong. His face contorted in agony, the veins and tendons standing out on his neck.

I had to do *something*. I remembered the vision of Vince's face covered in blood as the black shadow consumed him. The image was burned into my memory, and my insides quivered with terror.

In desperation, I summoned my magic and whispered,

"Magic above and powers that be,
Heal this man and set him free.
Release him from the pain within,
And free his mind from the prison therein."

My hands glowed purple, and Vince stiffened, his back arching and his eyes flying wide open. He sucked in a rattling breath as if he'd been holding it in. Then, his body slowly relaxed as he inhaled and exhaled deeply.

Color returned to his face, and he looked at me in shock.

"You okay?" I whispered, my heart still thundering.

"I—I'm not sure. My body, my mind . . . I couldn't breathe. It's like I wasn't here. For a few seconds, I was . . . somewhere else." His eyes darkened, and once again, he was that distant, closed-off dark angel. He wasn't the kind, innocent Vince I'd first met.

He was a creature of darkness.

"Vince." I touched his cheek. "Talk to me."

He blinked, and his eyes softened again. "Reapers are tethered to the Astral Realm. We can't be away for very long."

I stared at him, realizing what he wasn't saying. He had to go back.

And I had to let him.

A hard lump formed in my throat, and I swallowed. "Right."

Despair tugged at his expression. He took my waist again, and my heart beat an erratic rhythm against my ribcage. "I don't want to leave," he said, his voice low and agonizingly sexy.

"I don't want you to leave, either."

He kissed me, and I drew him against me again, savoring the warmth of his chest against mine, the hard planes of his muscles, the width of his shoulders.

He flinched away from me, his eyes scrunched up in

pain. He cried out through clenched teeth, releasing my waist to clutch his forehead again.

"Vince," I said, touching his cheeks.

Just as I was ready to cast another spell, he took a deep breath, his face clearing again. He released a half-groan, half-sigh and met my gaze with weary eyes. "It's all right," he croaked. "I'm all right."

"You need to go back," I whispered.

His eyes were tormented again. He shook his head. "I can't. I tried so hard to get back here. If I go back, I might not be able to return."

Grief and regret knotted in my throat. *Lilith, I can't do this. I can't send him away, knowing I might never see him again.*

But Future Vince's warning rang in my ears. *Something big is coming. Something bigger than even the mortal realm. Without him, the Reapers will be trapped.* It wasn't just him and me at stake here. There were so many others counting on him.

How could I be selfish enough to keep him here just because I wanted him?

"You—you cast a spell," Vince said quickly. "Can you use your magic to heal me? To keep me here? Maybe make a potion?" His eyes were alight with hope, and it tore at me, clawing at my insides.

"No, Vince."

He blinked at me, stunned. "Why not?"

"Because—" I thought about lying to him. Forcing him back by pretending I didn't care. That I didn't want him here.

But what good would that do except hurt us both? If Vince were like me, if he only looked out for himself, then maybe we would both agree to remain here together.

But Vince *wasn't* like me. He put other people first. He saw the big picture and always found a role to play. It was why I loved him.

He was a protector. Even when he didn't want to be.

I took a breath. "Your Mimic came to see me. From the future."

Vince's face drained of color. "What? What did he say?"

"He told me I had to send you back. That if I didn't, the Reapers would suffer. That you're the only one who can help them keep the dark forces at bay."

His mouth opened and closed. He licked his lips. "I —*what* dark forces?"

"He said something about . . . souls being lost. Magic being stolen. The gate between realms tearing apart."

Vince's face turned bone white. He took a shuddering breath. "Mother of Lilith." He ran a hand through his hair again.

The horror on his face made my chest tighten. "What is it?"

He pressed his lips together, his eyes wide. "Some of that stuff is already happening."

My blood ran cold. *No, no, no.* Again, I thought of Vince screaming and covered in blood while the shadow suffocated him.

I can't lose him.

"But—but you can stop it," I said, trying to convince myself more than him. "Your Mimic said your Teleportation powers can save the Reapers."

He grimaced. "How? I have *no control.*"

"Maybe you'll *get* control. Just like you did before."

He remained silent. I balled my hands into fists, hating this feeling of utter helplessness.

I asked, "What—what about Luke? Can he help?"

Vince's gaze snapped to me. "No. Well . . ." He sighed. "I don't know. He doesn't know very much about Reapers. But . . . he *did* help me get here." His eyes grew distant and full of sorrow.

"I haven't seen him," I said quietly, answering his unspoken question. "Not since the fight with Hector."

Vince nodded but said nothing. Another flash of pain tore at his expression, and he stiffened. He grunted and pressed a hand against the wall for support.

"Go back, Vince," I said, pressing both my hands against his face. "I trust you. I know you'll come back to me. But they need you more than I do."

Vince exhaled in a groan and looked at me with tortured eyes. "Cora," he whispered.

I pressed a firm kiss against his lips. His hands trembled as he wrapped his arms around me, bringing me closer. I rested my forehead against his, closing my eyes as we shared breath.

"I love you," he murmured.

I smiled in spite of the crushing agony in my chest. "You too."

Vince's eyes gleamed with that familiar spark, the same heat I felt coursing through me. His face was strained again as he turned away from me. With a small *pop*, he was gone.

CHAPTER 15

VINCE

Shapes and sounds surrounded me, vague and distorted. I was falling and flying all at once, my stomach dropping and rising. It felt like a roller coaster, but more frightening.

Then, I slammed back into the ground. I inhaled a sharp breath, and for the first time in what felt like hours, a rush of cold clarity burst in my mind. It was like a layer of plastic had surrounded me when I'd traveled, and now it was gone.

I breathed in again and again, relishing the fresh gulps of air. My lungs expanded, and all the tension in my body released.

"You okay?" asked a voice.

Warmth spread through me, but when my vision cleared, I realized the person in front of me wasn't who I wanted it to be.

Disappointment dropped like a rock in my stomach. I sighed, my body sagging.

Jocelyn sat in front of me, cross-legged in the middle of the room, just like I'd left her. She didn't seem panicked or afraid, so I must've only been gone a second or two.

"What—what happened?" I asked.

"You vanished for a second. I thought I imagined it, but . . ." She trailed off, her brow furrowing with concern as she looked me over. I had no doubt I looked like a disheveled mess.

My throat felt dry. "Joss, I . . . I *traveled*."

Her face drained of color. "*What*? Where? When?"

I quickly filled her in, leaving out a few details of what happened between me and Cora. My face felt hot just thinking about it.

Jocelyn raised a shaking hand to her forehead. "I don't understand. You were only gone for a second! I blinked, and you were back."

"Time passes differently here, remember?" I recalled what Cora had said—that it had been six months since I became a Reaper. It certainly hadn't felt that long.

Jocelyn opened her mouth to respond when a scream pierced the air, echoing through the tunnels. We both shot to our feet. A chill swept over me.

Another soul has lost their magic, I thought.

"What *is* that?" Jocelyn asked in a hushed whisper.

The scream rang out again, shrill and haunting. The hairs on my arms stood on end.

I looked at Jocelyn, remembering Mom's request to keep quiet about the magic thief. But Jocelyn was still herself. She wasn't closed off like Ellis.

At least, not yet.

"Come on." I grabbed her arm and led her out of the room.

The screams grew louder. Another voice joined in. Then a third. A cacophony of anguished cries and moans filled the air as if nothing but ghosts surrounded us.

I froze, and Jocelyn went rigid next to me. For a moment, we just stood there, numb with terror as the echoing howls floated around us like spirits.

This was *nothing* like the last time a soul's magic was stolen. This sounded like *dozens* of souls were being tortured.

Hurried footsteps shuffled behind us. Jocelyn and I darted out of the way as several Reapers in black robes rushed past us, their hushed murmurs echoing.

Their urgency snapped me into action. I guided Jocelyn down the tunnel, following the other Reapers.

If more than one soul needed saving right now, then we had to help. We had to try. Even if we didn't know how to reap yet.

"You know what's going on," Jocelyn panted next to me. "Don't you?" Her words sounded like more of an accusation than a question. Her gaze was full of suspicion.

I didn't answer.

At long last, we reached the room with the concrete altar. Several Reapers already surrounded it, their hands clasped.

But the mass of floating white souls flitting about the room like hummingbirds could not be contained.

The wisps hovered in the air, some remaining still and others zipping back and forth faster than I could keep track. Shrieks and moans echoed, making my ears throb. I resisted the urge to cover them and flinch away from the horrifying scene before me.

Red magic glowed from the circle of Reapers, but it flickered and vanished like a candle being blown out.

Their magic wasn't enough.

"Vince!" cried a voice.

I turned and found Mom, followed by Gwen. Their faces were pale, but Gwen's face went rigid with determination.

"What's going on?" I shouted over the noise.

Dark wings sprang out behind Gwen. Her fierce gaze was fixed on the ceiling, and her voice was cold as she said, "Our thief has finally emerged."

Emerged. He was *here*? In this realm? My heart lurched at the thought, and I glanced around as if expecting to find a shadowed figure with a dagger, poised to kill us all.

"Vince, get out of here," Mom said, her eyes wide with urgency. Fear struck her face, and she looked whiter than paper.

"No," Gwen snapped, her icy gaze pinning Mom in place. "Both of them must stay. We'll need all the help we can get. Cecile, you need to grab the other Reapers. Ellis, Gray, Joey—anyone else who's missing. It's all hands on deck."

Mom's mouth tightened, and I saw the brief conflict in her eyes at the thought of exposing this secret operation to stop the magic thief. But whatever her concerns were about discontent among Reapers, this was an emergency. She nodded before darting away. Her footsteps were drowned out by the spirits around us.

"What can we do?" Jocelyn asked Gwen.

"Come with me." Gwen swept past us toward the circle of Reapers, who were chanting in low voices. Red magic flickered again, but it wasn't strong enough. The anguished spirits were overpowering the Reapers.

"Has this ever happened before?" I asked.

"No." Gwen's voice was clipped. Her gaze moved from me to Jocelyn. "Your wings need to be out. Do whatever you can to make that happen." She inserted herself into the circle of Reapers, joined hands, and chanted with the others.

I met Jocelyn's terrified gaze and swallowed. "We can do this."

She nodded, her eyes uncertain.

I closed my eyes, focusing on the soul of the girl I'd seen last time. My wings had just popped out on their own that time. Something must have triggered it.

But as I struggled to remember, I randomly found myself on the lacrosse field again.

Not now, I thought in frustration.

I envisioned the girl's soul writhing on the slab of concrete. The pull of my Reaper magic when I pledged my vow.

Luke stood before me, his face pale. "Vince," he said.

"No," I shot back. "I can't—I have to—"

"Your Reaper magic is *here*, Vince. Don't push it away."

I stared at him. Slowly, my eyes shifted to look behind him at the empty goal. A faceless opponent stood there, waiting for me.

My heart rate accelerated. My vision narrowed. I focused only on the goal. All other sounds and distractions melted away from me.

Inhale. Exhale.

In a flash, the field disappeared from view. An explosion of sounds and smells slammed into me so forcefully my head throbbed.

The air reeked of ash and a sharp, earthy smell that was vaguely familiar. More souls had appeared. Bursts of wind and magic whipped against my face.

Feathers rippled behind me. My wings were out.

"How—how did you do that?" Jocelyn asked.

I stared at her in bewilderment. "I have *no idea.*"

"Vince!" Gwen screeched, her eyes blazing. She jerked her head to the left, indicating I join the circle.

I glanced quickly at Jocelyn. "You can do this, Joss. Remember how you felt when you pledged."

Then, I rushed forward to join the circle, wedging myself between Gwen and Joey, who had just arrived. As soon as I clasped their hands, a jolt of electricity surged within me, stinging my skin and rattling my bones. My body lurched forward in response like I was on a roller coaster. My teeth chattered against each other.

Darkness clouded my vision, and for a chilling moment, all the sounds around me died.

A voice breathed in my ear, *You are mine. All of you.*

A violent shudder quivered through my body. The voice vanished, and the sounds returned, but my insides felt ice cold.

What the hell are you? I thought, glancing around the room again.

"Get back!" screamed a voice.

A burst of red light appeared above the concrete altar so intensely it burned against my eyes. The glow expanded, rippling like it was alive. Within the redness, a dark and shadowy figure emerged, stepping onto the ground.

My blood turned to ice in my veins. Black shadows swirled around the figure, reaching for us. For one wild minute, I was reminded of Cora and her shadow elixir, how she'd seemed to be made of the shadows themselves.

The shadow man grabbed hold of Ellis, who was closest to the red glow. Ellis suddenly went stiff, his eyes bulging. The shadows coiled around him like a snake, and Ellis exploded in a mass of blood and organs. Flecks of blood spattered my face, and my mouth fell open in utter shock and horror.

Bile climbed up my throat, but all I could do was stare, wide-eyed, as an eerie red mist swirled in the space where Ellis had been moments ago. The mist funneled toward the shadowy figure until he absorbed it completely.

The shadow man had just taken Ellis's magic.

Horror filled my chest until I couldn't breathe. My head spun, and I thought I might faint.

This can't be happening.

The Reapers around me went still, their eyes pinned on the shadow figure. It was painfully clear no one had seen anything like this before.

The magic thief wasn't just stealing from souls—he was now stealing from *Reapers*.

And we were all in grave danger.

My pulse skittered, and my breathing turned sharp. Each inhale was like knives in my throat, and my head pounded with a sickening rhythm. Panic clouded my thoughts.

I can't do this. We're all going to die. I can't do this.

The shadowy figure drifted toward another Reaper, and something sparked in my memory.

What was it Cora had said? *You're the only one who can help them keep the dark forces at bay.*

A foreign determination coursed through me, melting away my fear. An eerie calmness settled over me, and my magic twitched in response.

I knew what I had to do.

"Everyone, *grab on*!" I roared.

Several Reapers jumped from my outburst. I squeezed the hands of those closest to me and shouted, "Now!"

Everyone joined hands. The shadow figure grabbed another Reaper, crushing him into oblivion. The screams and moans pounded against my ear drums.

When the remaining Reapers had all joined hands, I focused on the energy churning within me and spun in place.

We all vanished with a *pop*.

CORA

THE ONE GOOD THING ABOUT VINCE LEAVING AGAIN was it forced me to get work done. Desperate for distractions, I barely allowed myself a minute of rest as I eagerly dived into my responsibilities. Meetings, paperwork, inspections, interviews . . . My calendar was so jam-packed it was about to explode.

A week after Vince left, Benny strode into my office, his face pale and his eyes wide. I'd never seen him look like that before. He was always either smarmy or brooding.

Never afraid.

He shut the door behind him and slapped a stack of bills on my desk. I stared at it, then raised my eyebrows at him. "Um, thanks?"

"We—we have a problem." Benny's voice shook.

I was instantly on my feet. "What kind of problem?"

"Look closely at those."

I sighed and bent over the bills, flipping through them with my fingers. A small tendril of magic puffed in the air from the motion, and I staggered back a step.

The magic lingered in the air, warm and familiar. The smell alone brought back a rush of childhood memories.

My throat felt tight. Even without the smell, I recognized the purple magic.

Bloodcaster magic.

My gaze snapped to Benny, my jaw rigid. "What *is* this?" I demanded.

"You tell me."

My nostrils flared, and I shook my head. "No, we aren't playing this game, Benny. *Where did you get these?*"

"I put a tracker on some bills and followed them, hoping to find our money launderer. All I found was an empty apartment. Looks like the guy left in a hurry. But these bills were left behind."

My mouth felt dry. "Are you saying this money—this *magic*—came from . . ."

"The money launderer, yes."

I stilled. Alarm bells pealed in my mind. *Wrong, wrong, wrong.* My instincts screamed at me to get out, to flee. It was ridiculous, but I trusted my instincts for a reason.

This was *bad*.

"I—" I stopped, at a loss for words.

"Cora." Benny stepped toward me. "Did you do this?"

I glared at him. "*No.*"

He raised his hands in surrender. "Sorry. I had to ask."

I crossed my arms, then uncrossed them. Shifted my weight from one foot to the other. "So . . . so someone's trying to *frame* me?" But something in my gut told me that wasn't quite right.

"Isn't there a way for you to determine where the spell came from?" Benny asked.

"Maybe." I leaned over the bills again, sniffing deeply. The smell of fresh soil and lilacs. That was familiar. That was *my* magic.

But then . . . something else. Something like the morning dew mingled with pond water.

I straightened, and my blood ran cold. "This isn't my magic."

Benny's eyes locked onto mine. "What are you saying?" His voice was slow and purposeful, and the hardness in his gaze told me he already knew the answer.

"There's *another* Bloodcaster here," I whispered. Saying the words aloud sent a chill through my body.

Another Bloodcaster.

We were rare enough as it was. A Bloodcaster could only be born of two other Bloodcasters, and we were such a hunted species of casters that we usually didn't live long enough to find another, let alone *mate* with them. I'd never known my parents. I assumed they'd died.

Now, I wasn't so sure.

"Do you . . . *know* of any other Bloodcasters?" Benny asked, his eyes uncertain.

"No," I said shortly.

Benny nodded once. "Okay. A new player then. Any ideas?"

Panic and confusion coiled in my stomach. I couldn't breathe. Couldn't *think*.

Whoever it was, they obviously knew about my blood. They wouldn't be here if they didn't, and it wasn't exactly a secret anymore.

I was already at a disadvantage.

"Cora," Benny snapped.

"I'm thinking!" I shouted, rubbing my forehead.

Benny looked at me like I'd lost my mind. And I couldn't blame him. I'd always been the calculated killer. I'd always known how to get a mark.

But this was way beyond my expertise. I'd never hunted my own before. I'd always relied on my unique powers to give me the upper hand.

Not anymore.

I dropped my arms and straightened as an idea popped into my head. "I've got it. I'll cast a locator spell with my blood. It'll alert me to any Bloodcasters in a ten-mile radius."

Benny pointed at me, his eyes lighting up. "Good. That's good."

I nodded and shuffled through the drawers in my

desk, my hands shaking. After knocking a few corked vials over, I finally found the potion I was looking for.

"Cauldron," I said to Benny, jerking my head toward the filing cabinet.

Benny strode forward, tugging open the bottom and biggest drawer. With a grunt, he hefted my cauldron up and hoisted it onto the desk, which rattled from the impact. "Can't you just use a *bowl?*"

I shot him a sharp look. "A cauldron harnesses the power. It provides a stronger conduit to the magical energies." Muttering under my breath, I added, "Seriously, it's like you don't even know what magic *is*."

Benny snorted and crossed his arms, watching me as I combined ingredients. A familiar spicy aroma filled my nose, making my eyes water. I cleared my throat and placed my hands over the mouth of the cauldron.

Before I could utter the spell, an explosion knocked me off my feet. I flew backward, slamming into the wall and making the windowpane rattle. Benny yelped as he was thrown as well. Red and white light blazed from the center of the room, warbling so loudly it made my ears throb. Squinting from the glow and clenching my teeth against the pain in my limbs, I staggered to my feet, trying to make out the figure encompassed in the strange light.

Was it the other Bloodcaster? Had they decided to attack me?

Even as I thought it, I knew it was ridiculous. Blood-casters had purple magic, like me. The only person I'd seen with *red* magic was—

"Cora!" cried a familiar voice.

My blood ran cold. Urgency pulsed through me. "Vince?" I shouted, rushing toward the glow. But when I got close, a searing heat boiled through my skin. I shrieked and backed away, clutching at my arms as if I'd been burned. As soon as I moved away, the scorching sensation vanished.

"What the hell's going on?" Benny yelled over the roaring of Vince's strange magic.

I gaped helplessly at Benny, unsure of what to say— what to *do*.

"Vince!" I cried again. "What's happening?"

"I can't—hold on—" Vince's voice was strained, and it echoed as if he were in a vast cave.

Unbidden, the memory of Vince being attacked by a shadow appeared in my mind. I had to help him.

Raising my hands, I faced the glow and muttered,

"Magic above and powers that be,

Calm this force in front of me.

Settle the magic and the forces here,

And free the caster that he may appear."

Purple magic sprang from my fingertips, hovering in the air for a moment as if unsure of what to do. Then, they funneled toward the eerie red glow, mingling so the magic turned the color of blood. Gradually, the warbling faded, and several dark figures appeared. They stumbled into one another before collapsing to the floor in a heap.

The magic vanished. The air suddenly felt emptier even though my office was now packed with people.

My jaw dropped. Vince and more than a dozen other Reapers were lying on the floor, moaning. Some sported bloody wounds. Others were trembling severely.

My eyes locked onto Vince. There were flecks of blood on his face, but he seemed all right. His gaze met mine, and he scrambled to his feet. Once again, I was awestruck by the magnificence of his dark wings, but it was impractical for my tiny office. The small space was now filled with bodies and feathers, and it made it hard to breathe. Everywhere I turned, dark feathers tickled my face. I shoved past wings and limbs, making my way to Vince.

"What's going on?" I demanded, my legs still throbbing from being thrown across the room.

Vince ran a hand through his hair and offered an apologetic grimace. "Uh, we've just been attacked."

CHAPTER 17

VINCE

Cora's eyes were blazing, her jaw rigid. I rarely saw her as the hardened killer that she was, but here and now, she looked fierce and formidable. It took all my courage to look her in the eye.

"You were *attacked?*" she repeated, her eyes roving over the other Reapers. "I don't understand. Who attacked you?"

"A powerful caster," said Gwen, stumbling to her feet. In a flash, her black wings vanished, disappearing into her shoulder blades as she approached us. "Whoever he is, he has the power to travel between realms. And he possesses Reaper abilities as well."

"He's a *Reaper?*" Jocelyn shouted from behind me.

"We don't know for sure," Mom said hastily as she rose to her feet.

"Today's attack confirmed it," Gwen said in a grim voice. "No one else has the power to crush other Reapers like that. Once we pledge our vow, we are protected by our magic so light and dark forces can't destroy us. Whoever it is, he must've found a way around the vow. A loophole."

Cora straightened, her eyes glinting. "So you came *here*? What if this rogue Reaper follows you? Then *my* coven is at stake."

"The entire magical *universe* is at stake, girl," Gwen snapped. "This is bigger than you, than *any* of us."

"Hold on!" I cried, raising my hands before Cora interjected again. Her face was contorted with rage, and she looked like she was ready to gut Gwen herself. "Look, Cora, I'm sorry," I continued. "I didn't mean to come here. But my body was drawn here, probably because this is the last place I traveled to. I had no choice. My people were being slaughtered in the one place we were supposed to be safe."

Cora's eyes softened as she looked at me. "I just don't understand how you can stay here. When you were here before, you—"

"When were you here?" Gwen suddenly demanded, her voice icy. Her eyes were on fire when she looked at me.

Alarm raced through me. "I—what?"

"*When were you here?*" Her tone was lethal as she

stepped toward me. "You said you traveled here? When? How?"

"I—I—A few hours ago," I sputtered. "It was an accident. I was trying to access my Reaper powers, and—"

Gwen turned away from me, her lips tightening as she met Mom's gaze. I stared at my mom, whose face drained of color.

"What is it?" Cora asked, glancing between them, her shrewd eyes missing nothing.

"Most mortals and casters are unable to travel between realms because of the barrier we put in place," Mom said in a low voice. "But if *Vince* got out . . ." She trailed off and met my gaze. Her eyes were full of fear.

"Then you think he let the attacker in," Cora finished.

"Vince must've broken through the barrier somehow," Mom said, not meeting my gaze.

"What in Lilith's name were you *thinking?*" Gwen barked at me.

"Enough!" Mom shouted, slicing her hand through the air. "He said it was an accident. Obviously, he wouldn't have done it if he'd known. Instead, we need to focus on how to repair the barrier."

"It makes no difference," Gwen snarled, still glaring at me. "If that devil is in *our* realm, he can stay as long as he likes. We might as well find a new home."

Several Reapers started murmuring nervously,

exchanging worried looks. Jocelyn's mouth became small, her eyes wide as she looked at me imploringly. As if *I* could do something about it.

But no. I'd clearly done enough damage. My insides felt hollow.

Those Reapers were dead because of me. Because of my stupidity.

"Quiet!" bellowed a powerful voice.

The surrounding voices faded as a bulky figure stepped into view. I immediately recognized his gleaming yellow eyes.

"Benny," I said in surprise.

But he stared hard at Cora, his gaze intense. "The decision is yours. What do you want to do with them?"

"Did you not *hear*—" Gwen spat.

"*I said,* the decision is Cora's," Benny growled. White fur sprang on his arms and neck, and his fangs emerged.

Gwen looked startled as she took a hesitant step backward.

Cora sighed and rubbed her forehead. "You all can stay here with my coven. I can offer up some spare rooms in the motel for you. But I will need to share this information with my coven."

"You can't—" Gwen started.

"I *can*," Cora said with an edge to her voice. "You brought your problems to me, and I won't leave my people defenseless. They need to know their lives are at stake." She exhaled and looked at me. "How can you stay here? Won't you have those weird fits again?"

A few Reapers gasped and muttered in confusion and alarm. But I knew what Cora meant. How could the Reapers stay here when our bodies would pull us back to our realm? The pain in my head had been excruciating. We couldn't endure that.

"Leave that to me," Mom said, exchanging a glance with Gwen. "We built the enchantment surrounding our realm. We can tweak it so it doesn't make our brains deteriorate."

My blood chilled. *Deteriorate?* Lilith, what would've happened if I'd stayed with Cora? Would my brain have turned to mush?

My thoughts snagged on what Mom had said: *We built the enchantment surrounding our realm.*

Was it *Mom's* fault that we couldn't travel between realms? Had she lied to me about being unable to stay here?

"We can't stay with a *demon coven,*" Gwen said through clenched teeth.

"Why not?" Cora demanded.

Gwen's steely gaze shot to her. "You perform the vilest form of magic. You break the laws of nature with your thirst for blood. It goes against *everything* we vowed to do as Reapers."

Cora's gaze was lethal. She cocked her head at Gwen,

her eyes narrowing like she was a predator sizing up her prey. "I hardly think you're in a place to judge me and my coven. Do you have somewhere else you can go?"

An uncomfortable silence followed her words.

"I didn't think so. Benny will show you to your rooms." Cora gestured toward the door. "But in the meantime, I need to speak with *you*"—she jabbed a finger at Gwen—"to learn everything you know about this new threat."

Gwen's eyes flashed. "I will *not* share sacred Reaper secrets with some demon witch—"

In a blur of movement, Cora lunged and pinned Gwen against the wall, her hand pressed to the older woman's throat. Several Reapers rushed forward, gasping in alarm.

"Don't insult me in *my* territory," Cora hissed, baring her teeth at Gwen. "We'll offer you refuge, but only if you cooperate. This isn't some soup kitchen where we don't ask questions. These are *my people.* Your sacred secrets be damned. Take my offer or leave it."

Gwen made a choked, gurgling sound as Cora released her. Rubbing her neck, Gwen coughed and glared at Cora. "Fine," she said hoarsely. "I accept your offer."

Cora gave a tight smile, and admiration bloomed in my chest. Sure, she'd just attacked one of my superiors, but it had been sexy as hell.

"Take them away, Benny," Cora said, waving her hand.

"This way." Benny held open the office door, and the Reapers lined up behind him. "You'll need to retract your wings," he added. A few Reapers sighed, but one by one, the black wings vanished, making the room feel a little less cramped.

"Vince, a word?" Cora asked, widening her eyes at me.

I drew closer to her, shuffling past the Reapers as they exited.

"Are you sure about this?" she whispered. "I can't protect your clan here. If my people feel threatened—"

"I'm sure," I said. "We literally have nowhere else to go, Cora."

She nodded. "There's . . . something else."

I frowned. "What?"

Benny cleared his throat loudly. We both glanced at him. Only Gwen remained, her arms crossed like a cranky child as the rest of the Reapers' voices echoed in the hall. Benny watched Cora, his eyes burning with a warning.

I gazed between Benny and Cora, my frown deepening. It seemed like they were wordlessly communicating something. It made me feel oddly irritated.

Cora sighed. "I need to be up front with you if I expect it from your clan. We've discovered a new threat here as well. Another Bloodcaster."

My eyes widened. "A—*what*?"

Cora's mouth spread in a thin line. "A Bloodcaster. Someone with magic like mine. We don't know who it is, but I'll be casting a locator spell to find them. I just wanted you to be aware. We suspect this caster means to do us harm. They've been robbing us over the past several months, and we just discovered it."

I couldn't ignore the constant use of the word "we." I had to assume she meant her and Benny. A strange twist in my stomach made me suck in a breath.

"I'll handle it," Cora said, misinterpreting my response.

"I know you will," I said at once. "I just don't want you to have to fight one of your own."

She offered a smile. "I've been fighting my whole life. This isn't anything new."

I touched her cheek. "Thank you, Cora. We owe you. *I* owe you. You didn't have to do this."

She leaned closer to me. "Of course I did. It's *you*. I'd do anything for you, Vince."

Our faces were only a breath away. All I wanted to do was take her in my arms and kiss her senseless. But Gwen shifted behind us, sniffing loudly, and I felt Benny's eyes on us.

Maybe later.

"I'll, uh, be in my room," I said, my face on fire. Cora nodded, her eyes hot with desire as she watched me leave the office.

CHAPTER 18

CORA

I WAS *NOT* LOOKING FORWARD TO A ONE-ON-ONE confrontation with the gray-haired bitch, but it was unavoidable. I needed to assert myself *now* while she thought she was still in charge.

This was *my* turf. *My* people. She couldn't order me around like everyone else.

When it was just the two of us, I shut the office door and turned to face her. Her arms were crossed, her lips pinched with disapproval.

I waved a hand toward her. "I guess we should introduce ourselves. Cora Covington."

"Gwen Peters."

I nodded and pointed to the chair in front of my desk. "You're welcome to have a seat."

"I prefer to stand."

Of course she does, I thought irritably as I made my way

to my desk chair and sank into it. Just because *she* chose to remain standing didn't mean I had to. I leaned my chair back and clasped my fingers in front of my stomach.

Before I could speak, Gwen said tightly, "What's going on between you and Vince?"

I went still, my chair creaking. After taking a slow breath, I said, "I'm not sure that's any of your business."

"Anything concerning Reapers is my business. We have no personal lives, Ms. Covington. Our entire *beings* are devoted to our calling."

"That sounds rather rigid."

She offered a cold smile. "Only those with the strongest caliber are fit for the job." She raised her eyebrows pointedly.

"Oh, really? I was under the impression that Reapers were just Nephilim rejects. Leftovers."

Gwen dropped her arms, her lips quivering with rage. "How dare you—"

"No, how dare *you*? Keep your nose out of what doesn't concern you. I'm not one to offer refuge to *anyone*, let alone beings like you. But I care about Vince. You're lucky he's a kinder soul than you are."

Gwen's nostrils flared as her gaze drilled into me. I had no doubt her ice-cold glare would make many tremble with fear. But not me. I'd perfected that look myself.

Slowly, she exhaled and sat in the seat opposite me. Something in her expression deflated. Like the fight in her had vanished.

"When Reapers pledge their vow, they pledge their whole lives to the work we do," she said quietly. "Vince has made his vow. He made his choice."

"So this choice eliminates all other choices he might want? It turns him into an emotionless robot who exists only to fulfill orders?"

Rage blazed in her eyes. "*No*. But the work comes first. Vince knows this. Or at least . . . he'll understand it soon enough."

"Do you honestly think we're in some kind of relationship?" I scoffed. "I care about him deeply, but that's it. We live in different *realms*, Gwen. I know it's impossible."

"Do you?" she challenged. "Does *he*?"

I remained silent. I hadn't missed the heat that passed between us before he left the room. The feeling of hope and longing. The desire for something more.

"Why?" I asked softly. "What is it with you angels and swearing your *lives* over to someone else's whims? Can't Vince live the life he wants to live? Can't he do his job *and* pursue his own interests? It's all ultimatums with you people."

Gwen sighed. "The magic we possess is a heavy

burden. It requires more sacrifices than other forms of magic."

Well, I could understand that. But at least as a Bloodcaster, I still had freedoms. Even if it meant I was alone.

I cleared my throat. "Tell me about this attacker." We'd spent long enough talking about things that didn't matter.

Gwen leaned forward in her chair and filled me in on the shadow demon who had appeared in their realm, slaughtering Reapers like they were nothing more than dust. This demon had been stealing magic from passing souls before they'd reached the Astral Realm—before the Reapers could safely reap the magic and return it to the atmosphere.

"I have no doubt our thief knew exactly what he was doing," Gwen said. "The magic we reap helps keep the realm secure. It feeds the air and nourishes the world we live in. The Astral Realm relies on that magic more than the mortal realm does. When this thief stole magic repeatedly, our realm suffered for it. The barrier between realms weakened. He used this opportunity—and Vince tearing through it briefly—to make his move."

"What do you think he wants?" I asked.

"I don't know. But the Astral Realm possesses a vast arsenal of magic that could be used offensively if it falls into the wrong hands. If this demon has found a way to cross over to the other realms, it's possible he's learned how to take our magic with him. It would destroy our realm and create an unstoppable threat to yours. His magic would be unparalleled. Even Third Tier demons wouldn't be able to stop him."

I shuddered. After performing certain blood rituals, demons could Ascend to the Second and Third Tiers of dark magic, giving them more power. Damien had been Second Tier.

"Who could possibly have that much power?" I asked. "Who could do this?" Traveling between realms seemed even far-fetched for *me*, though I wondered if with the right spell and potion ingredients I'd be able to manage it.

"Someone with Reaper powers. Possibly a Nephilim, but he'd have to be powerful. Our realm is protected against the light magic of Nephilim. They aren't meant to cross over unless they've accepted the call of the Reaper."

I was stuck on the possibility of this being another Nephilim. Ice hardened in my chest as my gaze met Gwen's. "Could it be Hector Moses?"

Gwen frowned. "Possibly," she said slowly. "He *is* powerful. But the barrier's wards are firm and unyielding. If any high-ranking Nephilim could cross over, we would've seen this problem before."

A hard lump formed in my throat. "Hector is different. Before Vince joined you, he fought Hector. Vince—he *Jumped* using Hector as an anchor."

Gwen's brow furrowed. "I'm not sure what you mean."

As briefly as possible, I explained the process of Vince's time travel and the usage of anchors to keep him grounded. I glossed over Luke and the Timekeepers, since I wasn't fully certain who they were, anyway.

"The Timekeepers made it seem like he was some kind of deadly danger to the timeline because of it," I finished. "That he had the potential to travel just like Vince."

Gwen's face had turned ashen. "Merciful Lilith. Why didn't anybody *warn* us about this?"

I shrugged. "Luke implied this had never happened before. Anchors were only ever meant to be inanimate objects. Not living things."

Gwen groaned and covered her face with her hands. "Even if it *is* Hector, we have no way of finding him. Especially if the Timekeepers have him."

"What do you know of the Timekeepers?" I asked, narrowing my eyes.

"Not much. They like to keep to themselves."

"And I'm sure you have *no* idea what that's like."

Gwen shot me a flat look, but the corners of her mouth twitched. I was stunned this woman had any appreciation for humor.

"The Timekeepers and Reapers respect each other," she went on. "We have sacred vows to keep and protect. They preserve the timeline. We preserve the ebb and flow of magic. We don't interfere."

"Until now, it seems."

Gwen remained silent, her eyes contemplative.

I leaned forward, placing my hands on the desk. "I'll do some digging in the demon community. See if any rumors have popped up about this guy. If he's dark, I'll find him. But if he's not . . ."

Gwen nodded. "I'll reach out to my contact and arrange a meeting with the Timekeepers. This is beyond the Reapers now." She met my gaze. "You were right. I'm sorry I tried to shut you out."

Again, I was overcome with shock. This woman had completely turned her attitude around. It was unexpected and, dare I say it, *admirable*. I wasn't sure I would've come around so quickly if the roles had been reversed.

"Thank you," I said quietly, offering a small smile. "I'm grateful for your cooperation, Gwen. I swear I'll do whatever it takes to help you solve this."

She nodded and rose to her feet. "I know you will." She turned to the door, then paused and glanced over her shoulder at me. "There's no future for you two," she said, her voice barely above a whisper. "I hope you know that."

I stared at her, resisting the urge to snap that I *did*

know. How could I not? If this magic thief succeeded and siphoned magic from another realm, then this mortal realm was doomed. If he *didn't* succeed, then things would go back to how they were before, and Vince and I would be worlds apart. The thought made my heart twist and my chest tighten so intensely I couldn't breathe. Heat stung my eyes, and I hastily blinked away the emotion before it consumed me.

Something like grief tainted Gwen's expression. When her eyes met mine, it was with solidarity and understanding, not chastisement.

She'd experienced this firsthand. She'd lost someone. I could read it plainly on her face.

So instead of arguing, I nodded stiffly. A more affectionate person might've offered condolences or kind words. But Gwen and I were of the same mold. No nonsense. Shove our emotions away and get the work done.

Gwen nodded too, her eyes closing off once more before she left the room.

CHAPTER 19

VINCE

I GOT A FEW HOURS' SLEEP BEFORE THE INTENSE pressure built up in my chest, making it hard to breathe. To be honest, I was shocked it took this long. When I'd last been here with Cora, it had only taken minutes before the splitting pain struck.

A shrill ringing blared in my head, and I bolted from the bed, clutching at my head. My lungs closed off, and I couldn't breathe. Dark spots danced in my vision.

As quickly as it had come, it vanished, and I sucked in several deep breaths. But the air still felt thin. Insufficient. I remembered how clear the air had seemed in the Astral Realm when I'd returned.

We wouldn't last here. At least not for long.

A knock sounded at my door, and my heart lurched in my throat. I didn't realize how badly I wanted it to be Cora until I found my mom on the other side.

"Can I come in?" she asked.

I sighed and stood back to let her through. I closed the door and turned to face her. Her eyes were tired, and her hair was frizzier than normal.

"Are you all right?" Her gaze roved over me as if expecting to find injuries.

"I'm fine."

Mom exhaled with relief. "Gwen and I cast the spell to loosen the Astral Realm's hold on us. Hopefully, it'll buy us some time."

I fixed a hard stare at her. "So all this time, you could've just *magicked* away the restrictions keeping us tied to that realm?"

Mom blinked at me. "Vince—"

"It's just one lie after another, Mom. And I'm tired of it."

Her head reared back in shock. "What're you talking about?"

Anger boiled within me. My nostrils flared as I held up fingers, counting each deception of hers. "First, there was the whole *forgetting your humanity* thing. Then, the magic thief. Then, the fact that you just conveniently didn't care about me and Dad anymore. Now, you're telling me the one thing I wanted more than anything— *to go home*—was within your power the whole time and you couldn't even bother."

Mom's face turned ashen. Her mouth opened and

closed weakly. At long last, she managed, "I—I never meant to lie to you, Vince."

I nodded stiffly, not meeting her gaze. Deep down, I knew it was unfair of me to judge her so harshly. She was out of practice being a mother.

But whose fault was that? All she had to do was cast some spell and she could've come back to me and Dad. *I guess it just wasn't important enough.* My throat felt hot, and I blinked away tears.

Mom stepped toward me, her gaze pleading. "Vince, you have to understand what happens when Reapers stay in a realm they don't belong in. The fabric between worlds could tear apart, separating the realms permanently. We might not ever be able to get back."

"Is that such a bad thing?" I snapped.

Mom closed her eyes briefly. "We *can't* do our job here. We can't see souls or their magic in this realm like we can in the Astral Realm. The work *has* to be done in a neutral space between here and the Underworld. There's no other way."

I said nothing and clenched my teeth against the pain still coursing through my chest.

Mom took my hand, and I resisted the urge to shake it from her grasp. "I wanted to see you more than anything. But I also knew that if I did, I—I wouldn't want to come back. And I couldn't risk it." Her voice grew thick, and she swallowed, her eyes shining. "So much more was at stake than what *I* wanted. Sure, I could've been selfish and gone back to you and José. But if I had, the consequences would've been devastating. The separation from my realm would've torn me apart, killing me slowly. And that's the *best-case* scenario."

I frowned. "What's the worst case?"

Mom's eyes turned grim. "The souls would be trapped in limbo. Unable to cross over because the Reapers can't reach them. Eventually, the Underworld would crumble. The souls of the dead would spill into the mortal realm. It wouldn't be pretty."

Though my throat still felt tight, I found myself nodding. The rage within me subsided. When Mom put it that way, it *did* seem kind of selfish.

And I knew firsthand the agony of being with the one you loved and being unable to stay. If Cora *hadn't* pushed me away—if my Mimic hadn't told her to—I almost certainly would've stayed. Even if it killed me.

I exhaled. "I'm sorry."

Mom made a small, whimpering noise and gathered me in her arms, pressing kisses to the top of my head. "You have nothing to be sorry for. I should've been up front with you from the beginning."

I wanted to object to this, knowing that if she *had*, I would've demanded she send me back. But perhaps she was right. Perhaps plain honesty from the get-go would've been better.

When we drew away from each other, I cleared my throat and asked, "So, what do we do now?"

"Gwen says Cora's working on a spell to lure out our magic thief. Draw him back over to this realm. If it works, I'll go back to the Astral Realm and strengthen our wards to allow us to come back without his interference."

My stomach knotted. "You'll . . . go back there?"

Mom offered a soft smile. "I'll be all right, Vince. This is what I'm good at. The last time something like this happened, I held my own just fine."

"The last time?" My chest tightened with anxiety.

Mom gestured to the scar on her face, and my blood ran cold. "We've had magic thieves before. But none of them have been able to cross over. The last thief was hard to catch, and he tried taking a piece of me with him."

I shuddered. "How did you catch him?"

"Remember when I told you I'd been to the mortal realm for an emergency before? That was why. We tracked down the closest soul to death and lingered, waiting for the thief to show himself."

"Why can't we do that this time?"

Mom's face sobered. "Because he's in *our* realm now. We waited too long. If we'd acted sooner, maybe—" She broke off, her voice catching on the last word.

I took her hands in mine and squeezed. "What can I do?" My body felt restless with pent-up energy. I had to do *something*.

Mom blinked tears from her eyes and swallowed hard. "You can rest. We'll need all our Reapers at full strength if Cora's spell works."

Something within me deflated. Rest? Yeah, right. I was way too anxious for that.

But as Mom bid me goodnight and left my room, an idea formed in my head. There was one secret weapon of mine that no one else knew about. No one except Cora. And perhaps it would make all the difference.

I had to go find Luke.

"It won't work," Benny said flatly.

My eyes narrowed. "How do you know?"

He raised an eyebrow. "Because I've been doing this longer than Luke has. He can't interfere."

"Gwen says she's reaching out to the Timekeepers," Cora said from behind her desk, rubbing her forehead. Exhaustion tugged at her face. "Maybe they'll cooperate."

Benny scoffed. "I doubt it. That's why I never joined. They don't play nice with others."

"Even if the entire universe is at stake?" I challenged.

"Yeah. Even then."

I rolled my eyes.

Cora slammed her palm on her desk, and I jumped and looked at her. "Benny, take him to see Luke. It can't hurt. Besides, Vince needs to get out anyway—to see his dad."

My heart lifted at the words. *I'll get to see Dad.* I'd closed myself off from that hope a long time ago, thinking I'd never be able to speak to him again.

Cora met my gaze, her eyes softening as if she knew exactly what I was feeling right now.

"Thank you," I said quietly.

She nodded and stood from her desk. Her eyes flicked to Benny. "Call me if things go south."

Benny nodded, and Cora made for the door. Before she left, I blurted, "Wait. You aren't coming?"

Cora paused and glanced at me. Regret shone in her eyes. "I wish I could. But I've got too much to do here. I have to find *your* criminal *and* mine. Plus run this coven." She sighed, shaking her head.

I stepped toward her. "Let me help." When she opened her mouth to argue, I added quickly, "Please, Cora. I can't just be useless here. I have to do something."

Cora pressed her lips together and eyed me, her gaze contemplative. "Find Luke first. If he can help us, that's our priority. If you come back empty-handed, I promise I'll put you to work." Her mouth curved in an alluring smile that made my stomach turn to mush. I wanted to lean in and kiss her right there, but I knew this wasn't the time or the place.

Cora's eyes stirred with heat, and I wondered if she was thinking the same thing. "You two be safe."

I really didn't think I needed Benny's assistance, especially when he closed his eyes and confirmed that Luke *was*, in fact, at home. That would've been the first place I'd look.

But Benny insisted he should come in case there were any dangers lurking nearby—including the Timekeepers. He would get a heads up if there were.

Plus, Cora trusted him. For some reason. I tried not to let that knowledge bother me.

Benny admitted he didn't have a car and asked if I could Jump us there. Ordinarily, I would've told him no, since Mom insisted the Reapers needed to save their strength in case there was a fight coming. But I was so tired of feeling useless that I readily agreed. Besides, it meant we could get back sooner. I didn't want to be away for too long.

I held out my hand, and Benny grasped it tightly, his

eyes uncertain. "Have you ever Jumped with another person before?"

I shrugged. "A few times with Cora. We time traveled ten years into the past."

Benny's eyes widened, and his face paled, giving me a small slither of satisfaction. "Uh, any chance that'll happen to us too?"

I laughed. "Don't worry about it. I have a lot more control now." Although, that wasn't entirely true. I still felt like my Jumping happened by accident.

I closed my eyes, then faltered, my breath hitching.

Benny asked, "What's wrong?"

My eyes opened. "It's just . . . normally, when I Jump, I link minds with Luke. He'll know we're coming. Is that a problem?"

"Possibly. If he knows ahead of time, it means the Timekeepers will too. It's best to have the element of surprise, just in case." His jaw ticked back and forth in contemplation. "You can link minds with me this time."

I blinked. Discomfort swelled in my stomach. "Uh . . ."

Benny fixed me with a flat look. "Got a problem with that?"

I sighed. "No. It's fine." To be fair, I didn't know Benny that well. Then again, I'd been upset when I found out Luke and I were connected without my consent, so having *anyone* in my head felt like a violation.

"Relax your mind," Benny said. "Go to your mental bridge. I'll intercept you before Luke does."

I nodded, closing my eyes again. In a flash, I was back on the lacrosse field, stick in hand. I gripped it tightly, glancing around at the faceless figures that surrounded me.

Then Benny appeared, wearing the same T-shirt and jeans. He raised his eyebrows as he gazed up and down the field. "Interesting," he said with a smirk.

I shrugged, my cheeks warming. Why was I embarrassed by this? Clearing my throat, I asked, "So . . . since I'm back in the mortal realm, do I need to summon my Teleportation powers the old way?"

Benny shook his head. "Your Reaper magic is still the same. However you traveled last time, do that again."

I nodded, gripping the crosse tightly in my hands. My vision narrowed, isolating the goal in front of me. Everything else around me faded. It was just me and the goal.

My heart rate slowed. My mind sharpened with focus. Without realizing it, I'd moved. My steps were strong and purposeful. I only saw the goal. Only felt the weight of the ball in my crosse.

Luke's house, a voice in my head whispered. I visualized the location clearly in my mind, as if it were a normal afternoon and we were lounging on his couch after school.

A small *pop* jerked me back to reality. Benny and I

spun in place. The air whooshed around us. Gravity pressed in on me, squeezing the air out of me.

Then, we landed. It was much less forceful than the last few times. But, then again, I'd traveled much farther. This was just a few miles. And no time travel.

Benny released my hand, staggering forward with a clumsy "oof." His face was ashen, and he shook his head violently, his eyes dazed.

"You all right?" I asked, slightly proud of the way I'd managed to remain upright. I didn't even feel nauseous this time.

Benny sucked in a deep breath. "Yeah. I'll be fine."

I looked around, my chest tightening at the familiar sight. The houses were small, mostly single-family homes. Thin pine trees lined the street.

I'd Jumped us to the neighbor's house, just in case our arrival attracted Luke's attention.

My stomach twisted with anxiety. For some reason, I was worried Luke wouldn't want to talk to me. He hadn't seemed particularly eager to help the Reapers last time I asked. But maybe if Benny and I ambushed him, we could get him to agree.

Benny's gaze grew distant as he stared in the direction of Luke's tiny, run-down home. After a moment, Benny said, "I sense three people in the house. One of them is Luke, and he's undisturbed. I can only assume the other two are family members."

I nodded. Luke was the oldest. His younger siblings were probably at soccer practice with their dad.

Benny's eyes cut to me. "He'll know as soon as we step onto the yard. Are you ready?"

"Ready."

Together, we strode toward Luke's house.

CHAPTER 20

CORA

My head was throbbing by the time I finally went back to my apartment. I knew it would've saved time if I'd just brought my spell notes and books to the office, but some small part of me craved a solace away from the coven. A sanctuary that was just for me.

Even if it was after midnight and I was bone-weary, ready for sleep.

"Cora?"

I stilled, my keys jingling in my hand as a dark shape emerged from the staircase at the apartment complex. My body tensed until I recognized the figure. It was Dex, the vampire.

I relaxed. "Nice to see you again, Dex."

Dex nodded politely. "And you. Are you well?"

I smiled, amused by the cordial way vampires spoke. It always made me curious about how old they were.

They were probably accustomed to propriety and customs from hundreds of years ago. "I am. What can I do for you?"

Dex shoved his hands in his pockets and glanced around. Though shadows surrounded us, my instincts told me we were alone. "I have news." His voice was barely above a whisper.

My heart fluttered with excitement. I stepped closer to him. "Tell me."

Dex hesitated. "This can't get back to Hunter. He's too afraid we'll be killed for sharing information with you."

Dread mingled with excitement, building up inside my chest until I couldn't breathe. "You have my word. I'm good at keeping secrets."

He nodded absently. "It's Piper," he said in a whisper.

I frowned. It took me a moment to conjure the image of the girl with the purple hair. The one who had eventually sided with me in front of the mob after the fire. "*What* is Piper?"

"Your thief."

My frown deepened. "Piper's too young. There's no way she's working alone."

"You're right. She isn't. It's her boss that has Hunter too scared to talk. I don't know him, but Hunter does. He says all the vampires in the city answer to him. If you want answers, dig up dirt on Piper first."

I opened my mouth to ask more questions, but before I could, Dex vanished into the shadows. Gaping after him, I shuddered against a sudden chill that gripped me and made my way to my apartment.

Piper was stealing from the coven? Chronologically, it made sense; she'd joined us just before Damien's death. But . . . she wasn't a Bloodcaster. I'd seen her magic—it was black.

I trusted Dex's information. But if Piper *was* stealing from me . . . then, *why*? She was powerful, yes, but barely eighteen years old. She seemed so down-to-earth. So solid. Not at all like those untrustworthy weasels who always tried to double-cross me.

She had to have another motive. Maybe her scary boss was blackmailing her. I knew what that was like.

And if her boss was as powerful as Dex said, then he was probably the Bloodcaster I was looking for.

I rubbed my forehead as I entered my place, bolting the door behind me. My body ached with exhaustion, but I still had so much work to do. I hauled out the coven's Grimoire, which I had acquired soon after Damien's death, and got to the more pressing matter of identifying the Reapers' attacker. The old book was full of spells and potions I'd never heard of before. For the first few weeks after I got it, my body itched to test out something new. But the coven responsibilities soon overwhelmed me, and I hadn't gotten the chance.

After brewing some coffee and drinking a cup or two to get my body buzzed, I sat at the table and started leafing through pages in the Grimoire. At first, I searched under the "demons" section, thinking that whoever their attacker was had to have dark magic. Maybe he was Second or Third Tier. But after scanning the various passages about vampires, werewolves, and shapeshifters, I came up empty-handed.

Then, I remembered what Gwen had said—that this enemy seemed to have the powers of a Reaper. Frowning, I turned to the section of the Grimoire about Nephilim. After scanning the pages, I found only a small paragraph about Reapers: *Some dark Nephilim possess the power to reap magic from a caster's soul. This power can only be accessed if a Nephilim pledges a sacred vow, or if a caster brews the appropriate potion.*

I stilled. My entire body felt numb with horror. I read the line again: . . . *if a caster brews the appropriate potion.*

Obviously, it wouldn't have been as easy as just listing the potion ingredients right there, otherwise anyone could do it. But the fact that the book *mentioned* a potion at all meant . . .

My heart thundered as I jumped up from the table, rushing into my room to dive through my notebook of potions and their ingredients, handwritten by me over the years. Frantically, I turned pages and pages until I found a potion I hadn't made in years: a Nephilim elixir.

My breath turned shaky and ragged as I glanced over the ingredients. Then, my blood ran cold.

It called for a white Nephilim feather. And, right next to it, in my own handwriting, I'd added uncertainly: *can it be substituted with a dark feather for dark Nephilim powers?* The ink was fresher here. I remembered adding this note after I'd met Vince and found out Reapers existed.

A sour taste filled my mouth as I took another shuddering breath. If my theory had been correct, there was a potion that allowed someone to temporarily *become* a Reaper. All they needed was a bit of my blood.

Or . . . the blood of another Bloodcaster.

This was all connected: the thief, the hidden Bloodcaster, and the powerful demon taking over the Astral Realm. But *why*? Why would a Bloodcaster want to rob me *and* steal magic from the Reapers? It didn't make any sense.

Suddenly, my skin prickled, my instincts screaming at me that something was wrong. I bolted to my feet, my pulse skittering as I looked around the room. The air shifted around me, and I smelled something familiar and foreign. Something flowery mingled with ash and alcohol.

My eyes narrowed. In a flash, my dagger was in my hand as I crept toward the living room.

"Who's there?" I demanded.

A low chuckle echoed from the kitchen. Blood pounded in my ears as I inched closer. "Do you have any idea how *stupid* you are for breaking into an assassin's home?" I snapped.

A shadow emerged from the kitchen before I could step inside. As he drew closer, I made out the features of a tall, wiry man with gray hair and a goatee. His cold, dark eyes surveyed me with interest and curiosity.

I grew rigid, sucking in a breath. There was that smell again. This time, I finally remembered where I'd smelled it before.

The orphanage. The blanket I'd been wrapped in as a baby. I'd kept it for years, often smelling it to try to get a whiff of who my parents were and why they'd abandoned me.

This man smelled like that blanket.

A lump formed in my throat. The man cocked his head and smiled, his face sinister and predatory.

"Of all those fools scrambling to find me," he said, his voice low and gravelly, "I knew you'd be the first."

I staggered back a step. "Why are you here?"

The man's eyes glittered as he drew closer. "Really? That's the first question you ask?"

My nostrils flared. "Get out before I gut you."

He laughed. "Such *fire*. Your mother had it too. Even on the day of her death."

Ice trickled down my chest. The feral look in his gaze told me he wasn't at all sad about my mother's death. I wouldn't be surprised if he'd killed her himself.

My head was spinning. I couldn't process this. Couldn't think. I had to get *out*.

No, a small voice in my head whispered. *Focus. You're a killer. You know how to think on your feet.*

I had to distract him. At least until the shock wore off. Right now, I knew I wouldn't be able to hold my own in a fight. I was too stunned.

Which was probably exactly what he wanted.

"Why'd you kill her?" I lifted my chin. "Did you sacrifice her in a blood ritual?"

The man grinned widely, showing his jagged and stained teeth. "Smart girl. Yes, I did exactly that. You probably know how rare Bloodcasters are. There were so many possibilities. So many experiments . . . I had questions that needed answering."

I suppressed a shudder at the thought of my *mother* being subject to experimentation. "Why the Reapers?" I asked. "Why my coven? How are they connected?"

He took a step toward me, and I inched away from him, keeping a solid six feet between us. "Your coven is a means to an end. It's *you* I really want."

A means to an end? Then why—

I froze, suddenly understanding. "You needed cash."

The man smirked as if pleased I'd figured it out. "I'd already infiltrated my way into your coven. I wasn't ready to strike yet, and the cash opportunity was right there in front of me." He shrugged. "I figured, why waste it?"

He'd probably hired Piper to work on the inside. My blood boiled at the thought. "And the Reapers?"

He laughed again. "That should be obvious. *Power.* Being a Bloodcaster provides me with so much raw, unstoppable magic. It's unparalleled . . . in *this* realm. But the Astral Realm? Oh, so many possibilities . . . Enough power to create my *own realm.* To create a whole new society of casters!"

The hunger in his eyes made me sick to my stomach. This man was cold and calculating. No emotion. No affection. It was as if he completely lacked the ability to care.

He only saw power.

"You want to sacrifice me too," I whispered.

He grinned. "I just need a *tiny* bit more power. My associates are duds in that department, I'm afraid." He winked conspiratorially as if we were sharing grievances together.

Associates. "How many people are working with you?" I asked. It couldn't possibly be just Piper in his employ. Dex had mentioned *all* the vampires in Hinport answered to him. He could have an entire *army* behind him.

"More than you think. Some of them you've already met." His grin widened. He was enjoying watching me squirm.

This guy was a psychopath.

And I'd had enough of him.

I hurled my dagger at him. A burst of purple light momentarily blinded me, and a loud clatter told me my dagger had fallen to the floor. I lunged, tackling the man. He shoved his weight forward, thrusting me off to pin me down. I slammed my forehead against his. He groaned. I kicked him in the groin, and he groaned again. A weak chuckle burst from his lips.

"They said you were good," he said in a strained voice. "But not as good as me."

His mouth opened wide, and purple magic flooded from his mouth as if he were breathing fire. His eyes darkened until there was no white left. Black veins stood out against his skin. The room darkened and quivered.

I struggled to rise, but he held me in place. Long claws protruded from his fingers, embedding into my flesh.

He was transforming into some kind of beast.

My heart plummeted to my stomach. In that moment, I knew I would lose. So, I did the only thing I *could* do.

I screamed.

CHAPTER 21

VINCE

WHEN I KNOCKED ON THE DOOR, LUKE'S MOM answered. Her face split into a wide grin when she saw me.

"Vince! We haven't seen you in forever! How are you?"

"Fine, thanks. Is Luke home?"

"I'm here." Luke appeared behind his mom, his face stony and his eyes guarded as he gazed from me to Benny.

"Can we come in?" I asked.

Luke glanced at his mom. "Give us a minute?"

Her expression stilled, her eyes filling with concern. I wondered how much she knew. Did she know her son possessed magic? Or had he lied to her too?

Slowly, she nodded and backed away from the door. I heard dishes clattering in the kitchen.

Luke stepped onto the porch next to Benny and me and shut the door behind him. Rubbing his arms against the chilly air, he hissed, "You *can't* be here."

"Things are bad, Luke," I said. "We wouldn't have come if it wasn't urgent."

"I *know*," Luke snapped. "When are you gonna get it? My mind is linked to yours. I know *everything*."

"Then you know my realm is dying!" I shot back. "Someone is tearing it apart as we speak, siphoning all the magic my people have reaped. We need your help. We need the Timekeepers' help."

Luke's face drained of color, and he staggered back a step. "I—no. Vince, you can't—"

"Luke, *we have no other choice*," I said in a hard voice.

"You don't understand what you're asking!" Luke's voice shook with fear. "The Timekeepers, they—they have no concept of right and wrong. For all we know, they'd *side* with the guy you're trying to catch."

My eyes narrowed as I took in his clenched fists and wide eyes. There was more to it than this. I stepped closer. "This demon, whoever he is, will tear the world apart. Do you want that?"

"Of course not!"

"Then, *help us*."

"Vince—"

"Oh, enough already," Benny snarled. He shoved Luke

backward until my friend slammed against the front door. Benny raised his fingers and pressed them to Luke's temple. Luke inhaled a sharp gasp and then went very still. His body was rigid, like a stiff mannequin in Benny's grasp. Benny's eyes closed, his brows furrowing in concentration.

Horror pooled in my stomach. Benny was sifting through Luke's thoughts. Fishing for information.

"Stop it," I whispered.

Benny ignored me. In his grip, Luke's body went slack.

I shoved Benny off Luke. "I said *stop*!"

Benny grunted. Something electric crackled in the air when he broke contact with Luke.

Benny whirled on me, eyes blazing. "This is what we came here for! And he wasn't cooperating!"

"You can't just *invade* his mind like that!" I roared.

"Guys," Luke groaned. He'd slumped backward against the door, his face ashen and his eyes incoherent. "It doesn't matter. He knows."

I blinked, my gaze shifting to Benny. "He knows *what*?"

Luke shook his head. "Not Benny. Hector."

I stiffened. My blood ran cold. *Hector*?

A small *pop* behind us made me whirl, my heart pounding a warning rhythm in my chest.

Standing in the yard, his hands shoved in his pockets,

was Hector, his eyes gleaming. He wore the same green robe I'd once seen on the Timekeepers.

Shock froze my body in place. I couldn't move.

"Vince," Hector said pleasantly, striding toward us. "I haven't seen you in an age."

My gaze flicked to Benny and Luke. Benny's face had paled, and wolf fur appeared on his arms and face as if preparing him for battle. Luke closed his eyes, his face clammy.

I positioned myself in front of Luke. If it came down to a fight, he was too weak to defend himself. Finally finding my voice, I said, "What do you want?"

Hector raised an eyebrow, peering around my shoulder at Luke. "There's no need. I can't hurt him. We're colleagues."

Unease wormed through me. *No. He's lying. He has to be. I'm sure he just stole that robe and is trying to throw me off.*

"I said, *what do you want*," I growled.

Hector spread his arms, looking offended. "I want to talk. We're old friends, after all."

That was an overstatement. Hector was my enemy. He'd banished my mom to be a Reaper so he could take her place as leader of the clan. He'd worked with Damien to put a hit on me because I was stirring up trouble with my warlock powers.

I clenched my teeth. My hands formed fists at my side. In a flash, my dark wings burst from my shoulder blades, casting shadows on me and Benny. Luke gagged and waved a hand in front of his face as feathers smothered him. I shifted slightly so my wings weren't in front of him, then faced Hector again.

Hector, at least, had the good sense to look alarmed at the sight of my wings. Magic circled through me, and an eerie red glow emanated from my hands.

That was new.

Hector's eyes widened slightly. "Very impressive," he murmured, his expression serious. All humor and mockery in his tone vanished.

"You want to talk?" I shouted. "Then, talk."

"I came to warn you," Hector said.

My eyes narrowed. "I don't believe you."

Hector sighed. Something about his face seemed . . . *different.* I couldn't quite place what it was. "I'm a Timekeeper now, Vince. I see so much more than I did before. Someone is trying to alter the timeline. And I've finally figured out who it is."

I sensed Luke stiffen next to me. Even Benny froze, his yellow eyes fixed intently on Hector.

"Why should I believe anything you say?" I asked.

"Because I preserve the timeline now," Hector said, his eyes earnest. "I wouldn't be a Timekeeper if I didn't have the Call inside me."

"The Call," I repeated in a flat voice.

Hector gestured to Luke. "Ask him. You can't be a

Timekeeper unless you have the flow of the timeline within you. The urge to protect it."

I went very still, suddenly remembering those small urges I'd had when I time traveled. The quiet voice inside me telling me to stay hidden. To avoid being seen. To return to a certain point in time.

"He's right," Luke said, his voice a bit stronger than before. He looked at me with a grim expression. "Not everyone has the Call. Those who do go through a rigorous testing process before they become a Time-keeper. Hector's telling the truth."

I scowled. I didn't believe that for a *second*.

"I can prove it," Hector said quickly. "The man you're looking for is named Quentin Cox."

My brow furrowed. Where had I heard that last name before?

"Go to Cora Covington's apartment," Hector said. "He's there now."

Panic filled my chest, and realization slammed into me. Cox had been Cora's real last name. *Cordelia Cox.*

Quentin was her father.

My arms flew out, snatching Benny and Luke by their wrists. Luke yelped. Hector shouted my name. But I didn't even hesitate before Jumping, focusing intently on the apartment complex I'd only seen once before.

Gravity slammed into me, and the three of us toppled to the ground in a heap. My wings were still outstretched behind me, dragging me backward like weights were tied to me.

"Vince," Luke groaned, staggering to his feet.

"Stay here," I said. If Hector hadn't been there, I would've just left them both at Luke's house.

"Like *hell*," Benny snapped. In a flash, he'd shifted to his wolf form, a powerful white beast bigger than any dog I'd ever seen. He fixed his yellow eyes on me as if challenging me.

I sighed, glancing at Luke over my shoulder. "Stay hidden. We'll be back."

Luke's face was pale, but he nodded.

I followed Benny's lead, since I didn't actually know Cora's apartment number. A petty side of me *hated* that Benny had been to her place and I hadn't, but I shoved the thought away. Now wasn't the time for childish jealousy.

Cora was in danger. The Bloodcaster she was looking for was her *father*. The thought sent icy coils of dread pulsing through my chest.

Faster. Faster. My legs pushed on and on until I was practically flying. Benny easily kept a brisk pace in front of me, and I remained on his tail.

We climbed a set of stairs, darting down hallways until Benny came to a stop. I didn't need to ask if this was it.

The door swung off its hinges. Broken glass littered

the linoleum floor inside. A dark stain pooled in front of my feet. Crouching over, I leaned close.

It was blood. *Purple* blood.

Benny and I shared a horrified look before we burst inside.

"Cora?" I shouted, darting from room to room. More shards of glass. Broken furniture. Stains of blood.

No, no, no . . .

"The Grimoire's gone," Benny said. I jumped and whirled, surprised to see him in human form. White hair still coated his arms. His eyes were wild with rage. "So are all her potion vials."

I gazed numbly around the wrecked apartment, too shocked to say anything. This was *Cora.* How could anyone have gotten the jump on her? Even if her father *was* a Bloodcaster, she was a deadly assassin. People whispered her name and shied away from her, fearing even a deadly glance from the Blade of Hinport.

"Did you know?" I asked, finding my voice at last. "Did you know her father was alive?"

Benny's jaw went rigid. Slowly, he shook his head. "Are we sure that's who came for her?"

"It's my best guess. Cora was looking for a Bloodcaster, and they only get their magic if both parents have it too. Unless she happens to have a Bloodcaster uncle or something . . ." I trailed off. A cold, hard emptiness solidified in my stomach. Cora was gone. We were too late.

Benny inhaled deeply, closing his eyes. The wolf hair on his arms stood up.

"Can you smell her?" I asked.

He nodded and sniffed again. When his eyes opened, he growled, "Damn. He Jumped. I can't track her."

He Jumped. Cora had said Bloodcasters could essentially create a potion with every kind of magic available. She once told me she'd taken a Nephilim elixir.

I straightened, my heart racing. With a gasp, I raced toward Cora's room, searching her dresser and bookshelf for her potion notes. Unless Quentin had taken those too . . .

Then, I found it. The notebook was open to the page on Nephilim elixirs. As if Cora had been searching for the same thing I was. A shiver raced down my spine as I read her note: *can it be substituted for a dark feather for dark Nephilim powers?*

"Merciful Lilith," I breathed. The notebook shook in my hands. My skin suddenly turned cold.

A Bloodcaster could acquire Reaper powers.

Quentin was the magic thief. The one who'd slaughtered my people.

And now he had Cora.

CHAPTER 22

CORA

My head throbbed in a sickening rhythm that pulsed through me, each beat bringing a wave of nausea. My head was spinning. Icy darkness surrounded me.

I vaguely remembered the details of the fight with my father. Broken chairs. Shattered glass. I'd managed to cut him twice.

But once he'd shifted to that . . . that *monster* . . . I'd known it was over. I tried recalling the details of the beast, but my head turned fuzzy. All I could remember was fur, claws, fangs, and magic pouring from his mouth. I'd never seen anything like it.

I groaned, trying to rise. But chains rattled, and resistance pulled at my wrists. Though I was enveloped in darkness, I knew I was in some kind of prison cell.

"Ah, Cordelia, you're awake," said a soft voice.

I flinched. His voice—*my name*—jarred too many

memories within me. The dank orphanage from my childhood. The ragged blanket I'd finally thrown out when I'd changed my name. Everything I'd tried so desperately to put behind me.

My father chuckled. "Don't worry. The drug will wear off soon."

"What did you give me?" My voice was a low rasp.

"Just something to knock you out. You put up quite a fight earlier. I'm impressed."

I shifted my arms, trying to feel out my surroundings even though I couldn't see. There had to be a way out. No one knew I was here. No one even knew my father was alive. Until a few hours ago, I hadn't known, either.

As a child, I'd been told my parents were dead. All my life, I'd believed it. How could I not? My blood made me a constant target.

"You aren't the least bit curious?" my father asked.

I couldn't see him, but I glared at the space where his voice was coming from. "About what?"

"Who I am? Where I've been all this time?"

"No."

"No?"

"I said *no!*" I spat. "I don't care who you are or why you left me or what your life is like at all. I don't give a *damn* about you! You're just some asshole who wants my blood. Just like all the others. So you can go to hell."

He remained silent. I expected him to laugh again.

But instead he said softly, "It's difficult, isn't it? Always being hunted."

I said nothing. I would *not* bond with him over this. We were nothing alike.

As if reading my mind, he went on, "You and I aren't so different, you know. We both had to cope with a dangerous life, always being on the run. You became a skilled killer, using weapons and cleverness to best your opponents. I also became a skilled killer . . . but with my magic."

"I'm not like you," I hissed.

This time, he did laugh. His voice was closer than before, and I instinctively shifted away from him. "I know more about you than you think, Cordelia. You're no saint. So spare me your judgment. You and I both kill for our own benefit."

"That's not true," I said through clenched teeth. "Not anymore."

He scoffed. "Oh, really? What, because now you're a coven leader? You've changed your ways? Turned over a new leaf? You thirst for death, Cordelia. You always have. And you always will."

Agony lanced through me at his words. I didn't say anything, but I didn't have to. Part of me knew he was right. Even when I became a leader and set down my blade, I still longed for violence. It was a habit. It was *comfortable* for me.

Did that make me a monster like him?

"This is your only chance to ask the questions you've held onto over the years," my father said. "Hate me all you want, Cordelia. But I'm the only one who has the answers."

"Stop calling me that," I snarled.

"It's your *name*. Your mother picked it out. Said it belonged to her grandmother."

My throat felt hot. I tried swallowing, but something had lodged itself inside so I couldn't breathe.

"You look like her, you know," he went on. "She had the same dark hair and bright eyes. You've got my strong chin and jawline, though. Remarkable, really. The likeness to Henrietta."

Henrietta Cox. That was my mother. Another fresh stab of pain seared through my chest, like his words were physically assaulting me. "Please stop," I moaned, hunching over, trying to shut out his voice.

But he continued, "Her magic smelled like lilacs. Yours does too. But while I had ambitions for finding a way to Ascend, she wanted to form a Bloodcaster coven. She didn't care about power—only unity. She wanted to seek out more like us."

I crammed my eyes shut. I didn't want this—any of it.

"She was narrow-minded." His voice drew closer. "Weak. She didn't realize we had more potential on our own than if we had a full coven."

"So you sacrificed her?" I croaked. "Great solution."

My father was silent for a moment. Then, he said, "You of all people should understand how to separate your emotions from what must be done."

I barked out a harsh laugh. "*What must be done?* I seriously doubt you were *forced* to sacrifice your own wife."

"Her carelessness was going to get her killed."

"Keep telling yourself that."

"She knew from the beginning our relationship was purely platonic. We were only looking to further our bloodline."

I shook my head, my mouth twisting in a disgusted grimace. It was horrifying. The idea of mating with someone else just to produce offspring—and then sacrificing all of them. Slaughtering your whole family for power. I myself never wanted children because of the life I led. I didn't want to bring kids into a world like this, a world where I had to kill on a regular basis.

But desiring a family . . . *purely* for the intent to destroy them? It was sick.

"My name is Quentin, by the way," he said. "I thought you should know."

"I don't care."

Quentin chuckled. I heard him shifting, and I automatically tensed. But then his footsteps drifted away from me.

"I'll return shortly with a meal for you," he said.

My mouth fell open. "What? You're *feeding* me?"

"Would you prefer I left you to starve?"

"Just sacrifice me and get it over with!" I snapped.

Quentin laughed. "So eager to die. I admire your courage, Cordelia. But it's too soon. You're weakened from our little scuffle earlier. Your blood will be fresher if I let you recover and regain your strength."

Like I was some pig waiting to be fattened up for a holiday feast. "Go to hell."

"Enjoy your solitude, Cordelia."

I spat in his direction as he walked away. A tiny chink of light briefly illuminated the room, revealing what appeared to be a large basement. A long chain surrounded me, and a tiny cot rested on the opposite side of the room—too far for me to reach. I shuddered at the thought of Quentin sleeping down here with me chained to the wall.

Darkness swallowed the room again, and I blinked as my eyes adjusted. But there were no windows. No light source at all.

I was completely blind. And I had no doubt Quentin had done that on purpose.

Struggling against the chains, I wiggled my fingers, trying to summon my magic. As I expected, nothing happened. Quentin didn't strike me as the idiotic type to chain a Bloodcaster unless he had magic dampeners.

But . . . a sliver of hope slowly bloomed within me. I twisted my wrist, and a grin spread across my face.

These chains were loose enough. Not like the tight cuffs Vince and I had been trapped in just before I'd killed Damien. No, these were old chains. It disturbed me to think about *why* Quentin had access to chains like these and what other horrors lurked down here.

But for now, I had a way to escape.

I shifted my weight, grunting slightly. When my hands were gathered behind my back, I felt for my knuckles until I found my thumbs.

With a forceful grunt, I shoved my thumb backward into the socket, breaking the bone. Agony flared in my hand, shooting upward in my body and making me see white spots. My thumb hung limply, and my whole hand was on fire. Sucking in a breath, I shifted again, each movement sending stabs of pain through my body.

Then, I broke my other thumb.

I bit back a roar of anguish, my teeth cutting into my bottom lip. The last thing I wanted was for Quentin to return. I couldn't beat him at my best, let alone with two broken thumbs.

Moving gingerly, I slid the chains off my wrists and sighed with relief. Out of habit, I blinked several times, my eyes still working to adjust to my surroundings. But the utter pitch blackness engulfed me.

That was fine. I could work in the dark. I just had to get away from the magic dampeners first.

Struggling to remember that brief flash of light that illuminated the room, I rose to my feet, my legs trembling from disuse. My steps were slow and careful as I edged away from the chains. I ran into something solid and hissed before scooting around it. I brushed a few uninjured fingers against the surface. It felt like a small table. I found the edges to make sure I stepped around it. I felt for the wall that I knew was close by. When I found it, I exhaled with relief.

I can do this, I thought. *I can do this.*

After a few steps, I wiggled my good fingers.

There it was. A spark of my familiar magic. Thank Lilith. In a shaky breath, I uttered a spell.

"Magic above and powers that be,
Heal the injuries inflicted on me.
Use the strength and force of my power,
To strengthen my body here this hour."

A flash of purple light. I quickly scanned the room, drinking in as many details as I could before the glow vanished.

Bookshelves along the walls. A small set of stairs leading to a closed door. A washer and dryer in the corner.

Snap. I inhaled a sharp breath as my bones set into place. *Snap.* My other thumb was healed. A fresh flare of pain spread through me, followed instantly by numbing relief. Though my thumbs still throbbed, I could wiggle them easily. And the fuzziness from whatever Quentin had drugged me with was gone too.

With the sudden strength and energy coursing through my body came the confidence I needed. I would escape. And I would take down my father.

I was Cora Covington. And I was *not* weak.

I held up my hands and summoned my magic again, using the purple glow to focus on the room once more. Squinting at the walls, I determined there *were*, in fact, no windows. Something in me deflated. I was hoping they'd just been boarded up or something. But no—it looked like my only way out was through the door, which was probably locked. And I doubted Quentin would go far. Breaking through that door would draw his attention, and I wasn't sure if I could beat him if it came down to a fight.

My jaw ticked back and forth as I considered my options. Gradually, an idea formed in my head. I approached the bookshelf I knew was on the opposite wall. When my fingers grasped the edges, I gritted my teeth and threw all my weight against it until it tipped over. Jumping backward, I yelped as it crashed to the ground, the loud noise making my eardrums throb.

I hurried across the room, dodging books and various items on the floor before I reached the small table I'd run into earlier. I snatched it, raising it high above me as I crept underneath the set of stairs, waiting.

Someone unlocked the door. It swung open, bathing the room in light again. I slid backward, farther into the shadows as Quentin descended the stairs.

The footsteps faltered as he no doubt noticed I was no longer chained up.

When his shadowy form appeared in front of me, I lunged, swinging the table hard against his head.

A strangled shout burst from his mouth, and I froze.

This wasn't Quentin.

The figure fell to the ground, now illuminated by the small chink of light left from the open door.

My blood chilled as I recognized the vibrant purple hair. It was *Piper*.

CHAPTER 23

I SAID NOTHING AS I JUMPED LUKE, BENNY, AND ME back to Luke's house. A steely rage had taken over my shock and horror from earlier. Now, all I felt was the bloodthirsty desire to rip apart Cora's father.

But first, I had to find him.

I'd expected Hector to take off as soon as we'd left. But, to my surprise, he stood there, waiting in the yard where we'd left him, his arms crossed and his expression grim.

I dropped Luke and Benny's arms and strode toward Hector, fury coursing through my veins and making me see red. In a flash, crimson smoke pooled from my fingertips. I snatched Hector by the collar and lifted him high in the air. Behind me, Luke shouted something, but I ignored him.

"Where is she?" I roared, my arms quivering with

anger. "Tell me!"

Hector's eyes grew wide. He shook his head. "I don't know. I swear."

"*I don't believe you!*"

"Vince!" Benny shouted.

Footsteps echoed behind me. A swell of power flared within me. My wings prickled. A jet of red magic exploded from my wings, and a sharp grunt told me someone had fallen over.

Deep down, a small part of me marveled over the fact that my *wings* had just cast magic. And I was curious whether it was Benny or Luke who I'd just attacked.

But my gaze remained fixed on Hector, whose face had drained of color, and I thought of nothing else but hurting him. *Ending* him.

"You *knew* she would be taken," I hissed. "You knew we would be too late. So, *where is she?*"

"Vince, I'm on your side," Hector choked.

I growled, lifting him higher, my hold on him tightening. Hector's face turned purple.

"Vince, *stop!*" Luke shouted.

"You really think he's not playing a part in this?" I snarled without looking away from Hector. "He knows. And I'm not letting go until he tells me."

"You're *choking* him," Benny said. "If you kill him, he can't tell us anything!"

I was so full of rage, so raw and brutal it was all I felt,

that I didn't want to listen. Didn't want to submit to logic right now. My magic coiled within me, ready to strike, to tear Hector limb from limb . . .

Something heavy slammed into me, and I released Hector. A force pushed me to the ground, pinning me in place.

It was Luke. He hovered over me, his eyes dark with an intensity I'd never seen before. I struggled against him, but then his fingertips pressed against my temples, and I went still.

I was on the lacrosse field again, but instead of standing there with my crosse and my gear, I was wrestling with Luke—as if he'd *Jumped* us to the field.

"Easy, Vince, *relax!*" he shouted, still grappling with my arms as I tried to free myself. "This isn't going to solve anything! You won't get her back by killing Hector."

A feral roar tore from my throat as I shoved Luke off me. But when I rose to my feet, we were still on the field. Whirling to face him, I said, "Take us back."

"Not until you chill the hell out."

I stomped closer to him. "Luke, I swear to Lilith—"

"What? You'll kill me?" Luke crossed his arms. "We're on *my* turf now. I'd like to see you try."

I faltered, glancing uneasily around the field. *My turf,* he'd said. What *would* happen if I tried to attack him here? This place wasn't real. I assumed it was in my mind or his. I didn't want to think about it. We were wasting precious time.

"Hector knew Quentin would be there," I croaked. "He knew Cora would be kidnapped."

"That doesn't mean he's working with Quentin. Think about it, Vince. Why would he be waiting for us at my place if he was involved in this?"

I stilled. The logical part of my brain that I'd pushed away now resonated with agreement. But my fury still pushed back. "You expect me to just *trust* him?"

"Of course not. But he's not the enemy right now. You can settle the score with him later. There are more important things. Like finding Cora."

I huffed several angry breaths before the redness at the edge of my vision slowly vanished. My heart rate steadied, and I looked at Luke as if seeing him for the first time.

I inhaled, regret burning within me. "I—sorry, Luke." Grimacing, I rubbed the back of my neck. "I just—"

"He took your girl, man. I get it."

Knots of fear and anguish twisted through my stomach. What horrors was Quentin subjecting Cora to?

No, I thought, shaking my head. Cora was strong. She'd get out of this. I remembered her when we were imprisoned by Damien. She'd found a way out then. She could do it again.

Even so, Quentin was a Bloodcaster. I had to help

her. He was powerful enough to take out *Reapers*. I didn't want to think about what he had in store for Cora.

"Look, we outnumber Hector three to one," Luke said. "Let's just hear what he has to say. If you don't like it, I give you permission to kick his ass."

I snorted in spite of the situation. My humor faded as I scrutinized Luke—the tightness of his jaw, the hardness in his eyes. "You work with Hector now?"

A stiff nod. "Not by choice." The venom in his voice surprised me.

"What do you think of him? As a Timekeeper?"

Luke exhaled as if something in him deflated. "He's got the Call. I've seen it firsthand. I can't deny he's got what it takes to do the job. I just think he's a pompous dick, that's all."

Again, I choked out a laugh. "But . . . is he dangerous?"

"For the timeline? No. But that's all the Timekeepers care about. Now, would he turn you over to a coven of demons for his own benefit?" Luke shrugged. "Possibly."

"And this *Call* wouldn't stop him from doing that?"

"No."

So, what Luke was saying was that Hector could very well be luring us into a trap—that he could be behind Cora's abduction.

And the Timekeepers wouldn't care. The bastards.

"Why does everything have to be so damn one-sided?" I growled, running a hand through my hair. "With the Nephilim and Reapers, it's *all-or-nothing*. Your magic is the only thing that matters. Everyone else be damned. And you Timekeepers are just as bad! As long as it doesn't affect the precious *timeline,* then you could be a serial killer for all they care." I huffed a sigh. "Why can't people actually *care* about other things? Other *people?* These groups, clans, covens—they all believe the world revolves around them. That they're the only ones that matter. It's idiotic! *There are other people in this world*! Why the hell doesn't anyone else *care?*" My voice rose with each word until I was practically shouting.

Luke simply watched me, his expression calm but guarded. I exhaled deeply, realizing I was wasting time. But with my rant came a release of tension in my chest. I'd been repressing this anger and frustration for too long.

But something in Luke's face told me he already knew this.

"You good now?" he asked. It wasn't snarky; it was genuine. He knew I had to get it out of my system.

I nodded. "Yeah. Let's go back."

I blinked, and we were back in the yard, standing in front of Hector and Benny. I expected Benny to demand where we'd been, but his gaze was intense, the wolf hair still thick on his arms. Hector was rubbing his neck, his face still slightly purple. As if I'd been choking him only seconds ago.

I shared a glance with Luke. He shook his head slightly. Somehow, even though our conversation had lasted several minutes, we were only gone for the blink of an eye.

I crossed my arms, leveling a glare at Hector. "Okay. Talk. Tell us what you know."

I felt Benny's bewildered gaze, and I knew what he was thinking. My anger was gone. I was completely different from the guy he'd seen moments ago.

Hector was suspicious too. His eyes narrowed as he glanced between Luke and me. Then, understanding flickered in his eyes.

He was a Timekeeper, after all. He knew all about whatever crazy magic had come over Luke and me.

"How did you know Quentin would be at Cora's apartment?" I asked, my voice slow and deliberate. My blood pulsed with urgency, knowing every second we delayed was another second of pain for Cora.

"I saw it on the timeline," Hector said in a raspy voice, still massaging his neck.

I frowned. "What the hell does that mean?"

Hector sighed as if I were some four-year-old who wouldn't stop pestering him with questions. His exasperation made me clench my fingers into fists, remembering all the garbage I'd put up with from him in the Nephilim clan.

"Certain events jump out at us from the timeline," Hector said. "Events that shouldn't be there. That need to be corrected."

"And . . . Quentin showing up at Cora's place wasn't supposed to happen?" I asked, my brow furrowing.

Hector nodded. "Ever since he got his Reaper abilities, he's been sending up all kinds of red flags. He has unauthorized power. Any Reaper who hasn't pledged a vow is violating the laws of the timeline."

My stomach twisted. "What are the Timekeepers doing about it?"

"That's why I came to see you. They're not doing anything."

My eyes widened, and rage flared within me once more. "Why not? You just said—"

"My superior's hands are tied," Hector said in a tight voice. His eyes flashed, betraying his disappointment. "Quentin has powerful allies. Hunting him down would start a war between his people and the Timekeepers. To my superior, the threat isn't worth it."

"You're just going to let him run around, doing whatever he wants?" I roared.

"Easy, Vince," Luke muttered.

"*I'm* doing no such thing," Hector snapped. "But I don't have the authority to send the Timekeepers to war with Quentin Cox. All I have are my own powers . . . and you three."

Silence fell between us as Benny, Luke, and I shared an uncertain glance.

"What's in it for you?" Benny said in a sharp voice. Long claws protruded from his fingers. He looked like he was seconds away from tearing out Hector's throat. "I find it hard to believe you're here to preserve the *timeline*." He spat the last word.

Hector's nostrils flared as he took an angry step toward Benny. "You have no idea what it's like, to have the Call coursing violently through you, to have it *whisper* things in your mind that you can't ignore. It's different for everyone, but what *this one*"—he jabbed a finger at me —"did to me bound me permanently to the timeline. I hear it. See it. Feel it *constantly*. It's a living thing in my head. Like a ghost haunting me for the rest of my life." He broke off with a shudder, and a slither of ice crept into my chest. "I have to silence the voice. I have to correct this, or I'll go mad. My head can't take it." His face turned ashen, and he shook his head.

A conflict of emotions warred within me. Doubt because I *knew* Hector. He didn't do anything unless it directly benefited him. Shock at his description of the timeline as a living entity—and the small part of me that resonated with the idea that there was some innate instinct to preserve the laws of time.

And, surprisingly, *sympathy*. Despite what he'd done, the idea of Hector going insane from the voices in his head made me strangely sad.

"I don't buy it," Benny said flatly.

Fire burned in Hector's gaze, and he lifted his chin. "I'll sign a blood contract."

I stiffened, and Benny's eyebrows lifted. Though I'd been a light caster most of my life, I knew blood magic was dangerous and not to be trifled with. Only the darkest of demons practiced it.

But as Benny stared hard at Hector, deliberating, I knew we had no choice. We wouldn't trust Hector unless he swore by his blood to assist us.

And we were running out of time.

"Do it," I said quickly before Benny could respond.

Benny's yellow eyes flashed to me before he nodded. In his eyes, I saw the same desperation I felt. He cared about Cora too. The thought made my stomach twist with jealousy, but right now, Benny and I had the same goal.

Benny lifted his hand and wiggled his long, clawed fingers. His eyes glittered with malice as he stepped closer to Hector. "First, I'll need your blood."

CHAPTER 24

CORA

Feeling ridiculous, I brandished the small table higher, ready to slam it into Piper's face if I had to.

Piper's hands flew up. "Wait, *hold on*! I'm not here to hurt you!"

"Liar," I snarled, advancing toward her.

"I swear, *I swear*!" she shrieked, her arms shaking. "We're sisters, Cora. I won't hurt you."

I froze. My blood turned to ice in my veins. *Sisters?* It couldn't be true.

Piper took advantage of my hesitation, her dark eyes widening as she slowly lowered her hands. A small gash oozed blood on her forehead from when I'd hit her with the table. "Quentin is my father too."

Doubt mingled with disgust inside me as I considered her words. If she *was* telling the truth, then I pitied her. I was messed up enough, having grown up *without* Quentin in my life. But Piper? Had she been raised by him? Raised by a monster?

"And your mother?" I asked in a low voice.

"Dead. He sacrificed her. She wasn't a Bloodcaster. He wanted to see if he could carry on the bloodline with a normal dark witch." Piper lifted her chin. "It didn't work."

"So, why are *you* still alive?" I snapped, my eyes narrowing. My gaze slid to the open door at the top of the stairs as if expecting Quentin to burst in and shout, *Surprise*!

"He needs me to do his dirty work for him. He—he's holding my aunt hostage. Using her as leverage." Her voice broke, and she swallowed. "He'll kill her if I don't obey him."

Something within me softened, but only a fraction. I knew what it felt like to be strong-armed by someone who should have your back.

Even so. She stole from me. I kept the table gripped tightly in my hands, though my arms now throbbed from holding it for so long. "You infiltrated my coven," I said softly. "You manipulated my people and stole money from me. Why should I trust a thing you say?"

"Because—because I *didn't know* what he would do to you." Piper's eyes shone with tears. "I swear it, Cora. I was listening when he was down here earlier, and—" She broke off with a strangled sob. "I'm so sorry."

I stared at her. Emotion and concern swirled inside me, but I kept my face impassively smooth. "I still don't believe you. Won't he kill your aunt if he finds out you've helped me?"

Piper's expression cleared, her eyes glinting with determination. "I trust you to keep her safe more than I trust him not to hurt her."

I continued to scrutinize her, searching her face for the telltale sign of a lie. Grief and regret swam in her eyes, but there was a fire in her gaze I recognized in myself. Hurt, betrayal, an aching loneliness . . . It was like looking into a mirror.

Quentin had hurt her. Badly. I didn't know the full extent of it, but I could read the trauma in Piper's eyes. Perhaps she'd always longed for him to become a proper father figure. I shuddered to think what kind of harm he could have inflicted on her over the years.

The emotion within me warred with common sense until my heart won over.

"I can't promise to save your aunt," I said.

"I know that," she said quickly. "But . . . you'll try, won't you?"

I nodded and set the table down.

Piper's face softened in relief, but I jabbed a finger toward her.

"Cross me, and I'll kill you," I hissed.

To my surprise, she grinned back at me, her nose slightly red. "I'm counting on it."

I glanced up the stairs. "Is he here?"

"No. He went to grab takeout, but he'll be back any minute."

Takeout. The idea seemed absurdly ordinary, given the fact he had his daughter chained up in the basement.

"He's probably got wards around the place," I said, raising a questioning eyebrow at her.

"He does."

"Can you disable them?"

"No. It requires his blood."

I shot her a flat look that said, *Duh.*

She sighed. "*Bloodcaster* blood."

My eyes widened. Could it really be that easy? My jaw ticked back and forth as I contemplated this. Even if my blood *did* unlock the wards, I had no doubt Quentin would somehow sense when they were disabled. How fast could he get back once he knew? Would his Reaper powers give him supernatural speed? Or did he have a Jumping elixir on him?

My head was reeling, and I took a deep breath to steady my nerves. *I can do this.* I looked at Piper. "You got a phone?"

She shook her head. "He has a landline, but it's scrambled. Won't work unless he's here."

Something hardened within me. Piper was practically

a prisoner here like me. She might be free to roam, but she couldn't get out or call anyone.

With no phone, I couldn't reach Vince or Benny. No one knew I was here, and I couldn't Jump. Once we got out, the clock would start ticking. If Quentin caught us, we were done.

If I had more time, I would've tried to rummage through Quentin's ingredients to make my own Jumping potion. But he could be back any second.

"Come on." I grabbed Piper's arm and dragged her upstairs. A bright light momentarily blinded me when we exited the basement. As my eyes adjusted, I made out an eerily clean kitchen, the countertops and floors spotless and gleaming from the sunlight streaming in through the windows.

Squinting, I peered out the window. Quentin's backyard faced another neighbor's yard. Beyond that, I made out what looked like a cul-de-sac.

I led Piper toward the backdoor, pausing before reaching for the doorknob. Magic prickled against my skin, and a faint warbling sound thrummed from the door. I flicked the edge of the knob, testing it.

Nothing happened.

With a deep breath, I opened the door and waited, my senses straining. But no magic pressed in on me. The wards were still intact.

After searching for the sharpest steak knives I could

find and arming Piper and myself with them, I slid one against my palm and let my blood drip to the floor.

"Blood of my blood, disable the charm,

That's meant to keep out those who will harm.

Break the spell and release the wards.

Open the path so I may move forward."

My hands glowed purple. The warbling of the wards intensified until my ears were throbbing. Then, with a *zap* that stung me like an electrical shock, the wards went down. A cold silence fell in its wake. The scent of Bloodcaster magic tingled in the air, but it faded with each breath I took.

I stretched my hand forward, reaching toward the backyard. Nothing happened. I felt nothing but air and freedom.

I looked at Piper. "Move."

In a flash, we were sprinting, knives in hand as we bolted through the yard, climbing the neighbor's fence. *Keep moving, keep moving.* I didn't know where we were, but all I had to do was get to a main road and I'd be able to find my way. We just had to get out of Quentin's reach.

"Do you know where we are?" I panted as we ran.

"Ravenbrooke," Piper wheezed. "Suburbs."

Damn. I should've known better than to expect Quentin to keep us in Hinport.

"Can we . . . ask a neighbor for their phone?" Piper asked, clutching at her side.

"Too risky. I don't know how many people here are working with him."

We rounded a corner, and the sound of heavy traffic met my ears. Hope glinted within me. So close, so close . . .

A heavy force slammed into me, knocking me off my feet. The knife skittered just out of reach as my hands met solid concrete, my arm bending at an awkward angle. Piper yelped next to me just before she collided with me.

We scrambled to our feet. My arms burned from fresh scrapes, my heart thundering with fear.

Striding along the sidewalk as casually as if he were out for a stroll stood my father. His hands were in his pockets, his eyebrows raised.

"Well, I must admit, I expected your escape to take a bit longer," he said with a sigh. "Very impressive."

He didn't seem at all surprised. I stiffened and glanced at Piper, wondering if she'd tricked me. But her face had drained of color, and she staggered back a step, her wide eyes full of fear. "P-please," she whispered.

Quentin's eyes darkened. "I warned you what would happen if you disobeyed me."

I roared with fury and lifted my hands. Purple magic exploded from my fingertips, blasting into Quentin's chest and sending him flying.

"Help me," I urged Piper, who was frozen with terror. She nodded numbly, and we surged forward. Black magic pooled from her own hands, mingling with mine as we assaulted Quentin again and again until he was nothing more than a haze of violet ash. The power around us was so thick it suffocated me, but still I slashed my hands through the air, pushing more magic forward until I felt it drain out of me.

Piper suddenly cried out and stiffened. She clutched at her throat and made horrible gagging noises. Like an invisible hand was choking her.

I stopped, allowing my magic to recede back inside me. Staring helplessly at Piper, I reached out. Her eyes reddened. Her face turned purple.

"Piper!" I shouted.

The haze of magic slowly dispersed, and Quentin emerged, his hand outstretched and flexed. Though he was several feet away, *he* was somehow choking Piper.

"Stop!" I shrieked, rushing to Piper's side. I touched her neck, but nothing was there. Then, I noticed my knife on the ground. I swiped it and flung it toward Quentin. He dodged it easily.

"You'll *kill* her!" I screamed.

"I'll do more than that," Quentin said softly. "First, Piper dearest, I'll kill you. Then, I'll go after Juliet. And her children. And anyone who's associated with her. Soon, there will be no memory of you left on the earth. It will be as if you and your mother never existed."

Piper fell to her knees, her eyes rolling back. Her face was now beet-red.

I charged toward Quentin, ducking when he aimed a blow at my face. My knee jerked up to his groin. He groaned, hunching over, but his arm remained outstretched. From the corner of my eye, I noticed Piper had completely collapsed.

I smashed my forehead against Quentin's, and he stumbled, his arm finally dropping. Punch to the throat. Elbow to the gut. Knee to the groin again for good measure. I swung my fist toward his jaw, going for the knock-out, but he caught my arm and twisted. A shooting pain coursed through me. His other hand snatched my hair, ripping strands from my scalp. I screamed.

"You are mine, Cordelia," Quentin hissed. "And I'll prove it to you. But first . . . I'll break you."

CHAPTER 25

VINCE

Begrudgingly, I took Hector and Benny back to Cora's place. Luke elected to stay behind, since he was no fighter, but he promised he'd remain linked to my mind. The reminder was strangely a comfort to me. Suddenly, my friend's secret telepathic powers didn't bother me so much.

Not when Cora's life hung in the balance, and *Hector* was my only hope.

Hector claimed the scene of the crime was the best place to start, since that was where he felt the strongest disruption to the timeline. Once we got there, he strode straight inside as if he owned the place. I had to ball my hands into fists to keep from strangling him as he stomped over Cora's broken furniture and glassware.

Then, standing in the middle of her living room with

his arms outstretched, Hector closed his eyes like he was praying.

Benny muttered a string of swear words and rubbed his forehead. I crossed my arms, trying to quell the mounting urgency within me.

After a few minutes, Hector inhaled deeply. "I can—I can see it."

"See *what*?" I snapped.

"The timeline."

I fell silent. *See the timeline.* I'd only ever felt a subtle touch, a nudge inside me guiding me. But it made my head spin, trying to visualize the timeline like it was a living thing.

"And?" Benny said impatiently.

"Quentin leaves a trail," Hector said, his voice far away. His eyes were still closed, and his face had gone slack. "Like footprints along the timeline."

"Which direction?" I asked, my head whipping around as if I could somehow see these invisible footprints.

Hector was silent for a moment, his brows furrowing in concentration. He pointed toward the door. "West. Toward Ravenbrooke."

"Grab on," I said loudly, reaching out for Benny and Hector. To my relief, they both hurried to my side without argument. I grabbed their arms and spun in place, focusing on Glen Bridge. In a flash, we were there.

As soon as I landed, a shrill ringing pierced through me. Pain pulsed in my mind, and my body felt too weak to fight it. I groaned, sinking to my knees.

"Vince." Benny was by my side, his eyes wide. "You okay?"

Slowly, the ringing faded, but I was still weak. I wasn't sure how much farther I could Jump. Gasping for breath, I glanced up at Hector. "Can you . . . take us there?"

Hector shook his head, his expression grim. "If I Jump, they'll know. They'll stop us."

I didn't have to ask who he meant. Gritting my teeth, I rose to my feet, leaning on Benny for support. "Still see those magic footprints?"

Irritation flickered in Hector's eyes, but he nodded, pointing toward the massive bridge. The Glen River stretched beneath us, glinting from the sun's reflection. Cars whooshed past us.

My legs wobbled, but I took a step forward. "How far can you see?"

Hector's eyes narrowed as he stared beyond the bridge. His eyes went unfocused for a moment. "About a mile."

"Vince, you can't—" Benny started.

"*Which direction?*" I hissed through clenched teeth, ignoring Benny's protests.

Hector glanced between us, his lips tightening. "Northwest."

I nodded and grabbed Hector's arm again before Jumping.

This time, white spots danced in front of my vision. The ringing returned to my ears so intensely I thought my eardrums would burst. I clutched at my head and moaned. Torrents of agony flashed across my mind like a dozen migraines slicing through me at once. Hector and Benny's voices were muffled, and I couldn't see anything in front of me. Someone shook me hard, but all I felt was pain. The ringing persisted. I screamed.

Smack. Hector's hand connected with my face. My head swiveled, and a new kind of pain blazed through me. But the ringing vanished, and my vision cleared. I stared up at Hector from the ground. My face was covered in sweat. We stood on a sidewalk near the suburbs, the bridge a mere speck in the distance.

Panting, I stumbled to my feet. Hector and Benny stared at me with a mixture of fear and impatience.

"Better?" Hector asked.

I glared at him. *Of course* he'd been eager to hit me. But I couldn't blame him for it, since it had *worked.* With a deep breath, I nodded.

"No more Jumping," Hector snapped. "We're close enough now."

He turned and led the way down the sidewalk. Benny cast an uncertain glance at me before following. We turned left at Eastview Crossing, a neighborhood I recognized. We weren't far from my former Nephilim clan. The thought sent a whirlwind of confusing emotions coursing through me.

I forced my legs to match Hector's pace, refusing to slow us down. Cora couldn't wait. I could take a healing elixir later if I had to.

After a few steps, Benny slowed to walk alongside me, his brows creasing as he looked me over. "Save your strength, Vince. It may get ugly once we find her."

"Assuming he's leading us to the right place," I grumbled.

Benny's eyes went unfocused for a moment. "He is. I can see the footprints in his mind."

I stared at Benny. "You can?"

He nodded. "Quentin leaves a purple mist wherever he goes, marking his aura as something foreign in the timeline. Hector can see it more clearly than the other Timekeepers can." He cut a glance at me. "Because of what you did to him."

My chest felt hollow. I wasn't sure if I should feel *guilty* about that or not. Hector had been trying to kill me. Was this new ability of his a gift or a curse? Which did *I* want it to be?

"Here," Hector said suddenly, stopping in front of a polished two-story home with neatly-trimmed hedges and freshly-mown grass. If I didn't know any better, I'd presume a typical unassuming family lived here.

Which made it the perfect disguise.

I strode toward the front door, my body thrumming with energy, ready to rip Quentin limb from limb—but Hector threw out an arm to stop me.

"What?" I snapped.

Hector's face slackened. His eyes stared beyond me at something I couldn't see. Then, he murmured, "He isn't there."

I swore and ran a hand through my hair. "Then, *why did you take us here?*"

Before Hector could answer, a scream echoed nearby. I stiffened, and a chill raced down my spine. Squinting, I glanced around, searching for the disturbance.

About half a mile down the road, a tiny purple mushroom cloud exploded in the air.

In a flash, my dark wings were out, and I took off, spinning into the sky and soaring above Hector and Benny. Ignoring their shouts, I stretched my back and arms, easily finding the muscles connected to my wings. A groan rippled through me as I flexed my wings again and again, using the momentum to propel me forward. Within seconds, my shoulders and back ached, but I pushed onward. Wind bit at my face as I flew toward the purple magic. Three small figures came into view. One of them was on the ground, unmoving.

I landed on my feet, my chest heaving and my face covered in sweat. A gray-haired man—Quentin, no doubt —was wrestling with Cora. He had her arm twisted behind her. A few feet away lay an unconscious purple-haired girl.

Quentin saw me first. He straightened, one hand still gripping Cora and holding her in place. Recognition stirred in his eyes.

As soon as our gazed locked, a whisper tickled my ears. Something familiar pulsed in my body, responding to this man's presence. I smelled the blood of Reapers. I felt his shadowy presence as he slaughtered one Reaper after another.

A growl built in my throat.

And Quentin *smiled*.

Raw, brutal rage sliced through me, swift and merciless. Red crept into my vision and leaked from my fingers like a bloody mist.

For one brief moment, Quentin's eyes widened.

With a shout, I shot my magic toward him. An explosion of red crashed into him, knocking him backward.

Then, Cora straightened, twisting her arm back into place before she noticed me. Her jaw dropped, and shock and awe gleamed in her eyes.

I shot more magic toward Quentin. Cora whipped around and leapt for him, pinning him to the ground.

Hector and Benny arrived, surrounding Quentin.

"Benny, take his mind!" Cora shouted.

A muffled grunt. A shout. And then—

"I can't," Benny grunted.

Silence fell between us. As the red fog of my magic cleared, I realized why: Quentin had vanished.

VINCE IMMEDIATELY TOOK TO THE SKY TO SEARCH FOR Quentin. But Benny confirmed what I already knew: he was gone. Benny couldn't sense his mind within a mile.

Maybe he *had* had a Jumping elixir on him. The sneaky bastard.

Shooting pain still flared in my arm, but at least it wasn't broken. I glanced around for Piper, and my eyes fell on . . . *Hector*.

"What the hell is *he* doing here?" I shouted, waving my good arm toward Hector. My blood boiled, and every inch of me cried out for Hector's death. *Kill, kill, kill* . . .

Benny stood in front of me, blocking my path to Hector. "He's with us."

"Since *when?*"

"Since he led us to you."

I stilled, my eyes narrowing as I met Hector's gaze

over Benny's shoulder. Hector stared back, his expression unreadable.

I couldn't believe these guys actually bought the *I'm-here-to-help-you* act.

Vowing to snap Hector's neck the moment his back was turned, I moved toward Piper's inert form on the ground. Her face was bone white, and red marks surrounded her neck. As if Quentin had *literally* choked the life out of her.

Desperation crashed through me. I leaned closer and felt for a pulse. There it was. Faint, but it was there.

I exhaled, hanging my head. Relief poured through me, sweet and exhausting.

I hadn't realized how much I *needed* Piper to be alive. Which was ridiculous. I didn't even know her.

But she'd risked her life—her aunt's life—to help me escape.

I stood and found Benny watching me. A powerful emotion flared in his eyes, something I'd never seen there before. Something hot and urgent and wild.

It made my stomach churn, so I looked away before I asked him, "How much of Piper's mind can you access right now?"

Benny cleared his throat. "Her most recent thoughts would leave an echo in her mind. I can access those."

I nodded. "Can you find her aunt? Quentin was keeping her hostage. I want to grab her before Quentin kills her." *If he hasn't already.* My chest felt hollow at the thought.

Benny pressed his lips together and knelt next to Piper, pressing two fingers to her temple. I turned just as Vince landed in front of me.

The sight of him stole my breath.

Pure, untethered fury filled his face. His eyes were ablaze, and a sinister red smoke still surrounded him. His dark wings cast shadows on me, flaring behind him. It was both beautiful and terrifying.

My heart lurched as he stepped toward me. I opened my mouth to speak, but before I could, he gathered me in his arms, drawing me to his chest.

I yipped in surprise, my body going stiff. Then, with my face pressed into his shoulder, I let myself relax, welcoming his mint-and-soap scent, the warmth of his body, the rapid thundering of his heart that matched my own. His strong arms surrounded me, and though I didn't often need someone else's strength, in this moment, it was nice to know I had his.

"You came for me," I whispered against his shirt. My throat caught on the words.

"Of course I did." His breath tickled my neck. I was acutely aware of every place his skin touched mine. His cheek and mouth at my neck. His arms at the bare strip of my waist from my wrinkled shirt. His arm, climbing up my back so his fingers could tangle in my hair.

I wanted to press myself into him. To fuse my body with his.

When we finally pulled apart, I looked up at him. The intensity of his gaze, burning and smoldering, made my stomach turn to jelly.

"Vince—" I said.

Then, his lips were on mine, crushing me. His mouth drew a startled gasp from me. His kisses were insistent and firm. Unyielding.

I quickly recovered from the shock, my body responding with enthusiasm. Part of me faintly registered that this wasn't the time or the place, that there were more important things to worry about . . . But he was kissing me like we were the only two people in the world. Like he would die if he didn't kiss me right here, right now. His movements were deliberate and commanding—nothing like the gentle, careful, tender kisses we'd shared before. This left no room for negotiation.

And I loved it.

I trembled when his tongue flicked against mine, then grabbed his collar and yanked him closer. My lips matched his movements. My tongue entwined with his. Desire boiled within me until it consumed my entire body.

Someone cleared their throat loudly behind us, and I reluctantly pulled away, gasping for air.

"Found her," Benny said stiffly. I looked at him and

found a careful mask of apathy. His eyes betrayed nothing.

I knew that look well. It mirrored my own when I wanted to keep my emotions locked away.

A knot formed in my throat, and all heat left my body in an instant. Though he worked hard to hide it, I could read it plainly in his rigid body and tight expression. He'd seen me kiss Vince. And it bothered him.

"Where?" I asked in a strained voice.

"North side of town. Too far to walk." Benny raised his eyebrows expectantly.

Oh, Lilith. With a sigh, I turned to Vince. "Can you Jump him?"

Vince blinked. "Of course." He strode toward Benny, his wings tickling my face as he brushed by me. Benny continued to watch me with that achingly distant expression. I tried to offer an apologetic grimace, but he looked away, turning to face Vince instead.

After Benny told Vince the location, Vince took Benny's arm, and with a small *pop*, they were gone.

Leaving me alone with Hector and my unconscious half-sister. I shifted, moving between Hector and Piper in case he got any ideas.

Hector's eyebrows lifted, and he laughed. "What do you think I'll do? Dismember her right here?"

"You have a habit of destroying people when they least expect it," I said.

Hector's face darkened. "I'm not that person anymore."

I scoffed. "I find that hard to believe."

We stared each other down, neither of us giving in.

At long last, he asked quietly, "What do you know of your father?"

"Not much. Even if I did, I wouldn't tell you."

His eyebrows flicked up as if to say, *That's fair.* The gesture was . . . strangely *normal.*

My jaw ticked back and forth. "Why did you help them find me?"

Hector's dark eyes remained fixed on me as if he were trying to read the intent behind my question. As if he were trying to read *me.*

After a moment, he said in a soft murmur, "Because he's a threat to the laws of time."

My head reared back. I wasn't expecting *that.*

Another *pop* echoed, and Benny and Vince reappeared, dragging an unconscious figure with them. I hurried forward, inspecting the frail older woman. Her frizzy, graying hair fanned out around her face like a mane. Her expression was slack, and several bruises covered her face and arms.

But she had a pulse, thank Lilith.

"Here," I said. "Let's get her—"

Suddenly, Vince collapsed. A trickle of blood oozed from his nose. His face had drained of color.

I sucked in a gasp, dropping to my knees and touching his face. "Vince? Can you hear me?"

His face went slack, his eyes rolling back until they were all white.

"Vince!" I shouted.

His body started seizing. Terror lodged itself in my chest, stabbing through me. Panicked, I glanced up at Benny and Hector, but they both stared in horror at Vince.

Think, Cora, think! I urged myself. I shifted so Vince's head was in my lap. Then, I placed both hands on his head and whispered a spell.

"Magic above and powers that be,
Heal this man and set him free.
Release him from the pain within,
And free his mind from the prison therein."

My hands glowed purple, and Vince's body arched, his chest rising. A strangled scream tore from his throat, ringing in my ears and chilling me to the bone.

Slowly, his body relaxed on the ground with a long exhale. His eyes closed, his head lolling to the side.

He was unconscious. But still breathing. And the seizure had stopped.

I sucked in sharp, ragged breaths as tears pricked my eyes. I impatiently blinked them away and looked up at Hector.

"What's wrong with him?" I demanded.

Hector gaped at me. "How should I know?"

"You're really telling me you had nothing to do with this?"

"He's been killing himself to find you, Cora," Benny said softly. "He pushed himself too far." Benny jerked his head toward Piper's aunt.

My heart dropped like a stone. *Of course.* Even Jumping with one other person was difficult. But Vince had Jumped with *two* people—not to mention everything else he'd done to find me.

Warmth and suffocating regret stifled my breathing, and I half gasped, half sobbed. "You idiot," I moaned, leaning down to press my forehead against Vince's. "You stupid, beautiful fool."

It was difficult transporting all three unconscious people back to the motel in Hinport. But Benny communicated mind-to-mind with Luke, who sent for reinforcements. Several Reapers came to our aid, including Vince's mother and Gwen, both of whom shot me sharp and hostile looks as if Vince's condition were my fault.

To be honest, it kind of was. And it made my stomach twist with guilt.

Benny put a few wolves by Piper and her aunt's room in case Quentin decided to return for them.

As soon as we got back to Hinport, a girl assaulted me, demanding to know what had happened to Vince. She spoke so quickly, her face a mess of ginger hair and wide eyes, that for a moment, I didn't recognize her.

Then, realization hit me. An unpleasant feeling wormed its way into my stomach.

"Relax, Jocelyn," I said with a sigh, rubbing the back of my neck. My body ached in all kinds of places. "He's fine. He just exerted himself too much."

"Because of *you*, no doubt," Jocelyn hissed.

I stared at her. I'd never seen such venom in her expression before. She'd always been so calm, poised, and unassuming. "I didn't do *anything* to him," I said, my voice steady and cold. "Vince makes his own choices. If he decides to run into battle, then I can't stop him."

Jocelyn's nostrils flared, her eyes narrowing into slits. But she said nothing as she turned away from me, following the Reapers as they carried Vince to his room.

I wanted to follow, but Gwen made it plain this was a "Reapers-only" affair and I wasn't welcome. Seething, I plopped down on the carpeted floor of the hallway by Vince's room, determined to stay put until he woke up.

I wasn't sure *why*. He was well cared for, between Jocelyn, Cecile, and the other Reapers. And, as Benny curtly reminded me when he finally tracked me down, I had plenty of coven duties to attend to.

I stubbornly refused to leave my post outside Vince's

room and instead had Benny bring me the stack of papers waiting for me on my desk so I could work on them in the hall. Benny stood there for a long moment. I felt the judgment in his gaze but ignored his stare until he finally stalked off.

Before diving into the paperwork, I cast a quick protection spell on Vince's door that would alert me if anyone broke in. Then, I tethered it to my magic—so that if a Bloodcaster tried to get through, the entire coven would be alerted.

Better safe than sorry. Even if I accidentally tripped the wards myself.

A few people came and went as I signed paper after paper, reading through contracts and agreements, my eyes itching with sleepiness. Gwen shot me an icy glare when she left Vince's room. Cecile paused for a long moment, her penetrating gaze spearing right through me. And Jocelyn breezed past me without a second glance.

Hours passed, and Vince still didn't wake. Cecile and Jocelyn alternated staying in his room so he wouldn't wake up alone. I had Benny's men check in with me regularly about Piper and her aunt, both of whom were sleeping.

The longer I sat there, the more my body strained and exhaustion pulled at every muscle. And the more I avoided it, the more it stared me in the face: the truth of why I refused to leave the hall.

Guilt.

Jocelyn was right: this *was* all my fault. It was my fault my coven was in danger. My fault Vince had gotten hurt. And my fault the realms were being torn apart.

Because Quentin was *my* father. And it was me he wanted.

If I'd paid closer attention—if I'd actually *given* a rat's ass about my parents and who they were—I might have been able to stop this sooner. But no, like everything in my life, I'd run away from my past and whatever family I might've had, shoving the problem away to deal with later. And now, everyone else was paying the price for it.

I gritted my teeth through the aches and pains throbbing through my body, relishing in the discomfort because deep down, I knew I deserved it. I deserved so much worse.

CHAPTER 27

VINCE

Flashes of purple fire plagued my dreams. Mom screamed. Jocelyn sobbed. And Cora lay dead at my feet.

I woke in a cold sweat, my body shivering, though I was tucked under several blankets.

A small gasp made me sit up quickly, my heart thundering. As my eyes adjusted to the surrounding darkness, I made out a figure sitting next to my bed.

It was Jocelyn.

Lilith, I'd forgotten all about her. But perhaps that was a good thing. I shuddered to think what would've happened to her if she'd come with us to retrieve Cora.

Cora.

I shifted on the bed, but Jocelyn shoved me back down, her gaze steely. "You've done enough."

Her voice was so cold it froze me in place. I watched her warily. "Joss—"

"Don't," she said through clenched teeth.

My mouth felt dry. Why was she angry? What had I done wrong? When she turned on the lamp next to the bed, the light illuminated her stony expression. Worry mingled with anger, transforming the light, angelic features of my friend to someone almost unrecognizable.

"What—what's wrong?" I asked, fearing the worst. Had Quentin returned to the Astral Realm? Had he attacked the Reapers again?

"You're so thick-headed, Vince. So blind to what's *right in front of you*."

I shook my head. My utter confusion made my head throb. "I don't—"

"What is *wrong* with you?" she cried, lifting her arms and gesturing wildly at me. "You don't check with *anyone* before diving in like a complete idiot, almost *killing* yourself in the process even though Cecile *explicitly* said we should be resting, preparing for a battle we might have to face."

"I thought—"

"And not only that, but you manage to piss off the Timekeepers enough to completely butcher any efforts Gwen made to work alongside them."

My blood ran cold. *Oh, no . . .* "You mean—"

"Yeah. They sent a nasty message to Gwen just before their meeting, letting her know they didn't appreciate the

Reapers working alongside a rogue Timekeeper they've been trying to track down."

Rogue Timekeeper. That could only mean Hector. Bile climbed up my throat, and my mouth twisted. What had I done? "I—I didn't realize . . . Joss, Cora was abducted. She could have died."

"Oh, of course, because *Cora's* the only damn thing that matters in this world," Jocelyn spat.

My head reared back. I had *never* heard her talk like that. "Joss," I breathed in disbelief.

Jocelyn sighed, rubbing her forehead. "You're so clueless, Vince." Her voice was softer. More exasperated and less hostile. "You don't understand that what you do affects *everyone.* Did all those years living in a Nephilim clan teach you *nothing?*" She dropped her arms, letting her hands fall on her thighs. "The Reapers need you. Your mother needs you. *I* need you."

My tongue turned to sandpaper in my mouth. Numbness spread through my entire body as the sincerity of her words struck me hard. "Jocelyn . . ."

She raised a hand, her expression pained. "Don't," she whispered. "I know you don't see me the same way." She laughed, the sound harsh and grating. "Your actions today proved who you care most about."

My chest felt hollow. I wanted to deny it, but how could I? Everything she said was true.

I loved Cora. I didn't love Jocelyn.

And, as awful as it sounded, I cared about Cora more than I cared about the Reapers.

"I'm sorry," I said weakly. "So sorry, Jocelyn. I never meant to hurt you. And you're right. My actions today were . . . thoughtless. I should've been more considerate. I should've come to the Reapers first."

Jocelyn nodded, her jaw still rigid but her eyes softening.

"But . . . would you have done anything?" I asked quietly. "If I'd come to you and told you Cora's life was in danger, would you have done anything about it?"

Her gaze hardened again, but her silence answered my question. No, she wouldn't have done anything. She probably would've done everything in her power to keep me from going after Cora.

And I had no doubt Gwen and my mother would've agreed with Jocelyn. None of the other Reapers gave a damn about Cora, even though she'd given them refuge. Even though she'd risked her coven by protecting us.

"Lilith, I'm so *sick* of this," I groaned, leaning my head back against the wall behind the bed.

"Sick of what?" Jocelyn asked.

"This whole one-sided belief that our magic is the only magic that matters. Why is it a crime to look out for *everyone*? For all kinds of magic?"

Jocelyn's lips pressed together, forming a thin line. "We *do* care about everyone. That's the job of a Reaper,

Vince—to care for the magic of the universe and restore the balance between realms. But . . . our people come *first*. This is our family." She cocked her head at me. "Would you have gone after Cora if your dad had been mortally injured?"

I stiffened, and my eyes narrowed. "That isn't fair."

"Answer the question."

I shook my head. "*No.* I can't tell you *what* I would do in a hypothetical situation like that. But Joss, you have to understand—Cora *is* like family to me. I—I love her."

Jocelyn went very still, her eyes unreadable as she stared at me. Her mouth slowly opened in silent shock. Her gaze held mine, though my insides squirmed with discomfort, begging her to look away, to stop watching me like that.

Something shifted in the air between us. Something I hadn't realized was there at all. Whatever kinship Jocelyn and I shared was altered in this moment.

I'd always believed us to be good friends. But now I discovered she'd *always* wanted more. And perhaps that was all she saw in me: someone to love.

Now that I'd dashed those hopes to pieces, what was left?

Jocelyn's lower lip trembled, and she fled from the room, slamming the door shut behind her. I flinched as the door frame rattled, my eyes closing in pain.

But perhaps this was for the best. I couldn't give Jocelyn what she wanted, no matter how hard I tried.

Muffled voices echoed outside my door. I stilled, listening hard, but I couldn't make out any words. One voice grew louder, practically shouting.

I rose from the bed and cracked open the door just as thunderous footsteps stomped away from my room. Peering down the hall, I made out a figure crouched just outside my door, surrounded by piles of paper.

Cora.

She dropped her face into her hands, her body slumping forward. She looked exhausted.

A hard lump formed in my throat as I glanced at Jocelyn's retreating figure, then looked back at Cora.

I cleared my throat. "Uh, hey."

Her head snapped up, and her tired eyes met mine. She swallowed and shifted her weight. "Hey. How are you feeling?"

I rubbed the back of my neck, leaning against the door frame. "I was going to ask you the same thing."

A small smile lit her face. "I'm fine."

"Me too."

Silence fell between us. I wasn't sure why it felt awkward. We'd both sacrificed so much for each other. We knew we loved each other. But something tangible flowed between us, as if proving our love to everyone had changed things for us. Our feelings for each other had never been so . . . *open* before.

I watched her, my brows knitting together. "Why are you sitting on the floor?"

Cora blew air through her lips and shuffled papers around. "I, uh, wasn't exactly welcome in your room. But I couldn't bring myself to leave until I knew you were okay . . ." Her voice trailed off, her cheeks turning pink.

My own face warmed, and something hot slithered in my chest. But then I thought of my mom and Jocelyn. How could they treat Cora so horribly when she'd done so much for us? It didn't matter what mistakes *I'd* made—it wasn't like Cora *asked* to be abducted.

"Do you want to come in?" I gestured to the open door.

Hesitation lingered in her eyes as she looked between me and the door. "I'm not sure I should."

"Why not?"

"I'm pretty sure Gwen would skin me alive. If Jocelyn doesn't get to me first."

I winced, but Cora laughed.

"Relax," she said, groaning as she rose to her feet. "I'm used to death threats." Her eyebrows lifted.

"You shouldn't have to be," I said quietly, my gaze locked on hers. For a moment, we stood there, mere inches between us. Heat burned in our gazes.

Cora broke eye contact first, clearing her throat and

scrambling to pick up the scattered papers on the floor. I helped her collect them, and we went into my room together. We set the papers on the table by the TV and faced each other, that awkward, tangible *thing* still pressing in on us. Cora rubbed her arms and dropped her gaze. I licked my lips and crossed my arms.

At long last, Cora looked up at me. "You shouldn't have come after me."

"Cora—"

"You almost *killed yourself*, Vince." Her voice broke, and something inside me shattered at the sound.

I drew closer to her. "When I found out you'd been taken, I—I couldn't think. Couldn't *breathe*. Nothing would've stopped me from getting to you, Cora. Nothing."

Her eyes glistened, and she bit her lip, shaking her head quickly. "You risked too much. Your people—"

"I don't give a *damn* about the Reapers," I said through clenched teeth. "Not after how they treated you. Not after you opened your home to them and they turned their back on you when you needed help."

"They didn't turn their back on me. It wasn't their fight."

"It *is* their fight. Quentin is our enemy too. But Jocelyn just confirmed that if I'd come to them first, they would've done *nothing* to help you."

Cora touched my cheek. "You can't save everyone." Her voice was soft and tender.

I closed the distance between us until our chests were touching. "I don't care about saving everyone. I just want to save you."

Her fingertips trailed down my cheek, hovering over my lips. The gentle touch of her against my skin made me tremble. "I can take care of myself," she whispered.

"I know you can. But it wasn't just you who was in danger. You needed help, Cora. It's okay to admit that."

She nodded slowly. "Piper—she's my half-sister."

I blinked, stunned. "*What?*"

"Her mother was a dark witch. Quentin sacrificed her."

I flinched. "Merciful Lilith."

"He's a psychopath, Vince. You need to be careful. He has no feelings. He sees nothing but power. And he's strong. Stronger than me."

I arched an eyebrow. "*No one* is stronger than you."

Amusement danced in her eyes, but she stared intently at me. "Stronger with his *magic*. I'm a skilled fighter, but that means nothing against Bloodcaster magic. Especially when I'm so out of practice from hiding for so long."

My hands moved to her waist, tightening around her like she was my lifeline. "You're not alone anymore, Cora. I'll fight with you. We'll take him down together."

"How?" she breathed. "I saw you—you were broken. *Dying.* You can't stay in this realm for too long. And Quentin isn't someone we can take out easily."

A knot formed in my throat as truth resonated within me from her words. I'd felt the pain—the agony splitting through my head, similar to when I'd accidentally time traveled to Cora the first time. The incidents were more spread out, but they were still there. Which meant either Mom's magic was fading, or it wasn't strong enough.

I wondered if the other Reapers felt it too, or if I had just overexerted myself.

Cora wove her fingers through my hair, and my scalp tingled from her touch. "I can handle my own pain," she said quietly. "But I can't handle yours."

I inhaled a shuddering breath, wounded by the agony in her eyes and devastated to think *I* caused that. I made her worry, made her go insane with fear.

Just like she'd done to me when she'd been taken.

This love was a dangerous thing. It made us act irrationally. It made us careless, reckless, foolish . . .

Maybe there was a reason we'd been separated by realms. Because together, our love was too volatile. Too dangerous.

Cora seemed to read my thoughts. "We can't be together," she whispered. The words sounded more like a statement than a break-up. Like she thought I didn't know this.

I nodded. My throat felt tight. "I know."

"When—when we find Quentin, you'll have to go back with the Reapers."

"I know," I said again.

"We *can't*."

"You said that already."

We stared at each other. She drew in a shaky breath, and I leaned in as if she were drawing me in as well.

"Vince," she whispered.

"Cora."

Her mouth opened and closed, her eyes wide as they scanned my face. I'd never seen her like this before. At a loss for words. Frightened and anxious.

Cora wasn't scared of anything.

Neither of us moved. My hands were still on her waist. Her fingers were still in my hair.

Something electric moved through me, fueling a courage I didn't know I had. I leaned in, and my mouth covered hers. A small sound of surprise escaped her lips, but I drank it from her hungrily. My hands snaked up her back. Her trembling fingers slid around me, clutching at the nape of my neck. A burning, living presence stirred within us, brought to life by our passion. I broke apart only to gasp for air before my lips were on hers again. Her fingernails dug into the back of my neck, and I knew she felt it too. The urgency. The demand for more.

Our lips moved faster. Desperately. Her tongue

flicked along mine, and I groaned against her mouth. She tugged on my belt loops until our hips met. Together, we staggered until I had her up against the wall, my hands braced on either side of her. She cried out, and the sound drove me mad. My lips moved to her jaw, her throat, her collarbone. My tongue slid along her skin, and she gasped, the sound ragged.

As the heat between us churned and flowed like lava, as the agonizing desire built up more and more, I realized what had changed between us. Our love had shifted into something forbidden. Something impossible.

And yet, we were willing to give up everything to save each other.

A fiery, aching *need* pulsed between us. The need to protect. The need to touch, to kiss, to hold . . . Because we knew our time was limited. We'd be ripped apart again.

There was only us, here, and now.

Cora shrugged out of her jacket, her lips still locked onto mine. Her hands tugged at my shirt, lifting it higher and higher until her fingers trailed over the muscles of my abdomen.

I almost stopped her. Alarm flared inside me, a warning. We'd never crossed this line before.

But I needed her. I needed to feel her skin on mine. If I had to turn her away, if I had to watch her leave again, I felt like I would die.

Her fingers unfastened my belt. Unbuckled my jeans. A shudder rippled through me from her nimble touch, her swift movements.

She'd done this before.

But I hadn't.

"Cora," I rasped, the sound ragged and pleading.

Her hands stilled, and she pulled away to look up at me. Her eyes, usually icy, were now on fire. She blinked as if coming out of a haze, then dropped her hands. "I—I'm sorry. We don't . . ." She shook her head, her cheeks turning red.

The vulnerability and shame that crept in her face was almost too much for me. And the fire in my body didn't want us to stop. Even if she'd crossed this line and I hadn't, even if it wouldn't be as enjoyable as she was used to . . . The feverish pounding inside me demanded I keep going.

I loved her. She loved me. That was all that mattered.

In a swift movement, I lifted my shirt over my head and let it fall to the floor.

Cora sucked in a breath, her eyes wide as she gazed at my bare chest. My heart pounded a frantic rhythm inside me, but it was like a stranger had taken over my body. I felt no fear. Only one thought resonated inside me: I wanted her.

Cora removed her own shirt, tossing it onto the floor next to mine. My heart stopped for a full beat.

Her black bra stood out against her pale skin. Her chest rose and fell with heavy breaths that matched my own.

I took her waist, drawing her hips to mine. My fingers trailed along the bare skin of her back. Her hands pressed into my shoulders. Every inch of me burned with a raging fire that consumed me.

We were up against the wall again. Cora tugged at me, her legs lifting until they wrapped around me. I pressed into her, my hips grinding against hers. She moaned in my mouth, and I silenced her with lips and tongue and teeth.

"Vince," she gasped. She threw her head back, and I ran my tongue along her throat, my teeth finding her shoulder. Cora's fingernails dug into my back as she cried out.

Part of me just wanted to take her right here against the wall. Another part of me was almost brave enough to try it.

But it was my first time. I had no idea what I was doing.

Cora read the uncertainty in my gaze. She jerked her head to the left. "The bed," she whispered.

I nodded, carrying her to the bed and gently lowering her onto the sheets. She wriggled out of her pants and kicked them off. My own trembling fingers struggled with my jeans.

"Here." Cora scooted closer and unzipped my jeans before slowly pulling them off.

My pulse roared loudly in my ears as I stepped out of them and crawled onto the bed with her.

Her eyes met mine, searching. Questioning. I hovered over her, my hands pressed into the mattress on either side of her. Taking in her body—half-naked and barely concealed by the tiny black lace of her underwear—set my insides on fire. My nerves melted, leaving behind nothing but desire.

I kissed her, pressing against her, feeling her body arch into mine. The fierce pounding inside me urged us onward. More, more, more . . .

Suddenly, a heavy knocking sounded at the door.

It was like dumping a bucket of icy water on me. I scrambled off the bed, my blood running cold.

"Cora, you in there?" Benny's muffled voice asked. "Piper's awake."

I stilled, my gaze shifting to Cora. Her face was ashen, and she carefully slid out of bed before throwing her clothes back on.

More knocking.

"I'm coming," Cora rasped. In seconds, she was dressed. She turned to look at me, regret and longing filling her eyes.

Time seemed to stop, and for a brief moment, I wondered if I'd somehow triggered my powers. But no—

that was just reality slamming into me in full force, and my mind took a second to catch up. Cora and I stood there, watching each other. A dozen emotions passed between us. The same desire screaming inside me shone in her eyes too. The same conflict of *we-can't-do-this* mingled with *I-love-you-and-want-you-now*.

And then, the solid reminder that it *wasn't* just us and here and now. There were other things happening around us that needed our attention.

The thought sent a mixture of guilt and self-loathing wriggling through me.

I swallowed. "It's okay," I whispered to Cora.

She offered an apologetic smile. Leaning in, she pressed a soft kiss to my lips—so chaste compared to what we'd almost done. For a moment, that same heat thundered within me, demanding more.

But before I'd opened my eyes, she'd left the room.

CHAPTER 28

CORA

Idiot, idiot, idiot, each step seemed to say as I followed Benny to Piper's room. What the hell had I done? Or rather, *almost* done?

My coven was in danger. The Reapers' lives were at stake. Quentin was destroying another realm entirely.

Meanwhile, Vince and I were busy boning.

The heat of shame filled my face. Benny's stance in front of me was rigid, revealing nothing. Had he heard us? Was my hair a disheveled mess, completely giving me away?

Idiot, idiot, idiot.

Benny stopped, his eyes a guarded mask as he gestured to Piper's door. "She's waiting for you."

I didn't move. Benny held my gaze, but his expression betrayed nothing.

"Benny," I said weakly, stepping toward him.

He flinched, then composed his features again. In that half-second, agony flared in his face. I saw his grief. The still festering wound of losing his wife. His pack. *Everything.*

It was like that wound had been re-opened.

When he met my gaze again, a silent plea shone in his eyes. *Drop it,* he seemed to beg. As if saying the words would be too much for him.

I nodded once and knocked on my sister's door.

"Come in," a faint voice said.

I strode inside without glancing at Benny. Bright lights streamed from within the room, and I squinted against the glow, thinking Piper was summoning some kind of magic.

But no. She'd just turned on *every lamp in the room.* The floor lamp, ceiling lights, night lights, lamps on all the tables, the fluorescents . . . everything. I hadn't realized how dark it was in the hallway until I entered Piper's room.

I opened my mouth to crack a joke about it, but then I saw her—huddled on her bed with her knees pressed to her chest, her eyes wide and her breathing ragged.

My words died in my throat, and I saw the room through new eyes. She wanted every shadow illuminated. Every possible hiding place where her father could be lurking.

I couldn't blame her for that at all.

"Hey," I said gently, sitting on the edge of her bed.

"Hey." Her voice was hoarse. She rubbed her nose.

"Are you hurt?" I asked. *Stupid question.* Of course *she's hurting.* "I mean, do you need a healer? Or an elixir?"

Piper shook her head. "No, I'm all right. Thanks." Her eyes lifted to mine. "How's Juliet? And her kids?"

"Your aunt's fine. And I've sent my guys to the kids' school to look out for any trouble. They'll bring them here when school gets out."

Piper shook her head. "They need to get here *now*. Quentin—"

"Quentin will find them in a heartbeat if some strange yellow-eyed guys come and yank them out of school in the middle of the day," I said sharply. "It's too suspicious. A school full of witnesses is the safest place for them right now. When the final bell rings, and the whole campus is a chaos of kids getting home, *that* will be the time to slip away with them. It'll be easier for my guys to get to them during all the commotion. Trust me."

Piper's lips pressed together in a thin line, but she nodded. "Thank you."

Silence fell between us. I wasn't sure what to say. I'd never been good at condolences or affection. My job had always been to get in, get out, no questions asked.

But weeks of playing the role of coven leader, of forcing myself to *care* for my people—something in me broke at the lost expression on Piper's face. I thought of the dark witch I hadn't known very well and how headstrong and fierce she'd seemed.

But Quentin had broken her. Just like he wanted to break me.

I opened my mouth to speak, but before I could, Piper said, "I'm sorry."

I frowned. "For what?"

"For . . . stealing from you. Dragging you into this."

I offered a hollow laugh. I'd almost forgotten about the money laundering. "You didn't drag me into anything. He's my father too."

Piper winced. "I betrayed your trust."

I gave a half-shrug. "No harm done. I don't trust anyone, anyway."

In spite of the terror still etched in her face, Piper's lips quivered in the ghost of a smile.

I sighed. As much as I wanted to leave her here to sort out her trauma, I needed answers. Time was not on our side.

"I need to ask you about Quentin," I said.

Piper nodded again like she expected this.

"How long have you known him?"

"My whole life."

Everything inside me went still. *Oh, Lilith, no.* I'd been hoping it wasn't true, that he had just appeared in her life like he had mine.

"He raised me," Piper whispered, tears brimming in

her eyes. "I think he was waiting for Bloodcaster magic to manifest itself, even when I cast my first spell and it was black. He was always . . . hoping."

Bile crept up my throat. Piper had been nothing more than an experiment for him. Something to test and discard when he was done.

"And your mom?" I asked.

"I barely remember her. Flashes. Certain smells. Quentin sacrificed her when I was four."

Horror numbed my bones, and I swallowed down the agony clawing at my throat.

"I'm not sure when things changed," Piper went on. "But high school was when I saw him for what he really was. He used me for his dirty work, no longer caring that I wasn't the daughter he hoped I would be. I smuggled things for him. Threatened his enemies. Everything he needed to remain anonymous but powerful."

She was his weapon, I realized. *His Blade. Just like I was to Damien.*

"He never laid a hand on me," Piper said, meeting my gaze. "Never hurt me . . . n *that* way. He was too smart for that. He knew that abusing me would break me, and he needed me to be strong. But there was no love in our relationship. At first, that was what I wanted from him, but eventually, it was fear and not love that motivated me. Fear because I remembered what he'd done to Mom and that would be my fate if I became useless to him."

A survivalist. Again, something within me resonated with her words. She did what she had to in order to survive.

Piper continued, "Then, a few years ago, my aunt moved into town with her kids. Even though it was risky, I snuck out often to see her. And despite who I was and the terrible things I'd done, Juliet accepted me. She treated me like her own daughter. Every time I visited, I was reminded of what love *should* be. And I realized Quentin never loved me. And he never would." She took a shuddering breath, her eyes shining with tears.

My chest ached with sympathy. I knew how it felt to be alone and unloved. And to cling desperately to those who actually cared.

"I thought I was being careful," Piper went on, "but of course Quentin knew I was visiting Juliet. And as soon as he noticed my devotion to him was fading, he used Juliet as leverage." She paused, her lower lip wobbling. "I knew he would do it—he would kill her. I didn't have a choice, so . . . I kept working for him."

"What kind of jobs did he make you do?" I asked softly.

Piper's brows knitted together as she thought about this. "Mostly smuggling potion ingredients so he could make his elixirs. Occasionally, I helped him traffick powerful witches and warlocks for . . . for . . ." She trailed off, her voice trembling.

"For sacrifices," I finished.

Piper nodded, her expression crumpling. "At the time, I j-justified my actions, claiming it w-was either Juliet or them. I—I *had* to keep her safe." She shook her head, tears rolling down her cheeks. "But that d-doesn't stop the gnawing guilt from eating me up inside. Accusing me of b-being just as bad as he is."

"Piper, *no*." I took her hand in mine. "You aren't like him because you actually *feel* this guilt and sorrow. He doesn't."

Piper dropped her gaze, and I knew she didn't believe me.

"What else?" I prompted.

"I robbed a few places when he was low on cash. Took out some Second Tier demons who posed a threat to him."

My eyebrows lifted. She killed Second Tier demons? Impressive. "Which demons?" Maybe I could find a pattern of who he was targeting.

"Mostly dark warlocks. A werewolf alpha here and there."

"What kind of dark warlocks?" I asked, remembering Damien targeting Vince because he'd wanted his time travel ability.

Piper's eyes lifted to mine. "Thinkers."

I went still. Thinkers were Telepaths like Luke and

Benny. But Quentin wasn't just targeting normal Thinkers—but *Second Tier* Thinkers.

Benny was Second Tier.

"Why?" I asked in a hard voice, trying to ignore the terror that gripped my chest at the thought of Benny in danger.

"I don't know. He never shared anything with me. Just gave me assignments."

Yes, Piper was just like me. I'd never asked questions either. As soon as I had, Damien had blackmailed me into doing what he wanted.

"I know you're looking for weaknesses," Piper said. "But he doesn't have any. Even without his elixirs, he has spells he can cast by cutting himself and spilling his blood. He makes runes with it. Dampening cuffs can't stop him."

I already knew that. When Vince and I had been trapped, I'd used a healing rune on Vince, even though the cuffs on my wrists should've stopped my magic. It apparently didn't work on my blood.

"No one is unstoppable," I said, reverting back to my assassin mindset. "Everyone has a weakness."

"Not him. He doesn't love anyone. He only loves his power."

I said nothing. I didn't move, didn't breathe, as the barest form of a plan formed in my mind.

"Benny told me that Reaper saved my aunt," Piper said in a whisper.

I stilled and looked at her. *That Reaper.* Vince.

"Will you tell him thank you?" Piper asked.

Thinking of Vince sent knots of longing and sorrow into my chest. Slowly, I nodded. When I stood, Piper took my hand again, her eyes pleading.

"When you make your move, I want to be a part of it." Her eyes, once broken, now gleamed with the hungry haze of vengeance. "Let me come with you."

Once again, I knew that feeling down to my core. Piper and I were the same. Fueled by the fear of death. Burdened by a power-hungry father. Forced to hone skills that shaped us into brutal warriors.

"I will," I promised before I left the room.

I tracked Benny down in our new offices, a shabby alternative to what we once had. But, for now, it served our purposes. Benny sat at a tiny card table, surrounded by the papers I was supposed to finish.

When I approached, something unpleasant coiled in my stomach as I realized Benny must've returned to Vince's room to get the papers I'd left.

I cleared my throat as I approached, but Benny didn't even glance up. I stood in front of him and crossed my arms, eyebrows raised as I watched him sign a document.

At long last, Benny exhaled in exasperation and looked up at me, his expression closed off. "Yes?"

My brows knitted together. Benny had his moments, but he was never *this* irritable for this long.

I hated the tendril of dread inside me that told me it was *my* fault.

"I need your help setting a trap for Quentin," I said.

Benny stared at me, his face betraying nothing. Something sparked in his eyes, but it was gone in a flash. "Oh?" was all he said.

"You're not going to like it," I said.

Benny snorted without humor. "I'm used to that by now." There was an edge to his voice that cut right through me. He turned back to the paper in front of him, and for a second, rage shot through me. Was he *ignoring* me right now?

I snatched the chair opposite him and plopped down on the other side of the table. He merely raised his eyebrows at me.

"Out with it," I snapped.

"Out with what?"

"You've been pissy for days. Do you need to fight me or something? Blow off some steam?"

Benny fixed a cold gaze on me. "No. I'm fine."

"I don't believe you."

His jaw went rigid. "It isn't your business, Cora."

A mixture of anger and sorrow swirled in my gut. I took a breath to steady my nerves and said gently, "If you're a member of my coven, then it *is* my business. Talk to me, Benny."

"We don't have *time* for a therapy session," Benny snapped. "Didn't you come here to set a plan in motion? There are more important things than my bad mood."

I remained quiet for a moment, my perspective shifting. Instead of playing the role of the concerned coven leader, I put myself in Benny's place. How many days had I been in a funk and didn't want to—or *couldn't*—talk to anyone about it?

I sighed. "Like it or not, Benny, we'll have to *make* time. Because I need you at your best for this assignment. And no one understands more than I do the cost of fighting when you have something weighing on your mind. Whether you like it or not, it affects your performance. And I *need* you."

Once again, that unreadable *thing* stirred in his eyes. It lingered for a moment, and then I recognized it.

Pain. Raw, brutal, all-consuming pain. The sight of it blazing so plainly in his eyes was enough to make my heart stop.

"I assure you, this isn't something that can be fixed," Benny said, his voice low and quiet. "At least, not for a long time."

I raised my eyebrows, watching him. Waiting.

Benny groaned and dropped his head. "Cora—"

"I'm not moving until you tell me what's up. I don't care how long it takes."

He rubbed his forehead and blew air through his lips. "It's . . . well, it's a combination of things, really."

I cocked my head with interest.

His eyes finally met mine, full of anguish. "The anniversary of my wife's death is this week."

A heavy weight settled in my chest. *Oh, Lilith.* And here I was, thinking he had developed feelings for me. How self-centered *was* I?

"And I'm feeling conflicted about . . . so many things," Benny went on, lowering his gaze. "Anytime I find myself . . . attracted to another woman, the grief of that loss is so much more intense. Like I'm being punished for moving on before I'm ready."

My insides went numb. All I could do was stare at him as he expertly avoided my gaze.

"I'll be straight with you," Benny said, raising his eyes to meet mine. Small red splotches formed on his cheeks as he spoke. "I like you, Cora. Probably more than I should. And seeing you with Vince, it just . . . it messed me up."

Damn it all, I thought. "Benny—"

He raised his hand. "Don't. Honestly, it's nothing. It isn't you that's hurting me right now. It's *her*. Lynn."

Lynn. His wife. My mouth opened in surprise.

"It doesn't happen often, but since she died, if I ever find myself thinking about another woman like that, the guilt and agony are so crushing and intense that I can't breathe. And now it's even more difficult to bear with that anniversary looming closer and closer."

My mouth felt dry. I wasn't sure what to say.

"Even if I *did* want to act on these feelings and date you, I couldn't. I'm just not in the right headspace for it. I'm still grieving." He sighed, shaking his head. "But I'm also not a monk. I can't just turn those feelings off."

Lilith, what a mess. All I wanted to do was tell him I could fix this, that there was a solution to heal him. An elixir maybe.

But grief could only be healed with time.

"I'm sorry," I said, my voice breaking. "Really, I am."

Benny offered a wry smile. "You have nothing to be sorry about. If it wasn't you, it would've been someone else."

Now it was *me* who avoided his gaze. "I—do you, um, want to find another coven? Would that make things easier?"

His face slackened in surprise. "What? No, of course not! This is too important."

"But if you're in so much pain—"

"I told you, it isn't you. I'd be feeling this way no

matter where I went. And I can't let grief rule my life. There's too much for me to do."

I nodded, fully understanding this. "Well, if you change your mind, I won't begrudge you for leaving."

His smile turned more sincere. "Thanks."

I crossed one leg over the other and rubbed my palms on my jeans. Everything was so complicated now. What was I supposed to say?

Benny cleared his throat. "Well, now that *that's* out in the open . . ." He laughed nervously, and I joined in. Something loosened in my chest ever so slightly. Benny's expression sobered, and he asked, "Did you say you had a plan for catching Quentin?"

I nodded, leaning forward, eager for the subject change. "Yes. Piper was telling me about him and how he doesn't seem to have any weaknesses. First of all, I wanted to ask you about Thinkers. She mentioned Quentin was targeting them, specifically Thinkers who are Second Tier—like you. What do you know about that? Do you pose any threat to him?"

Benny frowned and rubbed his chin in contemplation. "There are so many different variations of Telepaths out there. For instance, Luke and I aren't exactly the same. No two Thinkers are." His brows knitted together, his expression growing distant. "But for a Bloodcaster . . ." He trailed off as something lit up in his eyes. "Can you make a Thinking elixir?"

My mouth opened and closed as I considered this. "Uh, no, actually. I tried once, but it didn't work. Nothing can replicate a Telepath's abilities."

Benny raised his eyebrows as if this explained it.

But I shrugged. "Why does that matter? Quentin has an entire arsenal of elixirs and power at his disposal. Why would he care that he can't duplicate a Thinker's power?"

Benny shook his head. "I don't know. Let me do some research and reach out to my contacts. There are covens of Thinkers out there who would know more about this than me. But if he's taking out Thinkers because he feels threatened, maybe there's something we can do that would wound him—or even kill him."

I nodded as Benny rose to his feet. I followed suit and cleared my throat. "Uh, that's not all."

He looked at me expectantly.

"I want to set a trap for him," I said, "using myself as bait."

CHAPTER 29

VINCE

MY MIND WAS STILL ABUZZ FROM THE HEATED MOMENT with Cora, and I needed to busy myself with something useful. After dressing, I tracked down Mom in her room a few doors down. I shuddered at the thought of her being so close when Cora and I almost—

Don't think about it, Vince, I sternly told myself before knocking briskly on the door.

I hadn't realized there were muffled voices until they abruptly went silent. With a frown, I wondered who was with Mom. Gwen, perhaps?

Someone shuffled around on the other side of the door before it finally opened, and Mom's wide eyes peered at me through a tiny crack in the door.

"Vince!" She sounded breathless and a bit startled. She glanced quickly behind her. "Uh, what do you need?"

"I wanted to know what I can do to help

with . . . whatever it is you're working on." I tried peering around her to no avail. "Do you need help with any spells or anything? Are the Reapers . . ." I trailed off, unable to concentrate on my words when Mom kept looking over her shoulder at something I couldn't see. "What's going on?" I asked, suddenly suspicious.

Mom sighed. "Please don't be angry with me. I wanted to tell you, but—"

"Tell me *what?*" Urgency flared in me, making my blood pound.

Mom stood back and held open the door. I strode inside, expecting to find a demon or something threatening.

Instead, I found a figure sitting at the small table by the TV, his face so familiar but so foreign. A face I never thought I'd see again.

"Dad," I croaked.

Dad stood, his face more tired than I remembered. His hair had grown longer and fell forward into his face. He wore a dress shirt and tie, as if he'd just come from work.

A lump formed in my throat. Mom shut the door behind me, and I shot her a questioning look. Her mouth opened and closed, her face redder than usual.

"What—what's he doing here?" I stammered.

"I brought him here," Mom said. "To keep him safe. I didn't want Quentin using him as leverage."

"I'm not *entirely* helpless," Dad grumbled.

Mom snorted. "Yes, you are."

Dad grinned.

Their easy banter—as if they *hadn't* been separated for over a decade—made my head spin. I leaned against the wall for support, my mind dizzy and throbbing. "But —*why* didn't you tell me?" I demanded, remembering Cora's insistence that I see my dad. Before everything exploded in our face and Quentin abducted her.

"Well, you were—I just—after everything that happened with Cora—" Mom stopped abruptly, pressing her lips together. Her eyes were guarded, as if she didn't want to be completely honest with me.

Everything that happened with Cora. I remembered Cora saying she wasn't welcome in my room while Jocelyn, Gwen, and my mom had been in there.

And Jocelyn's claim that I'd screwed everything up by going after Cora.

Ice hardened in my chest. "You didn't trust me." My voice was hollow. "Not after I ran off and nearly got myself killed."

"Your mom just wanted to wait until I was brought up to speed," Dad said. "You were the first person I wanted to see, Vince. But you were also injured and needed rest. We didn't want to overwhelm you."

"I'm not a child," I said, irritation prickling through me. "You don't have to coddle me."

Mom raised her eyebrows as if to say, *Don't we?* My blood boiled in response.

"Yeah, I was reckless," I grumbled. "I wasn't thinking." With a sigh, I ran a hand through my hair, my anger ebbing. "I get it."

"We weren't trying to hurt you," Mom said. Her gaze flicked to Dad, and warmth shone in her eyes.

Seeing that look—and seeing my dad return it—made all the tension inside me vanish. My parents had been separated for too long. Torn apart by the demands of another realm and my mom's Reaper responsibilities.

They needed to re-connect. Who was I to resent them for that? I'd only been away from Cora for a few months and it had been agony. We couldn't keep our hands off each other—clearly.

I slowly sank to the edge of Mom's bed. "Okay, so fill me in. What's our plan?"

Mom and Dad shared a look that made me reminiscent of my childhood when they were keeping something from me. Something a child shouldn't hear.

"Just tell me," I urged.

"We—the Reapers—are considering leaving. Finding a new home." Mom bit her lip and watched me hesitantly.

I blanched. "*What?* How? Where? I thought we could only stay here temporarily."

"We can. I don't mean here in the mortal realm. I mean . . . in the Underworld."

My blood chilled. *The Underworld.* I didn't know much about it. Only that the Astral Realm served as a bridge between the Underworld and the mortal realm.

"But you said only dead people could live there," I said slowly.

"That's not entirely true," Mom hedged. "Gwen may have found a loophole."

There was hope in her voice. It sounded as if she were giving up entirely on the Astral Realm.

And if that were true . . . did that mean I could never come back here? I would never see Cora or Dad again?

I shook my head in confusion. "Okay, so . . . you want to just run away? Instead of fighting Quentin?"

"He has the power of our realm at his disposal. He's unstoppable. The risk is too great. If we fight him and lose—which is highly likely—then our work can't continue. The souls of the dead will suffer, and the balance between realms will be torn apart."

"It sounds like that's already happening," I argued. "He's already *done* the damage! We need to stop him before he does any more! Do you really think he won't try to follow us to the Underworld and finish the job?"

Mom's face paled, but her expression hardened with determination. "This isn't an easy decision, Vince. We have to consider our duty as Reapers."

"I am *so sick of this*," I snarled, jumping to my feet. "We are not the only magical creatures that exist! There is an entire coven here—a damn *Bloodcaster* for Lilith's sake—who can help us fight this war. We aren't Quentin's only enemies. We need to unite with the others who are trying to stop him."

"Like Cora." Mom's voice was flat and full of sarcasm.

"Yes." My voice faltered. I didn't like the steely look in her eyes.

"Our problem escalated when you dragged her into this," Mom said.

Anger flared within me once more. "None of this is her fault."

"Quentin is *her* father!"

"Yeah, and unfortunately, we don't get much choice in who our parents are." My tone was biting and harsh, and Mom's head reared back in shock.

"Vince," Dad whispered in warning.

"Cora's a *demon*," Mom snapped, her eyes blazing.

"No, she isn't. She's a Bloodcaster."

"She runs a *demon coven*. She's on their side!"

"So?" I cried, raising my arms. "You're a *Reaper*, Mom! Who are you to judge? You became a Reaper because your light magic was taken from you. You don't get to turn your nose up at dark magic anymore."

"Look at the facts," Mom said, stepping toward me. "Over half of the demon population preys on humans.

Most of them can't even control the urge to kill. We turn our nose up at demons for a *reason*. They are killers, Vince."

I shook my head again and took a shaky step away from her. This *we're-better-than-them* garbage she was spouting sounded a lot like what Hector believed in when he thought Nephilim should be isolated from everyone else.

And honestly, were Reapers any different? So secretive, so private . . . They didn't want to share anything with Cora when we arrived. And now they wanted to look for a new home, *away from everyone* to carry on this "sacred duty."

My gaze shifted to Dad, who watched with a stony expression. The emotion in his eyes, the unease—it suggested he disagreed with Mom.

But he said nothing.

I clenched my teeth as resolve and bitter hatred hardened inside me. "Do whatever you want, Mom. But I won't be any part of it. I'm staying to fight."

Mom's mouth fell open. Dad's face paled, and he rose to his feet as if to stop me.

Before either of them spoke, I stormed out of the room.

I was halfway down the hallway when I collided with Luke.

My friend yelped as we both fell over. Laughing, Luke

extended a hand to help me up. When we both stood, and his expression sobered as he no doubt took in the rage etched into my face.

"What—what happened?" he asked.

"Don't worry about it. What're you doing here?" The edge in my voice made the question sound more like a demand.

Luke cleared his throat. "Benny asked for my help, and I've been doing some research. I think I've found a way to help you."

I raised my eyebrows. "Oh?"

"I'll need to talk to the other Reapers about it, though."

Something in me deflated. I rubbed the back of my neck. "Yeah, uh, that might be a problem. Mom says the Reapers want to flee and find a new home. But I refused. I'm staying."

Luke's eyes widened. "What? Can you *do* that?"

"No idea. But I can't just run away. I want to fight this asshole and stop him before he destroys everything."

Luke's mouth pressed together, forming a thin line. "I may be able to help with that."

I frowned. "With what?"

"Fighting . . . *and* fleeing."

Fifteen minutes later, the Reapers, plus my dad and Luke, crowded in the hotel lobby. A few of Cora's men stood guard around the exits, and Cora herself leaned casually against the wall across from us, watching intently.

I avoided Mom's gaze, though I felt her eyes on me.

"You have our attention," Gwen said, her voice firm and commanding. The coldness in her eyes suggested she had low expectations. "What is this plan of yours?"

Luke exchanged a glance with Benny, who nodded encouragingly. I'd forgotten they were both Thinkers. It was weird to think of them as friends.

Luke licked his lips, wringing his hands together in front of him. I remembered he'd always hated public speaking. He got terrible stage fright.

"Benny and I reached out to our contacts," Luke said, his voice trembling slightly. "We discovered something interesting about our Telepathic abilities. The strongest Thinkers can create a kind of mental prison. Impenetrable to *all* forms of magic." His eyes widened with significance.

"Even Bloodcaster magic?" Cora asked, straightening.

Luke nodded. "Quentin Cox was taking out Second Tier Thinkers because he knew this was a potential threat to his magic."

"You're not Second Tier," Gwen said, her eyes narrowing.

"Luke isn't," Benny said, "but I am."

I started. My heart lurched as I glanced at Cora. She met my gaze and nodded grimly.

Benny is Second Tier. How had I not known this?

Even Gwen looked shocked as she glanced from Benny to Luke.

"We have a few options," Luke went on, his voice gaining strength. "There's a binding spell we can use to bind the Reapers' magic and tether it to a single host—one lone Reaper—to keep the magic protected. Then, we can lock this Reaper in a mental prison to keep Quentin from getting to him. The only catch is, the Thinker has to stay alive. If Quentin finds out who's housing this Reaper magic and he kills the Thinker, the magic will be released and the Reaper will die."

I suppressed a shudder as my blood ran cold at the thought.

"You're suggesting we trap our *entire arsenal of magic* . . . in the mind of this demon?" Gwen gestured to Benny, who stiffened. The incredulity and scorn on Gwen's face was enough to make my blood boil.

"If you want to take Quentin down, you're gonna need to get over your bitchy prejudice *real* fast," Cora said, her eyes burning with fury.

Gwen's lips tightened, and her nostrils flared. Murmurs rippled around the room from Reapers and demons alike.

Before the arguing escalated, Luke jumped in again. "There is . . . another option."

The crowd fell silent and watched Luke attentively.

Luke swallowed and, for some reason, shot an apologetic glance at me. "Vince's mind is connected to mine. We're the only two people in this room with that kind of connection. It would take a powerful spell, but . . . I believe I can keep Vince and the Reaper magic safe in my own mind."

I stared at him, my body frozen with shock. It took a few seconds for me to register what he was saying.

I hadn't even reacted when Cora went rigid, her icy gaze on Luke. "Are you suggesting we *trap Vince* inside your head? Do you even have enough power to do that?"

"And are you even strong enough to fight off Quentin if he finds you?" Mom asked.

Neither of them asked in disdain or condescension. These were genuine questions.

But Luke flinched all the same. "I don't know. But it's either me . . . or Benny. We're the only two Thinkers who can help you."

Again, his gaze flicked back to me, and I understood what he was saying. He didn't want this for me. But he'd already ascertained that the Reapers wouldn't want to put their magic inside Benny. They didn't trust him.

But they *could* trust Luke.

My insides felt hollow. I already knew what the decision would be before Gwen spoke.

"We will use your bond with Vince," Gwen said to Luke. "Vince will be the vessel for our magic."

"No," Mom said, her voice even louder than Gwen's.

A stunned silence filled the room. Even the demons who didn't know Mom or Gwen seemed to understand the severity of this situation. Gwen's mouth tightened, her eyes spearing through Mom, who stepped forward.

Mom lifted her chin. "I will be the vessel."

My mouth fell open, and confusion and relief warred within me. "Mom—"

"The Reapers will fight," Mom said, her voice gaining volume. "I will guard our magic while the rest of you stay here to end the threat." Her eyes shifted to me, softening a bit. "Let Vince live his life. I'll bind myself to Benny willingly." She looked at Gwen, her gaze blazing as if daring her to defy this.

Gwen's nostrils flared, and her eyes were piercing as she stared Mom down. But Mom didn't shrink away. In that moment, I wondered who had the authority. I'd always assumed it was Gwen, given her legendary exploits as a powerful Nephilim. But Mom had also been clan leader.

It had never really mattered until now.

At long last, Gwen nodded stiffly. "Very well. Cecile will be our vessel."

CHAPTER 30

CORA

AFTER THE MEETING, THERE WAS A FLURRY OF ACTIVITY and questions. Many demons in my coven demanded to know why we were even helping these Reapers. Honestly, I'd asked myself the same question again and again.

But so much was at stake. If Quentin got more power, he could literally take over the world.

And, of course, there was Vince. I would do anything for him. Even fight a battle I would likely lose.

I extricated myself from the talkative demons who wanted to discuss this new threat with me. I found Vince sitting in the armchair of the lobby, his expression stony.

"Are you okay?" I asked.

He huffed a laugh. "No."

Slowly, I sank into the chair opposite him and leaned forward, meeting his gaze. "Your mom knew what she was doing. It was her choice."

"There is no choice," he said bitterly. "Nephilim, Reapers—they're all the same. Choosing your life for you. Taking away your freedom. It's all or nothing."

"You made the choice to become a Reaper."

His expression soured. "I know. And I've regretted it almost every day since."

The devastation in his face was almost too much for me. I took a deep breath. "I can try to find another way to—"

"There is no other way," he said glumly. "And we're out of time." He ran his hands through his hair. "If they could just *see* that allying ourselves with other covens— even with just *your* coven—would give us an advantage." He groaned.

I dropped my hands on my lap. "Stubborn fools."

"I know."

Silence fell between us. I shifted a bit in my seat. "What if your mom didn't have to do this at all? What if we could take Quentin out before Gwen even finishes the binding spell?"

Vince went very still as he watched me. I read the hesitant hope in his eyes, the guarded curiosity. "What do you mean?" he asked slowly.

"Quentin has no weaknesses," I said. "The only thing he wants—*craves,* even—is more power. He wants to sacrifice me to get that power because I'm the only other Bloodcaster he can find."

"Okay." Vince's eyes narrowed slightly. I could tell he didn't like where this was going.

I took a breath. "I want to lure him out, using myself as bait."

His head reared back, and he glanced around the lobby as if worried we'd be overheard. "Are you *insane?*" he hissed, leaning closer to me. "You'll get yourself killed."

"Not if I set the trap the right way. And I want you to help me do it."

He blinked, his face slackening in surprise. "You— you do?"

I nodded. "You're powerful, Vince. More powerful than you realize. And if you can use your time travel ability, it'll be an easy win for us."

Vince gaped at me, clearly stunned. The shock and pure disbelief on his face made me want to cry. He thought *nothing* of himself. No one had ever truly *needed* his help before.

I resonated with that—I'd been lonely for most of my life—but this was different. Vince thought himself incapable. Incompetent.

I put my hand on his knee, clasping his fingers in mine. "Help me do this, Vince, and it'll all be over."

He stared at me for a long moment, a dozen emotions filling his eyes. Hesitation, confusion, fear, surprise, affection, and then . . . resolve.

He nodded. "Tell me the plan."

Though it would've been helpful to march on Quentin with an entire army at my disposal, I kept our operation to just a trusted few of my coven: Benny, Piper, Vince, and Dex, the vampire. Dex had offered to convince Hunter to join, but I refused. For one thing, I didn't trust Hunter, not when he feared Quentin more than he trusted me. For another, I sincerely doubted Hunter would come. He'd been too afraid to offer me information. He likely would balk at the idea of attacking Quentin directly.

After securing the potions I needed and ensuring my crew was in position, I had Vince Jump me to Quentin's neighborhood—just a few blocks from where I'd been imprisoned.

Vince gathered me against his chest, and I savored his mint and soap scent, the feel of his muscular arms around me. The world shifted, and with a small *pop*, we arrived in the suburbs. I suppressed a shudder at the sight of the empty street, the sickening row of identical houses, and the eerie silence that swept over me.

"You don't have to do this, you know," Vince murmured.

I looked up at him. His brows pulled together, his jaw

rigid. Fire blazed in his eyes, and for a moment, he looked like that warrior angel I'd seen in my office—the first time I'd seen him as a Reaper.

I leaned up and pressed a soft kiss to his lips. He grunted in surprise but grasped my waist, pulling me against him. "I'm with you, Vince," I whispered against his lips. "Always. I'll fight for you. Kill for you. I'll slaughter anyone who gets in our way." I drew away to look up at him, relishing the hot desire stirring in his eyes. Not a whiff of fear of who I was or what I could do.

I loved that about him.

"Remember the plan," I said breathlessly. "Stay safe."

He nodded, pushing my hair behind my ear. "You too."

I touched his cheek, and then with a *pop*, he vanished, leaving me alone on the darkening street. A gust of wind tousled my hair, and I glanced up at the dark clouds, recognizing the warning of a thunderstorm.

Let it come. Let it rage around me.

I checked my daggers and potion elixirs before striding forward, remembering the street corner where Quentin had almost killed Piper. I didn't bother masking my steps or cloaking myself. Quentin needed to see me coming.

When I stood in front of his house, which seemed as pleasant and innocent as a docile kitten, I put my hands on my hips and raised my eyebrows. "I want to talk!" I shouted at the house.

A breeze rippled through the leaves on the nearby trees, but the house remained still. I waited, impatience throbbing inside me.

"Hello, Cordelia," said a quiet voice behind me.

I whirled, my heart thundering, to find Quentin standing on the street next to me. No sound, no indication of *how* he'd appeared there.

Swallowing down my alarm, I faced him and lifted my chin. "I want to negotiate a truce."

Quentin's eyebrows lifted. "Oh?"

I nodded. "I don't want anyone else getting killed."

Quentin's mouth spread in a wide, feral smile that made my blood run cold. "Is that so."

My instincts screamed at me to run, to get as far away from him as possible. But I shoved them down and said, "Yes."

I withdrew a vial from my belt and held it up for him to see.

"My shadow elixir. Consider it a sign of good faith." I tossed it to him, and he caught it easily, his eyes narrowing as he scrutinized it.

"What makes you think I can't make this myself?" he asked.

"I invented it. You can try, but it won't be the same without my blood."

His eyes glittered dangerously, and he pocketed the vial. "All right. I'll listen. Name your terms."

Keep him talking, Cora, I reminded myself. "I want my coven to stay out of it. No losses or casualties."

Quentin arched an eyebrow. "Very well."

"That includes Piper."

His eyes flashed, and his jaw went rigid. He inhaled deeply through his nose. "And . . . what do you offer in return?"

"I offer myself. Go ahead and sacrifice me, Quentin. It's what you want, isn't it?"

Quentin cocked his head, scrutinizing me. I held perfectly still as if he were a lethal predator.

At long last, he whispered, "No."

I frowned. "No what?"

"No, you wouldn't just come here out of the blue and offer yourself up. You're a fighter. You always have been."

I stepped toward him, gritting my teeth. "*You don't know me.* You may have heard stories about me, the Blade of Hinport, but things are different now. There are people I care about, and I have a responsibility to my coven. So don't you dare presume this decision was made lightly. That I wouldn't do this for my people."

The words were the truth. I loved Vince—I loved my city, my coven—enough to make this sacrifice if it should come to it.

Quentin watched me, his dark eyes cold and calculating. Though my insides churned with anxiety and fear, I remained perfectly still, holding his gaze.

"Take it or leave it, Quentin," I said. "If you don't give me your word, I'm walking. I need to know my people will be safe."

"Only my word?" he asked.

I shook my head. "A blood contract."

Something unreadable flashed in his eyes. "You would sign a blood contract with me?"

Hell no. But I nodded.

Quentin inhaled deeply—and then shuddered. A ragged groan burst from him, and he sank to his knees. He looked around, his eyes wild, until he stared at me in accusation. "What—what have you done to me?"

I lifted my chin. "It wasn't a shadow elixir I gave you. It was poisoned—set to activate with the absence of my body heat." My eyes shifted to the pocket he'd put the vial in. It had only taken a few minutes for my blood in the elixir to activate my spell, sensing that I was no longer in close range.

"Impressive," Quentin rasped.

I offered a cold smile. Then, I shouted, "Now!"

In a flash, my friends appeared: Benny, in wolf form, Piper, with black magic pooling from her hands, Vince, his dark wings spread behind him, and Dex, with his fangs extended and his red eyes gleaming.

Quentin clutched his side but managed a weak laugh.

"An ambush. A *trap*. Oh, well done, Cordelia. I couldn't have taught you better myself."

I stiffened, bristling at the pride in his voice. Hatred boiled through me at the thought of doing something he approved of. Above us, thunder rumbled, promising the storm I'd known was coming.

I drew my dagger, and Quentin's smile widened. "Are you going to kill me?" He choked out another laugh. "I'd be honored to become another one of your victims."

I stepped toward him, brandishing my blade. "You can't talk your way out of this, Quentin."

I slashed the blade through his throat.

Purple blood gushed from the wound. Quentin gurgled, spitting up more blood, his teeth stained with it. I watched the liquid run down his neck, pooling onto his clothes and the ground.

Until . . . the blood stopped.

The purple fluid receded back into his body, and the wound sealed itself, leaving nothing behind but smooth skin.

Cold horror chilled my body, and I staggered back a step, numb with shock. "What—"

"You aren't the only one with tricks up your sleeve," Quentin said, rising to his feet. His face was ashen, and he swayed slightly—indicating my poison still worked. "You think I wouldn't take a healing elixir before meeting you? Although, I must commend you for your ingenuity.

How did you concoct a potion to withstand the effects of healing?"

I took several deep breaths, trying to calm the raging panic within me. *How long does it take for a healing elixir to wear off?* I mentally calculated, trying to remember.

Benny growled and lunged for Quentin, tackling him to the ground. Piper and Vince followed, their magic mingling to form a swirl of black and red that consumed Quentin entirely.

A high-pitched whine pierced the air, and my heart jolted. *Benny.*

Something inside me snapped into action, and I dived into the fray. Thick magic filled the air, making it hard to breathe. I sliced a hand through the air. Purple magic glowed, and a narrow beam of light shone through the red and black haze, lighting my way.

I found Quentin poised over Benny with his hands pressed against the wolf's throat. Under his grip, Benny went limp.

I roared with rage and sliced into Quentin's shoulder, then again into his side. Quentin stiffened and cried out, releasing Benny. Piper slammed her magic into Quentin, knocking him backward. A small *pop* behind me made me whirl—to find Vince's Mimic arriving to join us.

This new Vince wasn't the scarred Vince I'd seen before. In fact, he wore the exact same clothes as *my* Vince. The two looked identical.

Which meant he'd come from the recent future.

I looked at my Vince, my eyes wide with surprise, and he offered a sly grin.

Together, we surrounded Quentin. He had nowhere to run. Even if he could heal, he couldn't take us all on at once.

Quentin stood, his eyes wide as he stared at the Vince beside me . . . and then his Mimic on my other side. "Interesting," he murmured.

I aimed a kick in the center of his chest, sending him flying. Then I pounced again. He couldn't heal if I stopped his heart. All I needed was one well-timed blow . . .

Purple magic burst against me as Quentin fought back. I grunted against the pain searing through my chest and ducked, avoiding another slice of his magic. I threw myself against his legs, and we both collapsed.

"Dex, *now*!" I shouted as I pinned Quentin to the ground.

Dex hissed, his fangs long and sharp as he buried them into Quentin's flesh, right at the base of his throat. Quentin screamed and then went still, his eyes wide and dazed as Dex drank from him. I watched, my knife raised just in case, but the longer Dex drank, the limper Quentin became.

Relief bloomed in my chest. It was over. It had to be.

Suddenly, Vince—*both* of them—bellowed in agony.

They clutched at their heads, their faces contorted with pain.

"Vince," I whispered, reaching for them. They both fell to their knees, their faces turning white.

Slowly, I faced Quentin, who now wore an insane smile. Though his eyes were clouded and his face had drained of color, he looked at me and winked.

"Dex, stop," I ordered.

Dex withdrew with a groan, wiping purple blood from his lips. His own eyes gleamed with hunger and awe, and for a moment, I found myself wondering if Bloodcaster blood tasted much different.

Striding forward and trying to ignore Vince's screams, I grabbed Quentin by the collar. "*What are you doing to him?*" I wanted to kill him right there, but I had no idea if killing him would stop Vince's pain.

Quentin laughed, the sound hoarse and feeble. Slowly, the puncture wounds on his throat healed, but I knew the blood loss would linger. "Do you think I'm an idiot? I stole magic from the Astral Realm—the very realm your boyfriend is tethered to. Of course I would use that to my advantage. Now, you get to watch while he dies."

CHAPTER 31

VINCE

Agony split through me. A searing ringing burned against my ears until I was sure my eardrums would burst. Beside me, a small *pop* told me my Mimic had vanished.

Good, I thought. *It means he's safe—I'm safe in the future.*

Which also meant I would survive this.

Something powerful coursed through my veins. Something familiar. A *knowing.* An instinct. What had once been a faint feeling now blazed inside me like a door had been thrown open. Light shone within me, piercing through the pain in my head. The ringing subsided.

All I saw was that brilliant yellow light, brighter than the sun. For one wild moment, I thought the sky had cleared, making way for the sun to break through—but then another crack of thunder split the air. Faint raindrops spattered on my face.

My senses returned, and I made out Cora's screams. My insides quivered at the sound.

"Please," Cora begged. "Quentin, *stop!*"

"I want what you promised me," Quentin said, staggering to his feet. "Give yourself up, Cordelia, and I'll spare him."

I searched within myself, looking for my Reaper magic—but instead, I found a steady stream of gold light flowing within me.

Somehow, I knew what it was: the timeline.

Cora was on her knees in front of Quentin. Tears flowed down her face as she nodded.

She was surrendering to Quentin.

For me.

I lunged. But instead of my magic reaching out, the *timeline* reached out, and I traveled. I went backward five minutes to when my Mimic had first appeared.

The presence of the timeline inside me was firm and powerful. It fueled me as I fought alongside myself and the others against Quentin. My presence here closed the loop I'd created. Just like before, there were two Vinces fighting—but this time, I was the second one.

Together, we surrounded Quentin. Then Dex drank from him. When Quentin lashed out with his powers from the Astral Realm, I knew what I had to do.

I crouched over and howled in agony, pretending to be consumed by the power of Quentin's Reaper magic. But the timeline had healed me . . . somehow. I felt nothing but calm.

No shrill ringing. No splitting pain in my head. Whatever side effects had crippled me before, whatever symptoms I'd endured being in the wrong realm, they were gone. It felt like I was an entirely new person.

It felt so *freeing*.

Pretending to stagger, I teetered forward until I was just behind Quentin. Then, I pressed a hand to his shoulder.

The timeline within me swelled, sensing something that shouldn't be there. Something that needed to be fixed.

The others were too preoccupied with my Mimic's screaming to notice me. Even Quentin, still lying there in front of Dex, focused all of his energy on the other Vince. No one paid me any attention.

I closed my eyes, pinpointing the source, the malady I felt the urge to correct. I found a huge, red presence within Quentin. The Reaper magic.

Come to me, I ordered. *Slowly. Carefully.*

Red magic seeped from Quentin, one drop at a time.

And I inhaled all of it. It swelled within me like a living thing, and I felt enlarged. Like my body was expanding to make room for it.

So much power dwelled inside me. My Reaper magic, my Teleportation abilities, the timeline, and now this— the reservoir of magic Quentin had stolen from the Astral Realm. I took several deep breaths, crying out in false pain every now and then to avoid arousing suspicion.

The transition was so slow that Quentin didn't notice. *No one* noticed as the last of the Reaper magic drained from Quentin's body.

When I finished, I spun in place with a *pop* and arrived right where I'd left. Right as Cora was nodding at her father, giving herself over to him.

"You want to try that again, Quentin?" I challenged.

Cora blinked and stared at me, her eyes wide. Quentin cocked his head at me, his eyes narrowing.

I raised my arms. "Go ahead. Kill me."

"Vince—" Cora cried.

Quentin only laughed. "You've got balls. I can respect that. But it'll be the death of you." His stare intensified, and I felt magic prickling along my skin.

But nothing happened.

Quentin's head reared back, his mouth falling open. His eyes went vacant, and I knew he was searching within himself for what wasn't there—the magic I'd stolen from him.

"You—*you*—"Quentin stepped toward me, his eyes full of rage.

Cora was on her feet again, a dagger in each hand as she blocked Quentin's path to me. "Take another step," she said through clenched teeth.

Benny twitched, and a growl built in his throat as he slowly climbed onto all fours. Behind me, Piper edged closer, though I felt her hesitation. She feared Quentin.

I couldn't blame her.

Quentin looked uncertain as we surrounded him and drew closer. Then, his eyes fell on me with sudden realization. "You're Cecile's son."

I stiffened, my entire body going still. *How does he know that?*

Quentin grinned. "The son of a powerful Nephilim queen . . . *and* my daughter's lover." His gaze shifted to Cora, and a disturbing hunger glinted in his eyes.

Cora looked at me, the blood draining from her face. And I saw what she saw: leverage. Weakness.

If Quentin had me, he could coerce her into doing anything. We'd just seen it happen. Cora would've sacrificed herself to save me.

Quentin chuckled. Then, a burst of purple magic filled the air, concealing him from view. Cora slashed her hand through the fog, clearing the way so we could reach Quentin—

But when the air cleared, he was gone.

"*Dammit!*" Cora roared, flinging her knives to the ground. "How—*how* does he keep vanishing like that?"

She whirled, her eyes ablaze as she stared at Piper, who stood a good five feet away from us. "And what the *hell* are you doing over there?"

Piper's mouth opened and closed, her face pale and her lower lip quivering. "I—I'm sorry."

But my mind snagged on something Quentin had said. *You're Cecile's son.*

He'd known my mother.

"Cora," I said urgently. "We need to get back to the coven. *Now.*"

Urgency flowed through my veins, gripping me tightly and making me impatient as I took turns Jumping back to the coven with Cora, Benny, and Piper. Dex insisted on walking on foot, even as rain poured from the clouds above. But I got the impression he enjoyed it. After all, he couldn't often walk around in the daytime. Perhaps being out here—even in the pouring rain—was a relief for him.

But as I Jumped back again and again, not trusting myself to Jump everyone at once, all I could think about was Mom.

You're Cecile's son.

Mom had offered herself up as the vessel. For *me.*

She'd known having my choice taken away would kill me. So she'd done it herself.

When would I wake up and *stop* letting people take the fall for me? My selfishness, my closed-mindedness, made me sick. How could I have been so blind?

I'd been so concerned with my own life—my freedom to make choices and live the way I wanted to—that I didn't bother thinking about other people. Jocelyn had chosen to become a Reaper because of me. Dad had given up his life of magic because of me. Cora had exposed her coven to Quentin because of me.

It was time for me to do the same. To sacrifice for others. To make that choice for myself.

Benny was the last one for me to Jump. When we arrived, I burst into the hotel lobby and climbed the stairs two at a time, desperate to get to Mom's room and ensure she was all right.

She didn't answer when I pounded furiously on the door. But with my frantic knocking, another door down the hall opened, and Gwen peered out, her eyes narrowing. When she saw me, her face slackened.

"In here." She jerked her head to invite me in.

I obeyed, entering Gwen's room to find Jocelyn, Mom, and Gwen hovering over a bowl of potion ingredients. A small gold amulet in the shape of an angel wing rested inside the bowl. It was already emitting an eerie red glow.

"Is everyone all right?" I panted, clutching at a stitch in my side from racing up all those stairs.

Mom's brow furrowed as she looked me over. "Yes, we're fine. What happened, Vince?"

I dropped my head and sucked in several deep breaths. The Reapers didn't know what Cora and I had just attempted. They didn't know we'd almost ruined everything.

"Quentin Cox knows you," I said, meeting my mom's gaze. "He identified me as your son."

Mom's face paled, and she exchanged a glance with Gwen, who stared at me, her expression severe. "How do you know this?"

"I just saw him. We almost had him, but—"

"Of all the idiotic things," Gwen hissed, stepping toward me, her fingers curling into fists. "When will you *learn*—"

"I know!" I shouted over her, but my eyes remained on my mom. "You can yell at me later. But I need to know, Mom: *how do you know Quentin?*"

The room fell silent. All of us stared at Mom expectantly. I held my breath as her expression turned grim.

"Years ago, I knew a Second Tier dark warlock," Mom said, her voice barely above a whisper. "He threatened the clan. We dispatched armies to intercept him, but he got away each time." She took a breath. "The more he evaded us, the stronger he became. He rallied forces alongside him. Light covens turned on us, fearing the power he possessed."

Gwen suddenly gasped. "The Demon War."

My heart lurched, and my eyes snapped to Gwen. "Are you—are you saying Quentin *started* the Demon War?" My voice was hushed.

Mom nodded slowly. "Well, not directly. But he put everything in place for it. Everything we needed to be defeated."

"And Hector?"

Mom shook her head. "I don't know how much he knew. Or who he was working with. He aligned himself with some demons, but it's possible he didn't know Quentin."

Like hell he didn't. Hector had connections everywhere. He *had* to know Quentin. Or at least know *of* him.

"Why didn't you mention this before?" Gwen snapped.

"I didn't think it was important," Mom said, her voice rising. "And I didn't even know it was the same person until recently."

"If he had enough power and foresight to start the Demon War . . ." Jocelyn said in a whisper.

"Then he's a lot stronger and smarter than we feared," Gwen said.

I looked at Mom. Her gaze locked onto me, her face stricken with terror. Like Cora, Mom knew what

Quentin would do. He would use me against them. And after Mom offered herself to be the Reapers' vessel in my place, I knew she would do anything to protect me.

I swallowed and turned to Gwen. "Let *me* be the vessel. I made a target of myself by seeking out Quentin. Now he knows me, and he'll try to use me as leverage. For Mom *and* for Cora. I can't let that happen."

Silence fell in the room. Jocelyn stiffened, her eyes wide. Mom closed her eyes, her expression filled with regret.

But Gwen stared me down, as if waiting for me to change my mind. "Are you *certain?*" she asked slowly.

I nodded.

"Can your Thinker friend handle this?"

I nodded again, feeling confident that even if Luke wasn't as powerful as Benny, our bond certainly was.

Gwen sighed. "Very well."

"No," Mom said, stepping forward, her eyes pleading as she looked at me. "Vince, *please.*"

"Quentin likes toying with his enemies," I said. "He'll lure you out. Play games with you. He *enjoys* tormenting people, Mom." I closed my eyes as anger and fear clawed at my insides. "I can't let him do that to you. Or to Cora. I can't let him use me to torture you."

"You have no idea what you're giving up. We don't even know how long you'll be trapped in there. It could be *years.*"

"I've made a mess of things since I got here," I said in a broken voice. "Most of this is my fault, anyway. Let me fix this."

Mom shook her head. "Quentin was attacking our realm even before you became a Reaper."

"But I made it worse," I said. I took her hands in both of mine. "Please let me do this. Let me make this choice for you. For all of you." I looked at Jocelyn, trying to convey the apology and regret in my gaze. Her eyes softened, and she pressed her lips together.

A deep thrumming pulsed in the room. The bowl of potion ingredients rattled. Every pair of eyes moved to stare at the bowl as the red glow intensified and then slowly faded.

Gwen was the first to break the silence. "It's done." Her voice was soft and hushed. "Any Reaper who touches this will be drained of their magic." Her eyes shifted to me. "If Vince wears this, he will hold *all* of the Reaper magic."

Something churned inside me as if coming to life, reaching for the amulet. I took a step forward. "And if I touch it?"

"It will take your Reaper magic too."

I swallowed. That *presence* still stirred in my chest. And with a jolt, I realized what it was: Quentin's magic that he'd stolen from our realm. It still lived inside me.

I'd completely forgotten.

My eyes watered from the intensity buzzing within me. My body lurched forward of its own accord until my fingers curled around the cold amulet.

"Vince, *no*—" Mom shouted.

Too late.

As soon as I touched it, I breathed deeply as if my lungs had been cut off until now. As if I'd never breathed before. The power inside me seeped out, funneling into the amulet. I wasn't sure what I was expecting—but it certainly wasn't *relief*.

I thought I'd feel empty. But instead, I felt free. Unrestrained. Like a weight had been removed from my chest.

I took several deep breaths, blinking tears from my eyes as I gazed around the room. It wasn't until I noticed Mom's face, slack with shock and hurt, that I realized I was *smiling*.

"Vince—" Gwen said weakly. I'd never heard her sound like that.

I blinked at her. "What?" Then, I looked down and found my *entire* body glowed red. I yelped and staggered backward in shock. As I watched, the redness receded until I was no longer glowing.

My breathing turned sharp. "What—what was that?"

"Where did you get that much magic?" Mom whispered.

"From Quentin."

"*How?*" Gwen demanded, the sharpness returning to her voice.

My mouth opened and closed. I wasn't sure how much to say. Something inside me warned me not to utter the truth about the timeline living inside me. That they wouldn't understand.

"I don't know," I said honestly. "I just touched him, and . . . the power came into me."

"You *reaped*," Gwen said, her eyes wide.

A stunned silence rippled over the room. Even Jocelyn's face had turned white, though she looked almost as confused as I felt.

"How?" I asked, my voice barely a croak. "I—I don't even know *how*!"

"Most Reapers train for weeks before they can fully access their abilities," Mom said quietly. Her eyes were full of awe and . . . pride. But also sorrow.

Because I'd just given it all up. Whatever potential I showed as a Reaper had been sucked into that amulet. And the blissful freedom I felt inside me roared at the thought of being tethered to the red magic again. Of being restrained.

I didn't want my Reaper powers back. I wanted to stay like this.

Gwen shook her head quickly as if waking from a stupor. "It doesn't matter how impressive his skills are.

Right now, we need to get every Reaper in here so we can move forward with this before Quentin—"

A deep rumbling shook the floor. The windows rattled. My world tilted until I fell against the wall, struggling to remain upright.

When I felt queasy enough to puke, the trembling stopped. The room righted itself, and we all stared at each other in confusion and horror.

Jocelyn hurried to the window and peered through the blinds. She sucked in a sharp gasp. Her hands trembled as she turned to face us.

"What is it?" Gwen and I said together.

"It—it's Quentin. With an army."

CHAPTER 32

CORA

I SENSED HIS MAGIC BEFORE I SAW HIM. I WASN'T SURE how. A presence shifted in the air around me, thickening and swarming like an invisible hive of bees.

The hairs on my arm stood up, and my skin prickled. Magic churned through the air, sweeping through me like my body was transparent—like there was nothing keeping me between me and him.

My father was here. And he wasn't alone.

Benny was by my side in an instant as we hurried out the office and flung open the front door.

Sure enough, there stood Quentin. Behind him was an entire pack of wolves, baring their fangs at me.

Benny gasped, his body going rigid. "Trent . . . *Michael*, what're you—"

"They work for me now," Quentin said with a wide grin.

My fingers curled into tight fists at my side. "What is this, a power play?" I demanded. "Congratulations, you've proven you're so terrifying you can coerce other demons to work for you. Great job."

Quentin cocked his head at me, his eyes narrowing. "You really don't get it, do you?"

I scowled at him, but my blood raced as if warning me. Something big was coming. Staring me in the face.

"What do you think I was doing while Piper stole from you?" Quentin asked, stepping closer. "You think I was just hiding in Hinport, biding my time?" He chuckled and shook his head. "I knew it would be a battle to take you down. No one had ever managed it before, and you had quite the reputation." He stopped when he was five feet in front of me, his smile feral. "So, I was busy recruiting."

"You mean *blackmailing*," Benny hissed, his body quivering with rage. "These wolves were my *friends*. They never would've joined you unless they had no choice."

My gut twisted at his words. I didn't doubt him. My mind circled through the different horrifying things Quentin could've threatened them with—like slaughtering their families.

Quentin only shrugged. "It doesn't matter *how* I recruit them. All that matters is they belong to me."

Like they were nothing more than possessions. Objects to be tossed around.

"You had your chance," Quentin said. "You gambled your coven's safety so you could trap me. Consider this my retaliation: a declaration of war. Surrender yourself to me, or I will rain hellfire down on you and your puny coven. You have one hour." He offered a jovial wave before turning on his heel and disappearing down the street. The pack trotted after him, though a few wolves lingered to stare at Benny before they followed.

Benny exhaled a low hiss through his teeth. "He's *baiting* you."

"And it's working," I snapped. "I can't keep my coven safe if he has every demon in the city under his thumb."

Benny turned to face me, his expression hard. "What're you saying, Cora?"

"I'm saying I need to surrender."

His eyes flashed with anger. "You *can't*."

"I'm just *one person,* Benny. If he brings a war, there will be casualties. People will *die*."

"And what will happen when you surrender?" Benny drew closer to me, his expression taut with fury. "Quentin will sacrifice you. He'll gain *more* power. And then he'll rule *all* the demons of Hinport. If you think the killing will stop with you, then you're more naïve than I thought."

"I can't have their blood on my hands!" I cried, waving my hand toward the neighborhood behind us.

"You are the *only* thing standing in the way of

Quentin taking over our coven. If you give up, their blood is on your hands anyway."

My head reared back at the bite in his words, the harshness of his tone.

"You are a *fighter*, Cora," he growled. "So *pick a damn fight with him*."

Fire burned in his eyes so intensely I thought it would melt my skin. And something roared within my chest at his words as if he'd awakened a beast.

The beast craved blood. *Quentin's* blood. The beast wanted to bleed him dry, to cut him apart . . .

I sucked in a trembling breath. I hadn't unleashed that beast in a long time.

"We need the Blade of Hinport," Benny whispered. "Bring her back."

My eyes felt moist, and I blinked rapidly to clear them. My chest swelled. My stomach churned. My legs itched to run, but that itch intensified until it spread through my entire body.

I needed to fight. To strain, to grit my teeth, to look death in the face once more.

I was coven leader, yes. But Benny was right: I was a fighter. Quentin knew it too. He expected it.

"He wants a war?" I said, my voice low and dangerous. "Let's give him one."

Clarity coursed through me, swift and powerful as I gave orders, never stopping to breathe or think. I sent Dex to gather as many vampires as he could, though I doubted there were any still on our side. Benny went to find Luke so they could mentally seek out any demons in the city who hadn't been taken in by Quentin.

We needed every ally we could find.

Piper rounded up those in our coven who couldn't fight—those who were too old or injured—and sent them to the bunker we never used. I'd called Damien paranoid for building it. But here we were, in desperate need of a shelter to keep our people safe.

I was busy rounding up soldiers and weapons. My people were trained in basic combat, but none of them were fighters like me. My whole purpose had been to do the dirty work so no one else would have to.

But we didn't have time to train. War was on our doorstep *now*.

I didn't know where Vince or the other Reapers were, but I had to trust they were keeping their heads down. Last I'd heard, Gwen was busy preparing the spell to bind their magic so Cecile could take it with her into Benny's mind.

The thought sent a jolt of realization through me. Relief and agony crushed my chest, making it hard to breathe.

Benny could *not* fight in this war. There was too much

at stake. With Cecile in his mind, he needed to be protected.

If he died, so would she. Along with all the Reapers' magic.

I'd just gathered my most vital elixirs when I sought Benny out to warn him to stay hidden. But he was already waiting in front of my apartment, pacing anxiously. I froze, the glass vials clinking in my arms.

Benny stopped when he saw me, his eyes burning bright and clear. "We're ready."

"How many?" I asked, fearing his response.

"Fifty. Twenty wolves, fourteen witches and warlocks, plus fifteen vampires with Dex."

I swallowed and nodded. Fifty was a lot—certainly more than our original coven—but if there were only fifty demons we could rely on in the city, that meant Quentin had *hundreds* on his side. Maybe more.

"You can't fight," I said.

Benny's eyebrows lifted, his mouth hanging open. "What? Why not?"

"You need to work with Cecile. Get her hidden and keep yourself safe."

Benny shook his head. "It's not me. It's Luke."

I frowned. "*Luke*? Is he strong enough?"

Benny stared at me for a long moment. Then, comprehension dawned, and a mixture of emotions filled his gaze. "You haven't heard."

"Heard *what?*" Impatience gnawed at my insides.

"Vince is going in instead."

My brows knitted together, and it took me a full minute to process what he'd said.

Vince.

Was going into *Luke's* mind.

To be trapped.

A hard lump formed in my throat. I couldn't breathe. Couldn't *think*.

I had to go to him. *Now.* Convince him not to do it.

He'd be chaining himself for *who knows how long* . . .

"It was his choice, Cora," Benny said quietly. "Quentin knows him and how valuable he is. To the Reapers and . . . to you." His voice tightened at the last word, and he dropped his gaze.

Guilt wriggled through the mess of emotions circling through me. It was too much. *Too much—*

A deafening *boom* shook the ground. Benny and I teetered, bumping into each other as we struggled to regain balance.

This tremor didn't last as long as the first one, but I knew what it meant.

Time was up. Quentin was ready to attack.

I inhaled a shuddering breath. My instincts were failing me. Internally, I was at war with myself—go to Vince, or save my people. Normally, I thrived on conflict. My body knew just what to do.

But not now. I stood there, frozen, while Benny watched me and waited.

It was his choice, Cora.

Vince had made his choice. Now, I had to make mine.

My breathing steadied, and resolve coursed through me. I handed three vials of potion to Benny.

"Healing elixirs," I said. "Give one to each division. Tell them to use it sparingly—it's all I've got."

Benny nodded, but he still watched me expectantly. "And what about you?"

The earth rumbled again in response. I gritted my teeth and barely managed to keep on my feet before the ground settled again. "I'm going to the front lines," I said, "to face Quentin."

Benny's eyes blazed with pride and determination. "I'll be there with you."

"No," I said quickly. "I need you to oversee the were-wolves. Rally them to the north side of town. That's where we're weakest."

"Cora, Quentin wants *you*. If you go to the front lines—"

"I'm not putting my people in the line of fire," I growled. "Not without me. I won't give in to him, Benny. I swear it."

Benny held my gaze for a long moment. Fire burned between us, and for one terrifying moment, I worried we would never see each other again.

Benny exhaled and dropped his gaze, then took my hand in both of his. "Be safe, Cora."

And then he was gone.

Finding Quentin and his army wasn't hard. The earthquakes intensified as I moved deeper into the city.

About a mile away from the ruins of our old office buildings, I saw a horde of demons, all wielding weapons.

And in front of them was Quentin.

As I'd instructed, my strongest men were waiting for me, led by Kent, a beefy dark warlock with tattoos all over his face. He straightened when he saw me.

"Is this everyone?" I asked, my gaze raking over the crowd. Something in my chest deflated. We had less than twenty. Across the street, Quentin had more than twice those numbers.

This would be over before it began.

Kent nodded, his bald head gleaming in the fading sunlight. "With nightfall, we'll have more. Dex is waiting in the complex for the vampires to emerge."

I wasn't sure we'd make it to nightfall.

"What's the plan?" Kent asked, crossing his arms.

I swallowed, feeling out of my element. I wasn't a soldier. Or even a strategist.

I was a cold-blooded killer. If this were a one-on-one combat, I would know exactly what to do.

You can do this, I told myself. *Just think of this as another assignment. Another mark. What would you do if your mark was surrounded by allies? How would you get to him?*

I took a deep breath. "We need to lure Quentin away from his men."

"How do we do that?"

I smiled. "Take something he wants."

Despite the frequent earthquakes and whatever turmoil was happening outside, Gwen managed to get the amulet in the hands of every Reaper.

And I was suddenly reconsidering my offer to hide away while my people fought—and most likely died.

Even *with* their magic, they were no match for Quentin and his army.

I should be fighting alongside Cora, I thought, gritting my teeth. But then my gaze shifted to my mom, who wrung her hands together with worry. Dad sat next to her, his face pale and drawn. He kept glancing at me, his eyes stirring as if he wanted to say something.

I couldn't leave without talking to him. In all the chaos that had been going on, I'd barely shared two words with him.

While we waited for Gwen to return, I strode toward

Dad. He instantly rose to his feet as if he expected my approach.

"I'm sorry," I whispered. My eyes burned with the threat of tears.

Dad stepped around the table and grabbed me in a tight embrace. "You have nothing to be sorry for."

"You must be so disappointed in me. I've made so many poor choices."

Dad drew back to look at me, his eyes shining. "I'm not disappointed. You're taking things into your own hands. You're keeping your people safe."

"I have no choice. I *have* to do this."

Dad smiled. "That's where you're wrong, Vince. There is *always* a choice. It's something you've struggled to come to terms with. But I think you're finally understanding."

I nodded slowly. He was right. Just like what Cora, Jocelyn, and Luke had told me. I had to make the best of my situation. Accept the consequences of *my choices*. And make a difference wherever I could.

I'd made the choice to become a Reaper. It was time to stop complaining and start *working*.

My gaze slid to my mom, whose eyes glistened with tears. I could give my parents what I'd failed to give them before: a life together.

The door opened, and Gwen strode in, her cheeks pink and her eyes wide. Her hands grasped a large piece of cloth. I knew the amulet was nestled inside. Gwen said it was dangerous to touch with your skin after your magic was gone. You risked losing your entire soul.

The thought made me shudder.

"The spell is complete," Gwen said quietly, approaching me. "The Reaper magic has been sealed. As soon as you put this on, you will feel the weight of the magic. *Don't* put it on until you're inside your friend's mind. The mind will provide a stasis, keeping you safe from the burden of the magic."

The burden of the magic. I swallowed hard. "What would happen if I put it on now?"

Gwen fixed a hard stare on me. "The force of the magic would likely kill you."

I flinched. I'd expected something like that.

Quentin's magic hadn't killed me, a small voice inside me said.

But I shoved the thought away. Perhaps that had just been a fluke. Or perhaps Quentin hadn't possessed *enough* magic to do me any harm.

A soft knock sounded at the door. Mom opened it, and there was Jocelyn with Luke behind her. Both their expressions were drawn with worry. Shouts and gunfire echoed in the distance, and the ground rumbled again. More fear and guilt wriggled through me. Was Cora okay?

This is the best thing you can do for her, I reminded

myself. *You're a liability, Vince. Quentin would use you against her. He saw her almost give herself up.*

I nodded to myself as the door closed behind Luke and Jocelyn.

"Are you ready?" Gwen asked me.

I met her gaze, my insides quivering from the severity in her eyes. To be honest, I *wasn't* ready. I hadn't fully accepted what this meant—what I'd be giving up.

And I hadn't gotten to say goodbye to Cora.

I closed my eyes, allowing regret to consume me for a moment. Reveling in that pain. Embracing it.

Because it served as a reminder for why I was doing this.

I opened my eyes and looked at Mom. Her face crumpled as if she were about to burst into tears. And next to her, Dad's face was ashen. But he offered a weak smile.

He'd already said goodbye to me once. This wasn't much different. I knew he could handle it.

"Tell her I love her," I said to Dad. "More than anything."

Dad nodded. He knew who I was talking about.

Mom sucked in a shuddering breath. Surprise and alarm flickered in her face before sorrow took over once more. I stepped toward her and embraced her. She clutched at me tightly as if she could ground me here by force.

It was different for her than for Dad. We'd finally been reunited after a decade apart. When I'd pledged my vow as a Reaper, she'd thought we'd be together forever.

We both had thought that.

"You'll get through this," I whispered. "You'll take him down in no time, and then I'll come back. This isn't goodbye."

Mom wept into my shoulder, the sobs so intense I knew she couldn't form words. Feeling her trembling as she cried made my own eyes sting with tears. I closed them, determined to keep it together. I would have plenty of time to break down inside Luke's mind—once I was alone.

When I drew away, I wiped the tears off Mom's face, and she gave me a wobbly smile.

"I'm so—so sorry," she breathed. "For everything."

A knot formed in my throat. "I've already forgiven you." And it was true. Whatever bitter feelings she had about Cora, whatever she believed about Reapers being the most important creatures in the world—I could forgive her all that. Because she was my mother. We didn't have to agree on everything.

I turned away as a tear trickled down my cheek. My lips trembled, and I couldn't look at my parents anymore. Not if I wanted to keep my composure.

Jocelyn flew into my arms and pressed a kiss to my

cheek. Before I could react, she'd withdrawn, rubbing her arms and avoiding my gaze.

"Stay safe," I told her.

She just nodded, still not looking at me.

Then, I faced Luke and took a deep breath. "What will happen to you?"

"Benny set me up with a coven of Thinkers in New York. They offered me shelter and will monitor my mind to ensure nothing—nothing happens."

"What will happen to my body?" I asked uncertainly, imagining a lifeless version of myself collapsing on the floor.

"My mind will absorb you," Luke said. "*All* of you. Your mind, your body—everything."

My face twisted with a grimace. "Will you—I mean, will it hurt? To have me and all this magic trapped in there?"

Luke smiled and shook his head. "With our bond, it'll be easy. A little heavy, but definitely doable."

My hands started shaking, so I focused on my breathing. Inhale. Exhale.

Then, Gwen was there, her hands outstretched. In her palm was the amulet wrapped in cloth. Gingerly, I grasped the corners of the cloth, careful not to touch the amulet, and tucked it in my hands.

"You all be careful," I said to the room at large. "Quentin is smarter than you think." I paused.

"And . . . please watch out for Cora. Even if you don't like her. She doesn't have many people to watch her back."

Gwen's lips tightened, and Jocelyn's nostrils flared. But, to my surprise, Mom nodded. There was no resentment in her face. And I believed she would look after Cora—for me.

"Ready?" Luke asked, stepping closer to me.

No, a voice inside me screamed. But I forced myself to say, "Yes."

"Close your eyes," Luke said. "Go back to the field."

It would be easy. As easy as breathing. That lacrosse field had become a mental haven for me. A place I could conjure easily.

But now, I was afraid of it. Afraid this monumental task would tarnish that field forever. That I would always see it as a prison from now on.

Steeling myself, I took a deep breath and closed my eyes, picturing the field. In a flash, I was there.

But it was different this time. There were no other players around me. And I wasn't dressed in my gear. I wore the same clothes as before—a T-shirt and cargo shorts. I still clutched the cloth and amulet with trembling hands.

Then, Luke appeared in front of me, his expression full of sympathy and understanding. "I'll be here. Anytime you need some company, just shout for me, and I'll be here."

"Thanks." The word sounded strangled.

Luke's expression went blank for a moment. "Uh, Gwen says to put the amulet on now."

I nodded, shifting the cloth so the gold gleamed in the sunlight. Inhaling deeply, I lifted the chain in my fingers and draped the amulet over my head. It settled in the middle of my chest, a heavy weight—a reminder of my task.

Protect the magic, I reminded myself. *If you're here, it means Quentin can't get this power. It's safe with you.*

When I let go of the amulet, the heaviness intensified, like it was an anchor dragging me down, down, down . . . I groaned, gritting my teeth against the strain, the tugging at my neck. I fell to my knees, hunching over.

Luke let out a sharp breath in a hiss. I weakly glanced up at him and found his expression strained. The muscles and tendons stood out on his neck. He clenched his fingers into fists.

"Gwen says . . . we will adjust to it," he panted. "But it's hard . . . at first."

I sucked in gulps of air, struggling to keep my eyes open. "It's fine," I grunted. "I'll be fine."

"I gotta go now, Vince. Before Quentin—"

"I know. Go. Be safe."

He nodded and then vanished. Leaving me utterly alone.

CHAPTER 34

CORA

GETTING CLOSE TO QUENTIN WASN'T EASY. I DOWNED my shadow elixir and made my way to his army. The front line of werewolves tensed at my approach. The benefit of my shadows was that they masked my scent, which was handy around werewolves. But they could still see the tendrils of black smoke surrounding me.

I weaved between soldiers. A few wolves snapped their teeth at me, but my shadows burst forward, blocking me from view. Vile dog breath stung my nostrils, but I remained unharmed.

Quentin sensed me before I reached him.

"So, *this* is your famous shadow elixir?" He chuckled as I drew closer. "I'm impressed."

Quentin gradually came into view, surrounded by demons on all sides. Werewolves, vampires, dark warlocks, and witches . . . He had his own personal squad to keep him safe.

The coward.

A dark witch lunged for me. I ducked to avoid her magic, then sent a burst of purple magic directly into her chest. She soared backward, colliding with another warlock and exposing Quentin.

I bounded forward, taking advantage of the opening. Even though Quentin only saw a rippling mass of shadows, he could still hurt me.

But I was prepared.

Once I stood directly in front of him, I pressed my hands together and murmured a spell.

"Magic above and powers that be,

Momentarily blind my enemy."

A flash of purple light, and then Quentin cried out, clutching at his eyes.

I moved quicker than lightning. Several demons surged forward, their faces taut with terror and confusion. I evaded them easily, sidestepping until I stood face-to-face with Quentin.

He froze, his eyes crammed shut. "I can still sense you. You think I'm powerless without my sight?" He swung a fist. I ducked, hooking my leg around his ankle and bringing him crashing to the ground. I pressed my knees into his legs, pinning him in place.

While he was down, I fished through his pockets. He

writhed and wriggled, trying to get away, but it was no use. A jet of purple flame seared against my face. Pain coursed through me, but I gritted my teeth, determined to get what I came for.

Then, I found it: a belt with holsters, similar to mine—though this reminded me more of a utility belt. The glass vials clinked together as I unbuckled the belt and rose to my feet.

Quentin blinked furiously, his eyes clearing.

Time's up.

I uncorked one of my own vials—a Jumping elixir—and swallowed it down. Before I could move, a splitting pain cut into my arm. Crying out, I wrenched my body free from the assailant before turning in place. I vanished with a small *pop* and reappeared a block away, where Kent was waiting. He frowned at the flurry of shadows surrounding me.

"Cora?" he asked.

I waved my uninjured hand, and my shadows vanished. Panting, I glanced at my other arm. Purple blood ran freely down my forearm, soaking my shirt. The wound pulsed and throbbed, and I hissed in pain. I didn't have time to take a healing elixir—and even if I did, I needed to save it for the other demons. They needed it more than I did. If I had more time, I could hunt for the healing elixirs Quentin probably had on his belt.

But time wasn't on our side.

I looked at Kent. "He's coming." I glanced at the crowd of demons behind him. "Everyone, get ready!"

I'd left a few of my strongest men on patrol around the city, but the bulk of my coven was here behind me. Ready to fight. Ready to die.

I could practically feel Quentin's fury. A dark presence stirred in the distance, raging. Drawing closer.

He was powerful without his elixirs. But he needed them, just like I did.

And, more importantly, I'd stolen from him. His pride was wounded.

A small smile quirked on my lips as I thought of his anger. But the satisfaction faded when an eerie purple mist seeped into the parking lot we stood in.

My heart lurched in my throat, and several demons shifted nervously behind me. A thrill raced through me, my once familiar companion: adrenaline. The excitement. The fight.

But it was different this time. It wasn't just me here. It was everyone I was responsible for protecting.

Fire burned in my veins, and my magic churned in response. Waiting. Ready.

When a figure emerged from the mist, I snapped into action. My magic swelled around me, gathering like a current that carried me forward. And I blasted the first figure until he fell to the ground.

It wasn't Quentin. I knew he wasn't stupid enough to put himself at the front.

Not like me.

Another blast. Another one down. But they were approaching quickly, and I couldn't hold back all of them. Dozens of demons emerged, racing forward, wielding their weapons. I sliced my magic into one of them and ducked to avoid a dagger in the face. Kick in the shin. Slice in the gut. Blood sprayed, demons screamed, bones crunched . . .

The air was a cacophony of sounds. The coppery tang of blood stung my nostrils, mingling with the thick smell of the various dark magic around me.

I heard Kent go down behind me. Then another one of my guys.

Agony pulsed through me, but I shoved it down. I could mourn them later. Now, I had to fight.

The demons didn't stop coming. It was like Quentin had Jumped his *entire army* right to us.

I'd hoped to lure him out—alone.

My plan had backfired. *Somehow* Quentin had Teleported his men right to me.

A scream echoed behind me. With a start, I whirled and found one of my witches being clubbed in the face.

My heart sank to my stomach. Behind us was another throng of Quentin's men.

Any second now and we'd be surrounded with no way out. We couldn't win this.

"Fall back!" I roared.

I urged my coven backward, dodging blades and gunfire. Shock rippled through me when I found Piper's familiar spark of purple hair. I snatched her arm, dragging her away from another demon's knife.

"What're you doing here?" I cried.

Piper's eyes widened at something behind me, and she shot her black magic over my shoulder, assaulting a demon. She fixed a fierce expression on me. "I'm here to fight."

"You can't—"

"I know I screwed up before. I can't fight my father head-on. But I can fight these goons, easy." She offered a grin before bashing her head backward into the face of another demon.

I raised my eyebrows, impressed.

"We have to retreat before they surround us," I said. Quentin's demons kept on coming as if they were multiplying. I no longer recognized the faces around me, except for Piper.

My coven was dying.

Were we the only ones left?

"For Hinport!" I shouted, raising my fist in the air. "My men, *on me!*" My voice cut through the haze of battle, and several demons shifted in response. I recognized Dex, blood dripping from his fangs as he feasted on a demon. He looked up at me, and I shot him a warning look. With a nod, he shoved aside the demon, whose throat was torn open, and made his way toward me.

Benny . . . Where is Benny?

I'd sent him to the other side of town with the wolves. But they should've been here by now.

"Cora," Piper said urgently.

Through the purple fog emerged one final figure I recognized. My father.

I shook my head. *No. If he joins the battle, we're all dead. We're already dying.*

The slaughter was so, so much worse than I'd feared.

I grabbed Piper's elbow. "Get to the bunker. Now."

"I'm not hiding!" she hissed. "I'm with you, Cora."

I didn't have time to argue with her. After grabbing the potion vial from my pocket, I quickly downed the rest of my Jumping elixir. My eyes flicked around the lot, squinting as I tried to make out anyone else on my side. Anyone I might have missed.

There was one more: Finn, a dark warlock. I hollered for him until he caught my eye and moved over to me. When we were all huddled together and Quentin's demons had us blocked in, I made sure we all had our arms linked.

"Hold tight!" I shouted.

I turned in place, gripping the arms of my last remaining comrades, and with a *pop*, we vanished from the battle.

Dust, dirt, and sharp concrete broke my fall. My hands were still tightly gripping the arms of Piper and Dex, so I had nothing to break my fall but my forearms. I grunted as the hard ground scraped against my skin. Around me, my comrades coughed and sputtered, waving dust out of their faces.

"Where are we?" Piper wheezed.

I squinted. A gloomy darkness surrounded me. As my eyes adjusted, I made out several dusty cardboard boxes and broken pieces of furniture. Dust tickled my throat. "An old storehouse. It's cloaked, and no one can enter unless they have—" I stopped. I was about to say *my blood* . . . but that now included Quentin. Shaking my head, I said, "We can't stay here too long. We'll have to move soon."

"And go where?" Finn asked.

A heavy silence fell around us. Our eyes met with grim realization.

We had nowhere to go. No home. No friends or allies.

Quentin and his army would hunt us.

We were on our own.

All I wanted to do was collapse in a heap and succumb to the despair. To do nothing but wallow in my defeat, in the horrible choices I'd made. I'd lost my coven, my city, my *family* . . .

But as I gazed at the bleak expressions of my last remaining allies, an unfamiliar fire burned in my chest. I yearned to triumph over this—but not for my own sake. For *them*. To save them. To bring them back home. To give them hope again.

Wiping dust from my pants, I climbed to my feet with a grunt. Even though my body ached and throbbed with injuries and exhaustion, I forced myself to stand up straighter and look each one of them in the eye.

"I don't know," I said, answering Finn's question. My voice was strong, but it crackled, betraying my fatigue. "I don't know where we'll go or how long we'll have to run. But this *isn't over*. I swear to you—on my life and on my blood—that somehow, we'll take our city back. One day, we will have our revenge. And I'll do whatever it takes to make it happen." I pressed my bloodied hand to my chest, my fingers forming a fist. "I'm with you. All of you. Until the end."

For a moment, silence followed, and I feared my words had no effect on them. But then, slowly, my friends stood, their eyes glinting with determination. One by one, they pressed a fist to their chests and echoed my words: "I'm with you. Until the end."

CHAPTER 35

VINCE

I had no concept of time in the field of Luke's mind. After what felt like an hour, the heavy weight of the amulet settled into something more bearable. I was able to straighten and even stand, though it was still a strain for me. Sweat dripped down my face, and my arms trembled.

After what I guessed was two hours, I could easily pace the length of the field. I even broke into a brisk jog, my legs aching to strain against something. Especially when everyone I loved was out there fighting—and possibly dying.

Were the Reapers helping Cora fight Quentin? Was Cora all right? What about my parents?

I didn't dare call for Luke. Not yet. He needed to get to a safe place first. I wouldn't jeopardize his safety by distracting him.

When I was too exhausted to keep pacing, I collapsed to the ground, propping my arms up on my knees as I twirled a blade of grass between my fingers. My heart thrummed rapidly inside me like the fluttering of a hummingbird's wings. My breaths were sharp and uneven, and sweat now coated my entire body. I vaguely wondered how I would take care of hygiene, sleep, food, and other needs . . . But I reminded myself Luke would be back eventually.

Perhaps I didn't *need* to eat. Gwen had said my body would be in a sort of stasis. Maybe time was completely frozen for me.

After another long stretch of time, the aching boredom started to gnaw at my mind. All I could do was fret about my friends and family, my brain circling through horrifying scenarios and dwelling on how helpless I was.

Something pulsed inside me the longer I sat there with my anxiety. At first, I thought it was simply the magic of the amulet. But the presence grew and grew within me until, with a jolt, I recognized it. Foreign, and yet so familiar.

The timeline.

It called to me.

As soon as I identified it, it surged forward eagerly. Power tickled my skin. I wiggled my fingertips. Even with my Reaper magic gone, I still felt *alive* inside. Not just the weight of the amulet, but the weight of my own powers.

My warlock powers. They mingled with the timeline, intertwined like two snakes enjoining. Like they fit together perfectly.

I stared numbly at the grass in front of me, finally facing what I'd been avoiding for so long.

The Call. The connection to the timeline. I had it. Just like Hector.

Something quivered along the timeline like a ripple in the water. I frowned. What *was* that?

There it was again, more insistent. Like a crisp, clear chord of music flowing through me.

My mouth opened, and before I'd even processed it, I spoke.

"Hector."

Hector appeared in front of me. And though my mind faintly registered I should be *shocked* at this . . . I wasn't. Deep inside, I knew I could summon him. Just like I could summon any Timekeeper.

Because I had the Call.

Hector only looked at me, also unsurprised. A heaviness stirred in his eyes—something I'd seen before but hadn't identified.

The timeline was a burden to him. Just as this amulet was a burden to me.

I rose to my feet to face him. My mouth felt dry. For a moment, we just stared at each other.

Then, I asked, "Did you know who Quentin was?"

Gold light flared inside me as if chastising me for asking this. The timeline, an unfeeling and logical side of me, warred with my emotions. It seemed to whisper, *This doesn't matter right now. And you know it.*

But I *had* to know.

"The Demon War," I said, my voice gaining strength. "Did you *know?*"

Hector swallowed hard. "Yes. I knew who Quentin was. But that was before."

I didn't have to ask what he meant. Before I'd marked him. Before he'd accessed the timeline.

"It was a fixed event on the timeline, Vince," Hector said quietly. "It couldn't be altered even if I wanted to."

My jaw went rigid. I said nothing.

"When Quentin was only a warlock, he wasn't a threat to the timeline," Hector went on, drawing closer to me. "He was merely another pawn in the grand scheme of things. But now . . . it's different."

The light within me resonated with his words. He was right. I'd time traveled to the Demon War myself. I hadn't been able to change anything. Not even my mother's disappearance.

It had been a fixed event.

Hector and I stared at each other, completely silent. Magic flowed between us as if we were simply conduits for the timeline. And though I *wanted* to remember this man was a murderer and a tyrant, the powerful presence within me recognized him as a kindred spirit. It was undeniable. So intense that I gasped for breath and tears pricked my eyes. The stunning realization of who I was and what I could do coursed through me like a strong current.

"You know, don't you?" Hector's voice was solemn.

I didn't need to ask what he meant—the Call. I knew about the Call.

I nodded. A tear rolled down my cheek, and I sniffed. "Yes."

"So, what will you do?"

I swallowed. Perhaps this was my way out. This was how I could help my friends and family.

I wouldn't be helpless any longer.

With a deep breath, I said to Hector, "Tell me about the Timekeepers."

Hector watched me for a long moment. Something unreadable stirred in his eyes. As I stared at him, I realized it looked an awful lot like . . . *regret*.

Before I could make sense of it, he asked, "Are you sure? The path to a Timekeeper is brutal."

I paused. I'd regretted my choice to become a Reaper. If I made another big choice like that, I had to be absolutely sure. "Can I keep this safe?" I gestured at the amulet around my neck. I'd given up everything for this task. I couldn't abandon it just because I was feeling useless.

Hector nodded. "Becoming a Timekeeper will give you immense power. Enough power for you to absorb that magic without a second thought." His eyes dropped to the amulet and then lifted to meet mine. "No one can take the magic from you once you claim it. It must be offered freely."

My insides froze as I processed his words. If I became a Timekeeper, I could use the Reaper magic—without the risk of Quentin stealing it. And when it was all over, I could just give it back to the Reapers and be done with it.

It seemed too good to be true. My brow furrowed, but before I could say anything, Hector spoke.

"There is a price," he said, his voice grave. "Nothing comes for free, Vince."

I licked my lips, trying to steady my racing heart. "What's the price?"

Hector's eyes tightened, and he said nothing.

My heart sank. "Can't you answer my questions before I decide?"

He shook his head. "No. The secrets of the Time-keepers are sacred. Once you open that door, you can't go back." Anguish filled his face, so raw and fierce that it made my heart lurch. I'd never seen him look like that before. "I didn't have a choice. Once I was marked,

I was thrust onto this path. There was no mercy for me."

Though the words weren't vengeful or angry, I still flinched. It was my fault. *I'd* taken that choice away from him. Hector hadn't asked to become a Timekeeper. But when the timeline came to life inside him, he'd had to respond. It had taken over his brain.

I clenched my fingers into fists and focused on my breathing. The timeline churned inside me, gaining momentum. Like it could *sense* it was so close to what it wanted.

I'd known for a while. I'd known there was something inside me, calling to me, keeping me on track. Something that preserved the laws of time, even before I understood why.

My jaw ticked back and forth as I considered my options. I could wait here indefinitely with this burdensome magic. Once Luke returned, I was sure he would give me answers.

But I would be stuck here. Possibly forever. I knew Quentin couldn't be defeated easily.

Would I just stand by and let my people die? Mom and Cora? Jocelyn?

"Will it help me stop him?" I finally asked.

Hector hesitated. "As I said before, it will grant you more power. And it will allow you to right the wrongs of the timeline. But you cannot change fixed events. If someone you love dies—if it is fixed—you can't alter it."

Despair swelled within me at the thought of Cora or Mom dying and me being unable to stop it. But . . . even if I remained here, I wouldn't be able to stop it, either.

"If his power remains unchecked, he will tear apart the realms," Hector said. "And that *will* threaten the timeline."

I swallowed. "But you defected. You went rogue. You aren't with the Timekeepers anymore."

Hector cocked his head, frowning as he considered this. "Yes and no. I will always be a Timekeeper. Nothing will change that. But not all Timekeepers work together. Some are part of a collective organization, like my former superior. But others . . . act on their own. Once you pass the test, you are free to monitor the timeline as you see fit. The organization might not approve, but . . ." He trailed off with a shrug that told me he didn't care.

Something in my chest lifted at his words. *Free. As you see fit.*

I'd never had freedom like that before.

I could operate on my own. Apart from the expectations of anyone else except the power thriving inside me.

The timeline had already been activated. Whether I liked it or not, it was a part of me. Even if I didn't become a Timekeeper, that wouldn't change.

I lifted my chin. I knew what I wanted to do, but I

waited a full minute before speaking. Waited for some instinct within me to stop me. To shout that this was wrong.

Nothing happened.

Resolve filled me. "I'll do it."

To my surprise, that same brutal regret struck Hector's face. He looked at me sadly as if I'd just accepted a death sentence. His voice grim, he said, "Very well."

My skin prickled. My heart dropped like a stone as if knowing something terrible was about to happen.

Then, a force struck my face, carving through my flesh. A bright light consumed me. The pain multiplied as if my head were splitting in two. My face was on fire. The agony tore through me, striking me again and again.

I screamed, and everything went dark.

Will Vince pass the Timekeeper test? Will Cora and the rest of her coven take their city back? Read *The Reaper's Call* to find out!

ACKNOWLEDGMENTS

A *huge* thank you to all my readers! Thank you for being part of the adventure. I am monumentally grateful for your support and encouragement. Thank you for loving these characters as much as I do!

A huge thank you to my beta readers: Tori, Ria, Kari, Melanie, Melissa, and Jenni. Thank you for your kind and helpful comments and the time you took out of your busy lives to help me. Your critiques have made me a better writer and have shaped these stories into the best they can be!

I'm so grateful for my fabulous ARC readers! Devika, Diane, Melinda, Tammy, Nicolina, Ana, Becky, Beba, Jeanine, Leila, Alwin, Dapoet, Erica, Darian, Kirstey, Pamela, Melissa, Scarolet, Robin, Krystal, Lane, Mary, Sarah, Jenny, Samantha, Beth, Anmarie, Allison, Gaby, Charly, Chad, Mel, Darcy, Kristin, Courtney, Kiranna, Alexander, Mary, Brittany, Missy Eybs, Kiandra, Lisa, Bianca, Malischa, Freya, and all my friends on TikTok and Instagram who promoted the book - thank you for always being so eager to read my books, and for your kind reviews. You guys are awesome!

And lastly, thank you to my loving and supportive family. Alex, Colin, and Ellie - you are my everything! All that I do is for you. To my kids, I hope you grow up knowing that no matter what, your dreams and goals are always attainable! You can do *anything*.

R.L. Perez is an author, wife, mother, reader, writer, and artist. She lives in Florida with her husband and three children. On a regular basis, she can usually be found napping, reading, feverishly writing, revising, or watching an abundance of Netflix. More than anything, she loves spending time with her family. Her greatest joys are her kids, nature, literature, and chocolate.

Subscribe to her newsletter for new releases, promotions, giveaways, and book recommendations! Get a FREE eBook when you sign up at subscribe.rlperez.com.

www.ingramcontent.com/pod-product-compliance
Lightning Source LLC
Chambersburg PA
CBHW051203190726
48288CB00006B/1791